LAUREL

WILLIAM HUMPHREY
Hostages to Fortune

"A desperate, impressive, astonishing book....All of his estimable earlier works pale before *Hostages to Fortune*....This remarkable book is the rarest of things —a book of adult life, of parenthood, the father's book and not the son's....Its structure is built on the way memory works, not the progress of a plot, though there is a plot, and it is adequately composed of twists and turns....Rich with pondering and extraordinary insights, and written with a mastery and ease of expression of complicated and difficult matters and feelings, it is nonetheless a book in the spirit of Chekhov, who in his letters cautioned another writer not to try to answer questions, but merely to pose them in the clearest and most truthful terms."

—*Chicago Tribune*

"A gripping triumph....A probing, at times devastating, trip into the soul of man. It raises tough, introspective questions that often cannot be answered as one grapples with pain and loss."

—*UPI*

"Sensitive, honest and wise....The voice in these books is intelligent, compassionate, civilized; we could hardly ask for more." —Jonathan Yardley, *Book World*

"*Hostages to Fortune* is a novel that grapples with pain and loss, that refuses easy answers. The story of Ben Curtis—whose determination to face tragedy and follow it into whatever depths it may lead—is deeply disturbing, a cleansing catharsis, a rare and timely triumph." —*Hooked on Books*, B. Dalton

"Chilling and intense....Through his effective and gripping use of language, Humphrey has painted a dark but beautiful portrait of an essentially good man...caught in the currents of fate, who somehow grabs hold of a dangling tree branch moments before tumbling over the falls." —*Richmond News Leader*

"*Hostages to Fortune* deals unflinchingly with matters of the heart and is written with intelligence and compassion. Humphrey has taken a difficult story and told it well." —*The Charlotte Observer*

HOSTAGES
TO
FORTUNE

WILLIAM HUMPHREY

A LAUREL/SEYMOUR LAWRENCE BOOK
Published by
Dell Publishing Co., Inc.
1 Dag Hammarskjold Plaza
New York, New York 10017

To Dorothy

PART ONE

He stood with his eyes shut tight and covered by his hand, holding his breath while the icy insect repellent dried on his skin. He had sprayed himself down to the waist, avoiding the palms of his hands, for the stuff could take the varnish off a bamboo fishing rod. He was allergic to the sting of bees, wasps, and hornets and to the bite of deerflies, of which, now in June, the woods were full. Unlike other people, he did not absorb and shed the venom; in him it accumulated, and he had been stung so many times now he was full of it. More stings, maybe just one more, could prove fatal to him, his doctor had warned. After all he had come through, that would be a senseless way to go. The doctor's advice was that he not take up fishing again.

Anointed against his enemies, he opened his eyes and breathed deeply, and with things just assuming form from out of the gray morning mist, it was like regaining consciousness, waiting for your faculties to return to you. He had begun the day before the day had begun. That way you sometimes got the jump on it. There was not a sound, near or far. The world seemed to be just emerging from the primal void and he was alone in it, as solitary as Adam on his first day —more so, for Adam had not known then that he was alone.

The rain that had come in the night, beginning at half past ten, had stopped at half past two, not to come again. He had been awake to hear it come and go and not come again, although in the old days just to imagine he heard it pattering on the sheetiron roof of the clubhouse along with the trilling of the frogs had been enough to lull him to sleep, no matter where he was. Now the earth slumbered on under a blanket of gray ground fog. Vapor overhung the river, and the trees lining its course were trunks with neither roots nor tops. He plucked a tuft of dead grass and loosed it. Straight to earth it fell through the windless air. It was a good day for fly-fishing.

He opened the trunk of the car and took out the rod case. From the partitioned cloth sack inside the case he took the butt section and one of the twin tips of the rod. He lubricated the male ferrule of the tip by rubbing it on the wing of his nose, introduced it into the female ferrule of the butt and, sighting down the rod, rotated the sections to align their guides, then pushed them together. They mated easily, rather too easily, and giving the rod a flex, he detected a slight wobble in the joint. The fit of even the finest of them loosened with time and use. He would have to have the ferrules replaced during the winter, out of season. That was, if he did take up fishing again. Assembled, the rod came alive, became an extension of him, an antenna, its sensitive tip aquiver, amplifying the steady tremor of his hand.

He seated the reel and threaded the line through the guides. He clipped off the old leader and replaced it with a new one, gratified to find that despite the tremor of his hands he could still tie a blood knot.

"How we doing?" he asked himself.

"Doing all right but it's better not to ask," he answered himself.

Come what might, for now, the fussy little ritual of ready-ing for a day's fishing reined in the mind, kept it in a channel between narrow banks. He attached his landing net to its ring on his vest and slipped into the harness of his creel.

From the transparent plastic holder pinned to the back of his vest he took his last fishing license. According to it he was Benjamin Curtis of Blairstown, New Jersey, Age 48, Height 6-1, Weight 205, Eyes Brown, Hair Black. He tore it in pieces and let them fall. From between the folds of his wallet, as he spread it to get his new license, fell the unopened letter given to him last evening at the club. He picked it up and replaced it and returned the wallet to his pocket. The new license gave his address as Stone Ridge, New York, Age 50, Weight 170, Hair White.

*

Both licenses had been bought in the same place, Kelly's Sporting Goods Store in Chalfont, the nearest village to the club. His every fishing license for twenty years had been bought there. It had signaled the opening of trout season, stopping at Kelly's on the way in to buy their licenses. The occasion was made all the jollier by the sight of the Kelly brothers' faces, for twins tickle something in us, perhaps elating us with the feeling that for once nature has been tricked out of her stern rule that a person shall have but one lone self. There were two Kellys, but like the twin tracks that make a railroad, the brothers were indistinguishable and inseparable and their lives ran parallel. Rotund, redheaded, white-faced, they were as alike as two radishes. Time in its countdown did not differentiate them; the winter that had passed since you last saw them had put identical marks on both. Either of them could have gotten away with murder, his friend Tony had once said: no witness could have sworn which of them had done it. They made you feel like you were riproaring drunk and seeing double.

That was how it used to be, but those two licenses of his told how long it was now since he had last seen the Kellys, and told something of what the interim had done to him. The brothers were together behind their counter when he stopped at the store late yesterday afternoon. Their double-barreled smiles were for some stranger.

"It's Ben Curtis," he had had to say.

It had taken them only a moment to recover themselves but for that moment they were aghast. *Aghast:* it came from the same root word as *ghost,* and that was what they both looked as though they were seeing. And so they were. He had become an embarrassment, a scarecrow, a specter. He frightened people, reminding them that not even the bond between two who had developed from the same egg could bridge over life's intrinsic loneliness. That image of himself mirrored in people's faces he had grown accustomed to in these past months; it was seeing it in duplicate that was so

unsettling, hallucinatory. It was as though his eyes would not
focus, like looking at a stereo picture whose halves refused to
merge.

With one voice (on a tape recording they themselves could
never tell which of them was speaking) the brothers ex-
claimed, "Ben Curtis!" trying to make their discomposure
seem like unexpected pleasure. Ben Curtis, of course! It was
the beard that had put them off. Then came their quick, their
too-quick recovery: the facial readjustment, the forced
smiles, the loss for words—the marks of illness-at-ease he had
seen so often but now was seeing double. In their confusion
the brothers sought each other out of the corners of their
eyes. It was as though they were trying to become one again.

They could not know this, but the Kellys were as much of a
shock to him as he was to them. There had been a time—the
very time he was here now to try to forget—when everybody
was twins to him, and, before that, a time when he himself
was.

*

His reception at the club was the opposite of this, for having phoned ahead and been told that his membership had
been kept active even though his dues had gone unpaid, he
was expected there, and when he appeared downstairs in the
bar it was evident that Eddie, the manager, had warned the
other members what to expect on seeing him. Eddie would
have done this with no more than an expression of the face
accompanying the words "Ben Curtis is back," or at most
with a shake of the head, for the club's motto, etched in the
mirror behind the counter, was "Thumbs Up!" and it was
considered bad form to bring your troubles here with you or
to remind others of theirs. A fisherman's luck was bad enough
without some unfortunate bringing more. To this temple of
the fish and the fly, people came for the weekend as though
to a religious retreat, leaving behind them all worldly cares
and concerns. "Think Trout," said their bumper stickers.
They spent their days alone on their own sections of the
stream and when all assembled at the clubhouse in the eve-

ning the talk never strayed far from the sport. Touchy topics
were avoided or were quickly dropped or were broken up by
others. Should a dispute over politics, for instance, erupt at
the bar, the disputants were served one on the house, and as
he set them down Eddie pointed both thumbs up. It was a
reminder and something of a reprimand, and it was all that
was ever needed. Sometimes friendships developed that extended beyond the club, sometimes love affairs originated
there, but for the most part members knew, or cared to
know, little about one another except as weekend fishing
companions. Perhaps the cheerful atmosphere of the place
was owing to the superficiality of their involvement with one
another. This was not a bar at which to pour out your troubles
at home to the bartender or to the patron on the stool next to
yours. Of him, most of his fellow club members knew little
more than met the eye. To be sure, that in itself was enough
now to put a momentary damper upon the customary conviviality of the place, but in keeping with the motto in the
mirror it was also enough to stop them from inquiring into its
causes. No condolences here. Sympathy could be taken for
granted; meanwhile, a stiff upper lip was expected of all.
Whether he could keep his stiff now remained to be tested,
but the club's house rule, its code of conduct, had been a
factor in his decision to risk a return. Studiously unnoticed,
he felt like a ghost come back to the scene of its former life.

Time was when Eddie would have served him his usual
without waiting for an order. But now Eddie had either forgotten what his usual was or he was leery of anticipating the
wishes of a man so changed from what he remembered. It
was as he served him his drink that Eddie gave him the
letter. A year's yellowing and dust it displayed. He took a
glance at the postmark and the date and put it away in his
wallet unopened. That was the spirit! Eddie signified by giving him the old club sign.

Most members, like him, up for the weekend, had arrived
within the hour and were still dressed for town, but now as
day waned others dressed for fishing came in. There was a
drifting in and out to the porch where, as their owners drew

off waders and cranked wet socks through the old clothes
wringer mounted on the rail, fish were laid out and admired.
This was the season for the big hatches of mayflies, a different
variety every few days, rising from the water at dusk as thick
as the mist that would rise from it later, and these members
had stayed out to fish the evening rise. The dinner hour was
set late for them.

The talk at the bar was of the hatches, the water condi-
tions, of which sections of the stream had been most productive lately. The Pale Sulphur Dun was the fly for twilight
these past several days. Last Thursday in Section Eleven a
catch of thirty-four, five of them keepers, fish over a foot
long, had been recorded. Yet another member had hooked
and lost the big brown trout that lived in the pool behind
farmer Frank Kemp's house.

While he pretended to listen to all this he stole glances
through the doorway into the sitting room. Nothing had
changed since he last saw it. Nothing had changed since he
first saw it twenty and more years ago. Not just the mounted
fish hung on its paneled walls but the entire place had undergone a kind of total taxidermy that stopped its clock at the
date of its founding: 1900. Grand Rapids chairs of stamped
wood from the Sears, Roebuck catalogue of that year furnished the barroom. Over its doorways hung the same trophy
trout that had always hung there and on the wall beneath a
mammoth bamboo rod, the tool with which the grandfathers
of today's members had subdued such monsters, hung the
same placard of snelled flies, their tinsel tarnished, the colors
of their feathers faded, in gaudy, bygone patterns that had
fooled a simpler generation of trout than today's more heavily fished and warier ones. A crazy, cranky old place it was,
determinedly anachronistic, proudly run-down—what Tony
used to call classy discomfort.

It was the sitting room that was the picture gallery, and
without doubt the photographs on the walls were still the
ones that had always hung there, with some additions since
he last saw them, for life goes on, but with no removals, for
that was not permitted. "Thumbs Up!" was their common

theme, too, and sooner or later, if this test he was putting himself to was to be a test and prove anything, he would have to take a look at them. For now, having taken advantage of moments when heads were turned so that the shaking of his hand would not be noticed, he had drunk his allotted martini and was as ready as he would ever be for the terrace.

It was just as it had been on another June evening long ago, except that he was alone now and that made all the difference. Introduced and proposed for membership by Tony Thayer, whose grandfather had been one of the club's founders, he had belonged to it for only a couple of years then. He was still living in the city, still doing newspaper work, and taking every opportunity to get away to the country. The Thayers' daughter, Christy, his godchild, had been weaned and could now be left with others, so Tony and Pris and he and his guest, Cathy Warren, had left the city at daybreak and driven up, breakfasting by the roadside on the way. It was a Monday and they had the clubhouse to themselves.

Now it was the evening of their first day. They had come in earlier and had hung their waders and their rods in their racks, had entered their catch in the club's record book, had cleaned their fish and had a drink, then gone upstairs to change and now they were down again for another drink before supper here on the terrace overlooking the stream. Then as now the rays of the setting sun turned the water to molten gold. In the shadows fireflies flickered and the chorusing of the first frogs of the evening was like the tinkling of innumerable tiny bells. The ladies were sitting, Tony and he standing at the parapet looking out, and when together they turned around he had felt that the moment, with these people, here in this place, was one he wanted to prolong for life.

He said, "Cathy."

She had looked up at him and it was like a flower lifting its head to the sun and, with her smile, blossoming.

"Marry me, will you?"

"Just name the day," she said.

"Be quick, Ben!" said Tony. "Before she has second thoughts."

"Yes, Ben, be quick!" Cathy said. "But as for second thoughts, I've had them already."

She had not minded his proposing to her publicly like this, for the public was Tony and she knew the depth of their feeling for each other. She was as proud to proclaim her acceptance as he was to claim her. She knew that this was not entirely the impulse of a moment. She had been kept waiting a good while for this and she had not minded that either. She knew he wanted to be sure of himself and of her, for he meant to marry only once.

Tony led them inside to the record book. Scratching out the 6 that he, Ben, had entered as his catch for the day, he made it 7. When he laid down the pen Cathy took it, scratched out her 3 and made it 4. This was preserved in the book for that year along with the others on the shelves going back to 1900.

They had all four been on the steps of the county courthouse before it opened its doors the following morning to buy the marriage license. They fished away the days of waiting. Here on the terrace Cathy and he had vowed before a local minister to love and to cherish one another till death did them part. Champagne had flowed like the stream below, and full of it, Tony, the best man, brought a blush to the bride's cheeks with his supplication, "Lord, bless this union of thy servants Benjamin and Catherine, and send them, we pray thee, an evening rise."

In just a week and a day their silver wedding anniversary was coming up.

Where was she now? he wondered as the bell summoned him to supper.

*

"Lazarus, come forth!" the bell cried to him with a loud voice.

"Lazarus stinketh, for he hath been dead four days," he said to himself.

He tarried on the terrace to give his fellow club members time to drain their drinks and go to the dining room and seat themselves without having to feel that they must invite him to join them at their tables.

Not all, but enough about him and his affairs was known here to force a role upon him. Before making his entrance he composed his face into a suitable expression. A delicate balance must be struck. He must look undaunted but not unfeeling. He must show that he had buried his dead but that he had not forgotten them. He must respond to smiles with a smile but not with a broad one; he must respond to looks of commiseration with a grateful look but not with one that pleaded for more. Even to people familiar with only a part of his story, like these here, he would be viewed with a combination of curiosity and caution of which he would be conscious every moment but of which he must appear to be unconscious. He believed he was up to this now. He believed he could show a brave face to the world. Unfortunately he could do nothing about the ravage to that face which aroused suspicions of there being even more to his story than was common knowledge.

The bar, its countertop covered with empty and half-empty glasses, was deserted. He passed through it and went down the hall to the dining room. It was not the pain of entering it for the first time alone or with nobody awaiting him there that arrested him on the doorsill—the pain would come later; at first it was the novelty of it. Forgotten were the attitude and the expression to suit it that he had so carefully rehearsed. Not since his troubles all began had he been among people, and to his long disused and still oversensitive organs the talk and the laughter, the lights, the glitter were a shock. He stood at the door dazed and irresolute. The pain of remembering Cathy made him yearn toward a happiness in which he had once shared. Old associations momentarily obliterated present realities: he forgot who he was now and remembered who he had been for so long—one like these, here on a holiday, surrounded by his family and his friends. It was lucky for him that he went unnoticed. Anyone seeing him there with that smile on his face would have thought him a monster of forgetfulness, morally and emotionally deficient.

He had already been served when Ruth Rogers appeared at his table. For a moment he thought that one of his secrets was out and that he was now to experience the mockery of being considered "eligible." The possibility of his patient's being exposed to a widow or two his own age had been the one aspect of this outing that his doctor approved of.

"Alone this evening?" Ruth asked.

"Every evening," he replied, though to himself, not aloud. Aloud he said, "Yes. I'm not very good company, I'm afraid, but won't you join me?"

"Cathy's not with you?"

She asked it disbelievingly. So she did not know. In this there was some relief, more painful irony. Ruth was one of those—like himself—who supposed that after what they had been through together Cathy and he could never again bear to be apart for a moment.

"No," he said. "Not this trip."

He helped seat her. He had forgotten the scent close up of a woman's fragrance and it dizzied him like a lungful of smoke after long abstinence. He seated himself. The waitress came and set another place.

"Don't wait for me," said Ruth, indicating his dinner. But he did wait, and she said, "It's good to see you here again, Ben. We've missed you." She was letting him know that she for one did not think it improper for a man who had been through what he had to want to enjoy life once again.

He thanked her. Said it was good to be back.

She said, "Actually I may not be coming back anymore myself after this."

"Oh?"

When she had been served she explained. "An old friend has recently proposed to me, and he's no fisherman—hates the thought. Besides, he lives out in Oregon. That all makes it sound like I've said yes to him, doesn't it? I haven't. But neither have I said no. If he asks me again—well, I'm not sure what I'll say."

"You're here to find out."

"Yes. Yes, I am," she said, wondering at his perception.

"Do you love him?"

"Love," she mused. "I'm not sure I know what it's supposed to feel like the second time around. Different from the first, I guess. I like him a lot. He's a good man. He says he loves me."

He looked around the room, then back at her and said, "This place meant a lot to your Jack."

"Yes," she said, and with her eyes expressed her gratitude for his understanding.

He understood that she wanted not to cheat this suitor of hers, not shortchange him. Her whole heart he could not expect, it was not hers anymore to give, but she wanted to make sure she was giving all she had left, not holding back any part of it. In this place that had meant much to her Jack she was hoping to commune with his spirit and either lay it to rest or else live in its thrall.

Which outcome she foresaw, her next words revealed. "When I lost him I vowed I would never marry again. But as I needn't tell you, Ben, life goes on."

She wanted confirmation of that. Wanted it particularly from him.

"Yes," he said. "Life goes on."

"And as I also needn't tell you, it helps to have someone to face it with."

In that, too, she wanted him to second her.

He managed somehow to say it helped to have someone to face it with.

With a sigh that had in it some regret but rather more complacency, she said, "I'll miss this old place. I was never all that keen on fishing but it was always fun to be here." She was fairly confident that her Jack's ghost, when she encountered it somewhere along the stream tomorrow, would let her off the hook, give her the old club sign, "Thumbs Up!" He hoped it did. A woman, he thought, could change her name—more than once. There was a boost toward getting a fresh start in life.

"It was a wonderful place for the boys when they were growing—Oh, Ben! How thoughtless of me! How could I? I'm so sorry. Oh, I could bite my tongue off!"

"Save it to say 'I do' another time. And of the first may you remember what you want to remember and forget what you want to forget."

To himself he said, "Do as I say, not as I do."

*

After supper, in the game room, the bridge and backgammon regulars were at it. From the poolroom came the click and clatter of the balls. In the sitting room women knitted, plied their petitpoint needles while sipping coffee and chatting together. Seated at the vise on the table in the corner a flytier had drawn a circle of onlookers. He remembered a fellow club member's once asking whether Tony and he tied their own flies out of season. That was before their son and godson began supplying them with his flies, but even then their answer had been no. For them there had been no out of season. Their year was a succession of sporting seasons, with closing day for one soon followed by opening day for another: salmon, grouse, ducks, deer.

He felt obliged to put in an appearance in the bar. Life went on; one paid one's dues by demonstrating that it did. Here was a good place to do it. Thumbs Up! Here he was safe from sympathy.

The looks the patrons turned on him showed him his mistake. The atmosphere of the bar had undergone a change; the falling barometer on the wall seemed to be its gauge. He had ventured into the very vale of tears just waiting for someone to shed them over. The weekend bachelors enjoying an evening free from their wives' supervision had arrived at a state of emotional unsteadiness, their sang-froid had thawed, and emanations reaching him from several of them made him feel they would be willing to exempt him from the strict application of the club's code, his being such a special case, and that they felt he was wishing they would. When one of them detached himself from the bar and tacked toward him he took refuge on the terrace. To be shunned by sober men was painful, to be sought out by maudlin ones was worse. It seemed it was to be his lot now to endure both.

A breeze had risen and set the trees sighing. Above the everlasting murmur of the stream the first of the evening's chorus of peepers was tentatively tuning up. The light from the barroom mixed milkily with the mist rising off the water as it cooled in the chill of the night. Overhead a half moon shone and the sky to the north was sprinkled with stars but to the south it was black and the blackness was spreading rapidly northward. The quickening breeze now carried the smell, or rather the absence of smells, of approaching rain. A first, far-distant rumble of thunder was like the yawn of some awakening beast of prey about to begin its nightly prowl. The barometer of his disposition was beginning its nightly fall, only tonight it was falling faster as his quickening memories marshaled like a gathering storm.

He felt on his forehead the first, premonitory raindrop and he went inside. As he passed through the barroom, Eddie, from behind the counter, said, "Good night, Mr. Curtis. And" —holding out a fist, thumb up—"welcome back."

He faltered only for an instant. "Thanks," he said, and to all he nodded good-night.

Passing the door of the room in which his wedding night had been spent, he considered this latest evidence of the changes in himself and of the wariness with which he must expect now to be treated. Eddie and he had called each other by their first names for years.

In his room, the duplicate in every detail of the one he had just passed, as flashes of lightning drew nearer and more frequent, he studied his reflection in the mirror. He recited to himself these verses:

> I look into my glass
> And view my wasted skin,
> And say, "Would God it came to pass
> My heart had shrunk as thin!"

For then, I, undistrest
By hearts grown cold to me,
Could lonely wait my endless rest
With equanimity.

But time, to make me grieve,
Part steals, lets part abide;
And shakes this fragile frame at eve
With throbbings of noontide.

*

The mist was lifting from the mountains now. From their
wooded slopes it rose in plumes like smoke from scattered
breakfast campfires. The moment had come for him to make
a decision. Whether to overhaul his long-neglected vest,
thereby delaying the fishing, or to start fishing, thereby delaying, or at least taking on one at a time, the memories
which the contents of the vest were sure to stir. A fly-fisher-
man's vest contained more things than a boy's pants pockets.
Even from the outside of it there dangled on strings a tackle
shop in miniature: nail clippers, folding scissors (a gift from
Tony, those), a surgeon's hemostat used to disgorge hooks
from fishes' mouths, the bottle of dope for making dry flies
float. His vest had been put away with no expectation of its
ever being used again and never looked at in all the time
since. That in its many pockets he carried on him an album of
images in the form of flies and gadgets, he knew, and in the
course of the day—if he stuck it out—he would, willy-nilly,
turn the pages of that album one by one. Better that, though,
than to turn them now all at once. Do that, and he might get
no further, as he had almost gotten no further than cleaning
out his locker earlier this morning at the club. The contem-
plative man's recreation, fishing's patron saint Izaak had
called it; well, contemplation was what he was here to get
away from. He must try to make this just a day's fishing,
forgetting the other days, especially the last one, telling himself that since then much water had flowed over the dam,
under the bridge, and other such threadbare phrases with
which people tried to cloak themselves against the sharpness

of fresh sensations and the chronic, incurable ache of memory.

Yet no matter how he tried, there would be no getting away from the knowledge that, as a pregnant woman was said to be eating for two, he would be fishing today for three. The consciousness of that had been with him since the inception of this outing. If it struck him now with the force of a fresh realization it was because he was here, actually here. Against his own belief—maybe against his better judgment—certainly against his doctor's, whose opposition was not because of his allergy to insect bites—he was here. That was not to say he was bound to stick it out. His room at the clubhouse might be reserved for the entire weekend but he could quit and leave at any time and be breaking no promises. He had made none, neither to himself nor to either of the ghosts he bore within him. Enough for now that he had made it this far. He was here—what was left of him. Now he must just trust to the current to bear him along. By going with it this morning maybe he would be able to go against it this afternoon. Get through one day and maybe it would be succeeded by another.

He donned his hair shirt, his many-pocketed vest heavy with reminders, and then, as in a dream, his felt-soled wading shoes making footfalls so silent he seemed to himself weightless, he crossed the meadow to the woods and the water, following his disappearing, reappearing feet through the fog blanketing the ground. The anthology of verse he carried in his mind supplied him with Spenser's lines:

> A foggy mist had covered all the land;
> And underneath their feet, all scattered lay
> Dead souls and bones of men,
> Whose lives had gone astray.

*

The club's ten miles of water was apportioned into twenty sections. A member's section, or his guest's, was his for the day. Customarily it was over breakfast, with much Alphonsing and Gastoning, that sections were assigned. Today, however, he had left the clubhouse before anybody else was up. As he pondered the assignment sheet his eyes disregarded his warning and he saw the newly hung frame on the wall above the desk. It contained, mounted on a card, a coiled leader to which a fly was attached and with the inscription "Tony Thayer/His Last Cast." The angler in him noted that when his friend hung up his rod at the end of that day the fly he had been using was the Gray Fox Variant. He put his name down for Section Seven. Not because he had overheard at the bar the evening before that it had been productive lately but because it was there that he had been fishing the last time. If today was to be a test then let it be one.

In its course the club's water changed its character several times. It was half a day's steep climb—he had done it once—to its source in a spring high on the mountainside above the clubhouse. At the start a mere trickle, fed by other springs and runoffs the stream soon swelled in size. Growing swift and burly, it carved gorges through solid rock. About halfway down the mountain it became a brook trout brook, and maybe it was the deeply evergreen-shaded water and the dark depths of it in which they lived and had adapted themselves to, or maybe it was the invigorating rigor of existence in those icy rapids, whatever the cause, the fish from there were uniquely pronounced in the brilliance and depth of their coloration, looking at all times of the year like other brook trout looked only in their spawning colors in the fall. Lapidary they were. To hold one fresh out of water and still glistening in your hand made you think of gemstones and goldsmithing, of cloisonné, of glazed polychrome porcelain.

The clubhouse pool with its concrete spillway placed upon the stream its first restraint and the leveling of the land below the pool further slowed and smoothed it. Over the next mile the water was stepped down over a series of log dams. A parklike stand of copper beeches bordered this stretch, and there, early in the morning, a fisherman sometimes caught his breath and froze at the sight of a deer at the water's edge, a shape only slightly darker gray than the enveloping atmosphere, so immaterial it seemed the ghost of a deer come to haunt the grove where it had died.

Once out of the shadow of the woods and in the sunlight the stream turned leisurely, meandering through meadowland, pausing in pools. Still cold, the water here was a few degrees warmer than it was higher up and the colder-blooded brook trout mostly left it to the more tolerant browns. The grassy banks were dotted with hawthorn, alders, osiers. Blue irises and yellow irises bloomed at the water's edge here early in the season; later on, cardinal flowers attracted hummingbirds to their scarlet stars. Nesting pairs of mallards burst off this water or the hen threshed the surface in her takeoff feigning a broken wing to lure the fisherman away from her hidden brood.

He had his favorites among the sections of the stream but he had made it a rule to fish all the other sections too. This had kept those favorites from becoming overly familiar to him, had made him study and master different types of water, to calculate where trout would choose to be in them and how best to approach their lie. Thus over the years he had gotten to know the entire stream. During his year away from it, on nights when he lay awake in bed, he had retraced it, sometimes from the top down, sometimes from the bottom up, recalling as closely as he could individual trees, boulders, shallows and pools, bends where the bank was undercut, fish he had caught and fish he had hooked and lost.

Section Seven was approached through a hemlock-covered hillside on its east. The shadowiness of the woods and the silence of his footfalls on the dead hemlock needles, the lingering reflection of himself in the eyes of the Kelly brothers and those of his fellow club members, the contradictory combination of familiarity and strangeness in finding himself here again, made it seem as though all this was from a former life, as indeed it was, and brought a sensation now grown frequent with him: a momentary disbelief in his own reality. He often caught such glimpses of himself, as though he had stepped outside his body and saw himself with eyes other than his own. Often it brought on this dizziness requiring

that he steady himself against something solid. At such times
the yearlong hiatus in his life seemed like a trance, a walking
sleep.

He reached the water's edge and stood looking upstream
and down. Just before stilling into a long, deep, and dark
pool, the water bubbled, effervescent, like champagne. Beneath the sweeping boughs of the hemlocks, their roots in
the current, tall rhododendrons grew in a tangle as thick as
mangroves in the tropics. They were coming into bloom
now. Vivid against its dark green, almost black leaves, each
pink-white cluster was a bouquet in itself.

Afraid to explore his pockets, he found what he needed
now by feeling the outside of his vest. It was a fly box. With
trembling hands he raised the lid and it was like opening
Pandora's box. Man-made imitations of insects though these
were, for him they were as menacing as a nest of hornets, the
sting of association in each and every one of them.

Even after a year's absence from it the stream bred memories in him as it did the mayflies that hatched as nymphs from
its bed and swam to the surface, metamorphosed and took
flight in swarms. One now reached the surface of his mind. It
came as he was choosing a fly. With that one, the Gold-ribbed
Hare's Ear, he had hooked and fought the biggest brown
trout of his life. His Anthony, his and Cathy's, Tony's godson,
had tied that fly, had been the witness to his fight with the
fish.

How some they have died, and some they have left me,
And some are taken from me; all are departed;
All, all are gone, the old familiar faces.

Maybe his doctor was right: he ought not to take up fishing
again. For him it was a dangerous recreation, fraught with
too many memories of a life now lost. Already he had been
stung repeatedly on this outing and not by insects, as his
doctor, who was not an allergist but rather an analyst, had
warned him he would be. But he had not really been talking
about insects either when he replied that the world was full

of them and that to live in it a man had to take his chances—
better to go out that way than to go on neither dead nor alive.

As for that fish, he had known from the instant of their
contact that it was no ordinary one. In the shake of its head
transmitted to him through the line there had been magiste-
rial disbelief in this effrontery. He struck and set the hook
and it was his turn to disbelieve when he felt the fish's
weight. What that was he could only approximate, for of
course, like all the big ones, the fish had gotten away, but not
before a fight lasting twenty minutes while Anthony, in his
waders, chased it toward him upstream and down. With a last
paroxysm of power it broke free at the landing net, leaving
him limp with excitement and disappointment. He did not
choose the Gold-ribbed Hare's Ear today. He was unlikely
ever to hook another such fish but if he should he had no
Anthony to help him now.

He had been left with a slight impairment of his vision,
which, when the operation was one as delicate as threading a
4X monofilament leader through the eye of a number 14
trout fly, not even his new half-moon spectacles could entirely correct. Even with one eye shut it was still two gossa-
mer strands he was trying to put through two pinholes, and
the effort was not made easier by that other lingering legacy
of his troubles, the incessant, ungovernable trembling of his
hands.

> But yield who will to their separation,
> My object in living is to unite
> My avocation and my vocation
> As my two eyes make one in sight.

The halves of his divided world had almost reunited now—
at least they had moved closer together again than when
they were split asunder into separate, identical worlds—but
still, displaced slightly to one side of everything he saw was its
simulacrum.

Finally he succeeded in tying on the fly and then at last he
was ready to take the plunge. The shock of the icy water on
his feet and legs sufficed to dispel from his mind those trou-

blesome words of Frost's *my object in living*. He noted that
the rain in the night had not been enough to muddy the
stream or raise its level appreciably. Should he stick to his
plan and work his way back upstream this afternoon that
would make for good, meaning demanding, dry-fly fishing.

He stood absorbing the chill as it rose upward beyond the
water level and waiting for the old thrill to rise in him, to see
whether it would once again. For half his lifetime this had
been for him the rites of spring. The poet who said that April
—when trout season opened—was the cruelest month, was
no fisherman. January, February, and March, when earth was
covered in forgetful snow, when streams were still and there
was not much hunting or none at all, that was his *morte
saison*. In April the streams threw off their ceremental lids
and purled once again. Two thirds of the trout in them would
have been winter-killed but that remnant third survived to
perpetuate their kind. The insects buried in the river bot-
toms stirred and rose to the surface and the trout rose to
them and he rose to the trout, coming out of hibernation to
find them still there and himself still there with them. Here
he was once again but now his sap ran sluggish.

Sunlight struck the tops of the hemlocks making the raindrops among their needles scintillate like a shower of emeralds and providing him with illumination to scan the surface
of the long quiet pool with which Section Seven began for
any hatch of insects there. Not that he would have known
which of his many flies to match it with if he were to see a
hatch, unless it was one of the half-dozen commonest vari-
eties. How his by-guess and by-gosh approach to fly-fishing
had exasperated Anthony! A fisherman for so much shorter a
time than his father, Anthony could nevertheless tell you the
Latin name and which of your artificials to imitate it with for
any of the myriad insects the stream bred.

Between the two schools of fly-fishing, as in everything
else, there was a generation gap. He never knew it until
Anthony told him, but he was a presentationist. To him the
important thing was not the pattern of the fly so much as it
was the accuracy and the delicacy with which it was pre-

sented to the fish. Oh, even his sort recognized that there were times when your artificial had to be realer than the thing itself if it was to fool the fish into taking it instead of one of the swarms of naturals coming off the water. But most of the time he relied not upon the exactness of his imitation but upon his skill in stalking the fish and casting the fly. When Anthony called him a presentationist he was calling him an old fogy.

Anthony was an imitationist. He was one of the new breed of scientific anglers. With the same intensity he applied to everything, he had plunged into the vast field of trout stream entomology. Not that he was any the less skillful in presenting his fly for all that, but when he did so it was as near a copy as could be made from fur, feathers, and tinsel of the one he had caught on the wing and identified out of the hundreds known to him. The demon of encyclopedic knowledge had always beset that boy. He would, if you insisted, tie and sell you a gaudy Royal Coachman imitative of nothing in nature like the one his entomologically innocent father had just selected, but he would both pity and scorn you.

Well! If presentation was what he must rely upon, then Lord help him! His first cast of the day looked like his first ever. The line fell upon the water like a serving of spaghetti. It was not that the line was kinky. It had been but he had attended to that. Wound on the spool of the reel, long un-used, it had been coiled like a spring when he removed it last night. Looking for something to occupy himself with at the witching time when churchyards yawn and hell itself breathes forth contagion to this world, he had dressed the line and looped it loosely on pegs on the clubhouse porch to relax and straighten. The kinks were in him. It was years since he had made so sloppy a cast. Instead of annoying him it tickled him. It tickled him so he laughed aloud. His inexpert-ness had carried him back momentarily to an earlier, more carefree time in his life. Then he stood listening to the silence as though for the call of some uncommon bird to be repeated and identified. It took a while for him to realize that the once familiar, now forgotten sound had been that of his own laughter.

*

By one o'clock in the morning it had been evident that this was turning into another of his nights. As drugs to induce sleep were forbidden to him, the passing of the eye of the storm was his signal to get up and in his pajamas creep downstairs so as not to disturb the slumbers of his fellow club members whose tranquil snores penetrated their bedroom doors. He knew what he would find downstairs, but the reality was no more to be dreaded than his lone pillow thoughts about it. The reality, being real, and thus suggestive at least of other, alternative realities, would even be preferable.

Not memories but moisture and mosquitoes kept him from the terrace now. Light from a single lamp illuminated the barroom. The door stood open and through the screen door fog had drifted in from outside and deepened the murkiness. He drew himself a mug of beer from the tap and marked it down on his long-inactive charge account. He sipped it slowly, for he had a long wait for the dawn.

The peepers had multiplied and now the night belonged to them. Their drone was pierced at fixed intervals by a screech owl uttering its long-drawn, broken, all-too-human-sounding sob. It was a nocturne he knew. He too was one acquainted with the night. On many like this one he had walked out in the rain and back in the rain, outwalked the furthest city light, looked down the saddest city lane, and passed the watchman on his beat and dropped his eyes, unwilling to explain. He had stood still and stopped the sound of feet when far away an interrupted cry came over houses from another street, but not to call him back or say good-bye.

He sipped his beer and listened to the patter of the raindrops from the leaves of the trees and the distant rush of the water over the spillway of the pond, the steady trill of the frogs, the ululation of the owl like a banshee prophesying doom, and when his mug was either half empty or half full he wondered which was better, to have had sound sleep at

night, appetite and good digestion, love, friendship, father-
hood, if only for a while, or was the pain of losing them such
that it would have been better never to have known them?
According to the poet, it was better to have loved and lost
than never to have loved at all, and he supposed that went for
all of life's blessings, to none of which had we any claim or
assurance of, but it was like asking a man deafened and
blinded in midlife whether he would not rather have been
born that way. Having heard Mozart, having seen a sunrise
and Chartres cathedral and the paintings of Picasso, one
could cherish the memory, but not without pangs of regret if
one must do so in silence and darkness that would never
again admit them.

> Oft in the stilly night
> Ere Slumber's chain has bound me,
> Fond Memory brings the light
> Of other days around me.

No other spot had for him more fond memories of other
days than this one, but to complete that very verse:

> The words of love then spoken;
> The eyes that shone
> Now dimmed and gone,
> The cheerful hearts now broken!

This unlikely hour was the one at which he knew the barroom best, though not as now, alone in it. After everyone else
had said good-night and gone upstairs, after Eddie had rinsed
and dried the last glass and mopped the countertop and left
them, Tony and he had sat here talking oft and late in the
stilly night. Tony had begrudged time lost in sleep, and when
with Tony so had he. In those days, before their troubles
began, the two of them had always met bubbling over with
news for each other, questions to ask, books to recommend,
jaunts to plan, amusing encounters to relate, nuggets of non-
sense to share. The one would learn the latest sayings, interests, and accomplishments of his godson, the other those of
his goddaughter. So as not to disturb the sleepers overhead

they spoke low, and that quiet and intent intimacy was a part
of his recollection of those nights. Tony was not only a good
talker himself, he made a better one of you. When, often at
an hour later than this, they switched off the last light and
climbed the stairs to their sleeping wives, he went always
with the afterglow of a stimulating conversational workout. If
only he could recall now some of the many sparkling sayings
he had been sure he would never forget! Good things in
abundance cheapened themselves; where so many came
from there would always be more. Now for company in the
night he had the peepers and the owl.

His thoughts turned—no stopping them—to a night that
he had not spent here with Tony. A night under this roof but
not in the bar. Another June night but one with no threat of a
storm, another sleepless, long night but one not nearly long
enough. His wedding night. The words of love then spoken,
the eyes that shone, the cheerful hearts, now broken . . .

The days of their banns had brought the week to Thursday.
The Friday would bring an influx of other members and their
guests for the weekend, but for the wedding ceremony and
the supper afterwards their little party still had the clubhouse to themselves. There in the sitting room he, his best
man, and the minister had waited for the bride and her
bridesmaid to come downstairs. She wore the cameo brooch
that had been Eddie's grandmother's and the wristwatch
they together had bought her just that morning, a pearl neck-
lace borrowed from Pris, and a blouse the blue of her shining
eyes. She carried a bouquet of lilies of the valley gathered in
the locust grove beyond the pond, and whenever in later
years he looked at Tony's wedding picture of them hanging
on the wall here he smelled again their heady, hypnotic
perfume. Pris played the wedding march on the old upright
piano and then joined them on the terrace for the service
and the exchange of vows and of rings—to avoid embarrass-
ing observations he was wearing his now, although now, following his loss of weight and the thinning of his fingers, he
could, for the first time in years, slip it off. The cook had
produced a wedding cake. After supper a conspiracy of

thoughtfulness and delicacy had emptied the place. The kitchen staff had hurried through their cleaning up and betaken themselves home, Eddie had given himself the night off, the Thayers had chosen a distant section of the stream to fish the evening rise, and now at nightfall the newlyweds had it all to themselves. So determinedly out of this world, care banished, pleasure decreed, it was the perfect hideaway for a honeymoon. Cathy declared she would not have exchanged it for any other.

The sun had shed over everything its last alchemical glow and then withdrawn, the dusk drew around them its sheltering curtain. By moving her things into his room, their first domestic arrangement, they transformed it into their room. The early nightcap he mixed for them was not entered on the charge account; at Eddie's insistence, everything was on the house tonight. He put a record on the phonograph and counted his blessings while, to the sobbing of saxophones and the keening of clarinets, Frank Sinatra lamented his lucklessness in love. For him there *were* friends waiting to throw shoes and rice. He was thankful for the hours she'd blessed, but thankful that *he* wouldn't have to dream the rest. The fullness of each moment made it seem that time had stopped to attend upon them. A moon the color of honey beamed down on the flagstones of the terrace. Their hymeneal, the multimyriad murmur of the peepers, with no discordant owl to screech that night, was like some sustained celestial hum, like the voices of the stars, of which the sky was so brim full that the fireflies flickering in the shadows seemed to be a shower of them fallen from the superfluity.

"Alone at last, Mrs. Curtis," he said.

"Mrs. Curtis. Mrs. Curtis. Mrs. Curtis." She seemed to turn the name one way and another so that its facets might all sparkle like a gem. "That's me. Mrs. Curtis. That's my name. I've been trying it on myself all afternoon but you're the first person to call me by it. Oh, dear, I hope I'm not about to spoil things by crying."

"It will take a little getting used to," he said.

"Mmh, but already I like the sound of it," she said.

"Maybe it will seem more like your own when it's something more than just a name," he said.

"Yes," she agreed, then, comprehending his meaning, colored so deeply it was visible by moonlight.

He took her drink from her, set it beside his on the parapet, and there they left them, unfinished.

Upstairs he swept her off her feet and carried her over the threshold, marveling to himself at her tininess, and then feeling some apprehension over it. She closed the door behind them and he set her down. As he undid her buttons, unzipped her zipper, she said, "I feel like a present being unwrapped. I hope I'm what you were wanting."

"You are a present," he said. "And just what I've always wanted."

She closed the distance he had put between them so as to admire her, took him in her bare arms, and with her lips just touching his, said, "I shouldn't tell you, but you needn't have waited for this until now, you know. I could never have resisted you. Does that make me sound like a wanton woman?"

"I'm counting on your being wanton, woman," he said. Then, "Thank you for saying that, my love. It was knowing I didn't have to wait that made me want to."

"Thank you, my love, for saying that," she said.

*

Two boys it was who met in the clubhouse kitchen late that night. Two boys on the same errand, appetites aroused by their exertions in satisfying another one, there to raid the icebox for a midnight snack, both in their pajamas, each barefoot so as not to disturb the other. Two men it was who, minutes later, returned upstairs together, each bearing his offering on a tray.

Like boys caught in some midnight mischief they had grinned guiltily and leered at each other and then simultaneously both had sobered, sensing something unworthy of them as husbands, something disloyal and degrading to the wives waiting for them overhead, in that suggestion of male clubhouse smuttiness. So much could pass in a look, so much more in a look reconsidered and revised on the spot, within the blinking of an eye. In just that fraction of time he felt he had been admitted into another of his friend's clubs, with all the privileges and all the duties of membership.

*

Oft in the stilly night now time came to a stop. Clocks, like the one on the wall here—where every effort was made to put a stop to time—ticked on, their hands advanced, but for him the night stood still. It passed for those asleep and unconscious of its passage. He got up now to limber his stiffened joints and he shook his head like shaking a watch to make it run. In the sitting room another lamp burned low. By its soft radiance he could see the big mounted fish hanging over the mantelpiece. He had been present to witness that one caught. There was a fond memory of other days when cheerful hearts were still unbroken.

As an angler Tony Thayer had been complete. He knew intimately the ways of his wily prey, was versed in stream entomology, could cast like a tournament champion, and he was blessed with that without which all these talents and attainments would have been for nought: he was lucky. It was not to detract from his skill to say that in fishing, as in everything else, Tony was lucky. Take the affair of that big trout in the clubhouse pool—or formerly of that address, now in everlasting repose here on its plaque above the sitting room mantelpiece. No peer of the dusty leviathans hanging over the barroom doors, to be sure. Those harked back to the days of yore. Their like would not be seen again, no more than would the men of mighty mold who had hung them there. But for these mean modern times Tony's was a big fish.

Big when first reported, he had for years been getting bigger, as though he throve on all the threats against him and the vain attempts upon his life, until now he was the length of a fire log and had a maw like an alligator. It had been resolved in solemn session that the health and future of their pond depended upon the fish's being removed forthwith,

before he cannibalized every other fish in it including those
of his own get, but so much water had flowed over the dam
since then that sons of club members were becoming members themselves and still the fish declined all inducements to
self-destruct and by now his brain was a computer pro-
grammed with every pattern of artificial fly ever to come
from the tier's vise plus projections of the permutations still
possible using the world's available materials. They tried for
him without expectation of outwitting him but just so as to
keep any fellow member from chancing to do so, and each
was content not to catch him as long as none of the others did.
For although they cursed him and denounced his wicked-
ness, the truth was he was their pet, their mascot; they admired the old reprobate and didn't really care how many of
their smaller fish he ate, were glad to have him to talk about,
were thrilled whenever he allowed them a glimpse of himself, and would miss him when he was gone. The place would
not be the same without Old Jumbo.

The season that Tony did it, the club's determination to
catch the fish ceased to be sporadic and halfhearted and
became a mania, a fixation. Even the sacrosanct and inviolable rule, their First Commandment, THOU SHALT FISH WITH
ARTIFICIAL FLY AND WITH ARTIFICIAL FLY ONLY, carved
upon their brains as though in stone, was waived.

"Spinning rods and lures are permissible," a heresy there-
tofore unspeakable within those walls, one punishable by
expulsion without even a hearing, was now openly urged by
one and all. "Minnows! Mice! Frogs! Night crawlers!" they
clamored, shuddering, and their voices rising in shock at
themselves. "Anything to get him out of there!"

In reality the fish was doing no more depredation than
they had winked at for years and they knew it. The flurry to
catch him came about because he was getting old, this season
might be his last, and being sportsmen, they wanted not to
see him go to waste by dying a natural death and thereby
furnishing sport to nobody.

One Sunday afternoon in August—the least likely month of
the season as the hour was the least likely of the day—as

members were packing their cars for the drive home, Tony, himself ready to go and only waiting for their wives, using an unsuitably light rod and a leader with the finest of tippets, both revelatory of how unprepared he was for what happened, made an idle cast and watched the fish float up from the depths of the pool, growing bigger by the moment, to inspect his offering as he had done countless times before only to spurn it and sink from sight again. The water that windless day was low, clear, and still, enabling the fish to detect even more easily the deception being practiced upon him, and the fly was one with which he was so wearily familiar that to present it to him again was nothing less than an insult. Known after its inventor as the Wulff, it had been a great killer, adopted by anglers everywhere, cast upon the world's every accessible inch of trout water, and there was scarcely a fish living that had not fallen for it, once. A close imitation of nothing in nature, it looked more like a moth than anything else. Unlike mayflies, moths make motions on the water, and it was this that prompted Tony that day to try giving his fly the tiny twitch, as though it were about to take flight, which provoked the fish into taking it before it should get away.

Instead of raising his rod and rousing the fish's resistance, Tony promptly lowered it. To do that took a denial of the angler's every instinct, but by doing it the pressure and the panic were taken off the fish. But for a prick lingering somewhere inside his mouth he could hardly have known that he was still hooked. So as to be less visible and thus less alarming to the fish, Tony sank slowly to his knees, come what might to his white flannel trousers. On this signal, as though they were his congregation and he their priest, every member of the audience already beginning to gather promptly knelt. In this prayerful posture was the contest fought and witnessed to its finish.

And they were as hushed and reverent as though silently at prayer. None had the presumption to offer advice. They were there to observe a master, or rather, a match between two masters: the fish, the idol of their common cult, and the man performing, the celebrant of the rite that bound them together.

But although Tony's was the textbook treatment of a fish that size, and although it sometimes worked by sapping the strength of the fish so insidiously he never knew it until too late, he was tied now to one that seemed to have read the book, one not to be finessed and finagled that way. This fish suspected that a sneaky attempt was being made to abridge his freedom, sensed that he had something foreign embedded in his palate, and was determined to rid himself of it instanter. Maybe he even knew he had drawn a gallery and felt called upon to show his mettle.

He was a brown trout, one of that breed that takes to the air to fight its battles, unlike the brookie which burrows when hooked. Now with first a bulge then with a burst of spray he broke the surface and rose out of water to his full length like a performing porpoise leaping for a reward. Luck was with Tony that day. Four times the fish showed himself in all his spotted splendor, in his multicolored coat of mail, threshing on air, and still the hook held. Again and again he dove to the depths and there stubbornly sulked, and still the leader withstood the strain. He gained the sanctuary of a sunken log only to find when he confidently quit it a quarter of an hour later that he was still in tow. For one who had had so little practice in them he knew all the tricks and he tried them every one. And he never surrendered. When he was netted at last and laid on the grass he needed no coup de grâce. He was dying. He could not have been revived and released even if that had been the common will, as well it might have been, of those who now rose stiffly from their knees and gathered around and in respectful silence looked down at him with bowed heads.

What they had witnessed was a demonstration of angling virtuosity, yet none of them but had tried for the fish themselves, many with the very same fly, and as Tony was the first to admit, his taking it that day had been pure luck. Forgetting what they above all should have kept always uppermost in mind, that without luck no fish is ever landed, they agreed.

They were used to saying that about Tony. He was born lucky and he had had the best life had to offer. Perhaps that was why, when his luck changed, he had been unprepared for it, or been unwilling to settle for anything less than life's best.

*

Fishing was in Tony Thayer's blood. His town, the old town of Hudson, New York, had been home port for his great-grandfather's fleet of whaling ships. That Thayer, Jason, had been among the last of the Nantucket whalers to leave the island for Hudson. The first and second detachments had come after the Revolution and the War of 1812 in search of a port sufficiently far inland to be safe from the marauding of the British. The later ones followed those because the need for ever-longer voyages in search of whales had made the ships of that day too big for Nantucket's little harbor.

When kerosene for illumination sent whaling into decline Jason Thayer converted his whaling fleet into refrigerator ships. What they carried was ice itself. During that era, the latter part of the nineteenth century, the cutting of ice was a major industry on the Hudson River. Jason Thayer insulated his ships' hulls with sawdust, a by-product of the Catskill Mountains logging industry, and such a thorough good job he did of it that months after being packed, after rounding the Cape and coming through the heat of the South Pacific and the Indian Ocean, they arrived in Calcutta or Bombay with better than half their cargo still in solid state. There where ice was a wonder, a miracle, hot thirsty maharajahs paid for it with rubies, emeralds, gold, silks. Riverside, the country house Jason Thayer built for himself on a promontory where, from the captain's walk on the roof, he could tally his outgoing and incoming ships, contained the finest private collection in the country of East Indian arts and artifacts. In the portrait of him that hung over the dining room mantelpiece, one of the few ever done by his friend and neighbor, the celebrated landscape painter Frederick Church, Jason Thayer looked genteelly piratical.

Lucky the man who had a spot of earth dear to him, that

sustained and supported him as it did the primeval oaks
rooted in the soil of Tony Thayer's ancestral acres. Tony
himself was a product of the river as surely as was one of its
shad.

The river dominated life along it, and helped somewhat to
democratize that life. Without it the gulf between the haves
and the have-nots there would have been as deep as the river
was wide. Water seeks its own level and there all men, rich
and poor alike, must seek it. Hudson river rats found one
another out across the barriers of caste and class, and the boy
from beside the tracks who poled the sports in their punts
through the windings of Tivoli's South Bay in quest of ducks,
who knew which of the railway trestles to fish from for
striped bass, who knew how to pickle and to smoke the ale-
wives that, on their spring spawning run, paved from bank to
bank the river's tributaries, grew up to hobnob with the heirs
of Astors, Livingstons, Van Rensellaers, and Thayers.

You can never ascend the same river twice, we are told; the
Hudson, being tidal ("the river that flows both ways," the
Indian name for it meant) was even more changeable than
most. For those who lived along its banks its tides were an
additional clock, regulating their activities from early childhood on. Riverbank children found their way down to the
water with an instinct like ducklings. Christy Thayer was
given a boat of her own almost as soon as she was trusted out
of sight. She taught herself to sail in the bay, to run and when
necessary to repair an outboard motor; only when the river
was iced over was she to be seen out of a flotation vest, and all
summer long she was as brown as toast. The river's seasons
dictated its people's pastimes. In spring, when the ice broke
up and floes of it drifted down and out to sea and left it open
once more and the flights of wildfowl used it as their flyway,
you went fishing. In summer there was boating and picnick-
ing along its banks and on its islands. As the days began to
shorten you built a duckblind to replace the one that had
been broken up and swept away in the spring thaw. Then
when, in the morning before the sun had touched it, there
was rime at the water's edge and thistledown from pollinat-

ing cattails like a hatch of insects on the surface, you punted
in the shallows for snipe. When the season opened in late
October you shot the ducks that had summered there, then
wintry weather up north sent them south sometimes as thick
as bees in swarm and long undulant ribbons of geese sounded
like a pack of slow-footed hunting hounds high overhead.
Then the river congealed and looked and sounded underfoot
like steel and there were iceboat races on the bays and at
night skating parties around big bonfires on the ice.

The river instilled in its people not only a second clock and
a calendar but also a compass. It compelled the eye. It was
the river you looked out on the first thing in the morning, and
finding it there was your reassurance that you were too. It
was toward the river that on a summer evening with drink in
hand you strolled out on the lawn to watch the sun sink in fire
behind the cobalt and cerulean Catskills.

To Tony his river and its bounty was the greatest gift
within his giving. He was generous with it, expecting in return only that it be appreciated and respected. He responded to people in a measure by their response to it. For
you to become an intimate part of his life the river had to
become a part of yours. Of his best friend's it had long since.

It was in May when the herring made their run upstream
to spawn in their native tributaries that the Hudson reawoke.
In this annual rite honorary river rat Ben Curtis was an eager, an impatient participant. The sign to watch for was the
blossoming of the shadblow. On a day soon after this event
would come a call from Tony announcing that the herring
were in. He would drop whatever he was doing and point
himself northward. Cathy and Anthony came along, for so
prodigious was the catch, and such the quantity of work it
entailed, that all hands were needed. Besides, it was fun for
all; they would not have missed out on it. It was spawning
time for the Hudson's shad too, and knowing that the river
was pulsating with fish in their headlong millions bound for
their orgiastic rendezvous, he could feel mount in him as he
drove alongside it an anticipation akin to theirs.

Like subway riders headed home at the evening rush hour

the herring sped upriver and surfaced at their separate sta-
tions, their spawning grounds, creeks with old Dutch names
like the Kinderhook, the Claverack, and the Roeliff-Jan-
senkill. To get over the rapids in which the creek, whichever
it was, ended, they needed a full tide in the river. Tony knew
the river's tides to the hour every day. It would be rising
when their party seated themselves among the plastic pails
and scap nets and rubber boots in the bed of the old pickup
truck and rattled off, and it would be at the full when they
arrived.

The blossoms of the valley's many orchards were hardly
more numerous than the herring. From near and far people
came not to catch them but merely to marvel at the sight.
Even after years of experience of it you were still awed by
this example of nature's prodigality. For the first few minutes
after getting down the bank with all their gear they too stood
and watched. No fear that the families already there, the
father hauling up a full net with every dip of it, would leave
an insufficiency for you and yours.

All across the creek's broad mouth, from their party's van-
tage point all the way down to the river and for a hundred
yards upstream to the first impassable falls, the surface bris-
tled with fishes' fins. Beneath these were more layers like
stacks of coins. They packed themselves in so closely they
rubbed scales off one another. The fins were aquiver as the
fish struggled in the current and were thrust onward by those
behind them and as the spawning urge wrought them to a
frenzy. The water was shallow and clear and the throngs of
fish were a silvery and scintillant stream like the stars of the
Milky Way. Here, there, and everywhere, around some female running ripe, a swirl of bucks made the water boil.
Then, before the one found the other and the two sank together to the bottom, the mingling milt and roe turned the
water milky.

Excitement succeeded wonder and while Tony and he
were still rigging the nets Anthony and Christy were already
in hip boots and in the water catching fish with their bare
hands and tossing them onto the bank.

Unchanged since antiquity, a scap net was simply a stout pole some ten feet long with four staves hanging from it to which was attached a square net of fine mesh six feet long to the side. On days when the fishing was slow the fisherman threaded a line through the nose of a herring and with it decoyed others over his sunken net. That fish was his "stoolie." No need of a stoolie on good days. Tony and he waded into the water, dipped their nets, waited a couple of minutes, and it was all they could do to hoist and swing them ashore to be emptied. A hundred herring bellied the net, strained its staves. Others were making similar catches and the bank glittered with threshing mounds of silver.

The full nets strained their muscles too, but tired as you soon were you worked on, for the herring must be harvested while they were there. Already around your feet spent fish were washing tail first back to the river, back to sea. You slithered and slipped among the rocks, fell in over your boot tops, and still you dipped and hoisted, dipped and hoisted until the plastic pails were brim full. Struggling back up the long steep bank with one of those in each hand you stopped often to rest, catch your breath.

At home all hands fell to scaling, gutting, trimming, washing, salting down the fish in kegs and crocks. That evening you ate hearty—of anything except fish. That night you slept the sodden sleep of one drugged by hard repetitive labor and next morning you woke stiff and sore in your every cell. Waiting for you would be a breakfast prepared by Tony featuring scrambled eggs and herring roe.

Their hands would be still a mass of cuts when the Curtis clan came back days later to help with the second stage, and the salt stung. Soon the cavernous old kitchen reeked of boiling vinegar and onions and pickling spices and above all, as these were chopped in pieces, of fish. When the work was done every surface was covered with glistening jars.

The herring to be smoked were left whole. They were skewered through the eyes on metal rods and hung in racks in the smokehouse. The firebox was outside the smokehouse, connected to it by a stovepipe. Throughout the night Tony and he took turns getting up and feeding the fire with corn-cobs and green hickory. In the morning the fish had been transmuted overnight from new silver to old gold. For days afterwards you smelled of fish and smoke and spices and vinegar and through the year the taste of herring brought back to you memories of the fishing and the fun, the fellow-ship.

If it should be an autumn visit to Hudson that he was on then it would be still dark when Tony knocked on his bed-room door in the morning and recited:

> Waken, lords and ladies gay!
> On the mountain dawns the day;
> All the jolly chase is here
> With hawk and horse and hunting spear;
> Hounds are in their couples yelling,
> Hawks are whistling, horns are knelling;
> Merrily, merrily mingle they.
> Waken, lords and ladies gay!

Relieved of his weight, the old canopy bed gave a groan. He washed but he did not shave. This morning was a holiday from shaving and whiskers were protection to the face against the wintry wind from off the water. He pulled on long silk underwear and, over these, long woolen ones, a wool shirt, and thick wool pants. The odor of mothballs in his clothes was another association with this season and this house. Going down the paneled and tapestried high-ceil-inged hallways with their family portraits and pedestals and all that old oriental opulence, you felt as though you were living in Sir Walter Scott's time and were on a weekend at a laird's great country estate.

Tony, at the kitchen range, would be just easing an om-elette onto its back. Kippers in a crucible—a prosaic skillet, really—were undergoing alchemy. An early riser, restless for each day to begin, Tony cooked breakfast for himself and whoever else was up each morning. Now he would intone:

> Louder, louder chant the lay:
> Waken, lords and ladies gay!

They would finish it together:

> Tell them youth and mirth and glee
> Run a course as well as we;
> Time, stern huntsman, who can balk?
> Staunch as hound and fleet as hawk;
> Think of this, and rise with day,
> Gentle lords and ladies gay!

How lightly they had said it then, and now youth and mirth and glee had run their course, and time, stern huntsman, had hunted down Riverside's gentle lord, but in those days they were full of mirth as Tony took a stone bottle from the freezer and the two of them tossed down with a toast to the day their time-honored eye-opener, a jigger of Dutch gin, icy in the mouth, fiery further down.

"What's our weather, gentle lord?" he would ask.

Tony always knew. His first act on getting up in the morning was to step outside and, while relieving himself, assess the weather. Not even a blizzard could stop him.

"Dark, dreary, dank, and dismal."

"Ducky!"

The lunch hamper would be already packed, so, breakfast finished, they would go to the den to get their guns and their gear. For years he had left his here at Riverside, Tony being his only duck-shooting companion. Men with whom you looked forward to spending all day in a duckblind no bigger than an outhouse were few.

It was fitting that he leave his gun here. This was its home. It was an under-and-over double-barrel made expressly for Tony's father by a famed London gunsmith. The finely checkered walnut stock had the figure and the finish of polished agate, the engraving of the metal displayed its breeding by its lack of display. The gun that had fit the father did not fit the son, so Tony said. It pained Tony to shoot a better gun than his friend. He offered this one to him.

"But, Tony," he had said, "I'd be afraid to shoot a gun that fine."

"Oh, just be careful where you point it," said Tony.

Day would be dawning, the light straining through the tent of clouds stretched low overhead. The wind out of the north would be laden with mist. In hip boots and down-filled jackets spotted in camouflage, carrying guns, hamper, shellboxes, they went down the path that parted the dense growth of periwinkle. Nero, the black Labrador retriever, bounded and frisked ahead of them.

At this time of year the boathouse sheltered the Thayer clan's entire collection of vessels. Boats were handed down in that family the way clothes were in others. Resting on saw-horses, suspended from beams, were sailboats for every age and level of competence, punts, skiffs, sculls, even a kayak, and there were the iceboats. In addition to those accumulated by his ancestors, Tony owned several that he had been given as the popularity of the sport among the river families, once great, declined. Stripped down to nothing more than a pair of crossed sticks, a mast with a set sail, a tiller and two shallow trays, one for the driver and one for a single passenger to lie prone upon, the whole thing poised on runners, an iceboat had but one purpose: speed. In a high wind one of those things could attain a hundred and thirty miles an hour; that, held by Tony, was, in fact, the current record. He had them in sizes from eighteen to thirty feet long. Trim, lean, even gaunt, and so strictly limited in function they brought to mind his Anthony's hawks, the little merlin up to the big goshawk, which, even at rest on their perches, seemed instinct with swiftness, with the same inherent capacity of an inert cartridge to explode into flight. After seeing it but before trying it himself he had urged his friend to give up iceboating as too dangerous. A man with a wife and child owed it to them to forgo some forms of fun. To this Tony replied that he had heard of a woman's being thrown over-board once and fracturing an arm but that it was a sport for which no fatality was recorded. And after experiencing it, bounding over the frozen waves with a noise like a galloping

herd, flying sometimes a foot above the glazed and dazzling
surface and feeling in his face the sting of the icy spray
thrown back by the runners, he himself had surrendered to
its appeal.

But today it was onto the water, not onto the ice. Their
punt, double-pointed for getting out of dead-end windings
too narrow to turn around in, was waiting on the ramp. They
stuffed two canvas bags with decoys and hauled the boat
down to the water. Nero leaped aboard and seated himself in
the bow: a fitting figurehead. He took his place amidship and
Tony launched them. The motor responded to the pull of the
cord, the bow rose high out of water and they planed across
the cove headed west. The rising tide was near the full. To
pass under the railroad trestle they had to duck their heads.

Inside the cove, separated from the river by the railway
embankment, the water had been smooth but on the river
the wind funneling down the valley raised waves and the
ride was rough as the boat crested and bottomed, crested and
bottomed. A southbound freight train, its length lost in the
mist, overtook them and clanked alongside with a noise like
the links of a chain being dragged over the ties.

The train's caboose had disappeared into the mist when
they turned from the river and passed under the trestle into
the bay. Under reduced power they crossed the open water
to the marsh. There Tony cut the motor and took it aboard
and stood with his long push-pole. In their jump-shooting it
was always Tony who poled. There was a knack to it, a final
twist of the pole against your hip, gondolier fashion, that
momentarily turned the pole into a tiller and steered the
boat through the tortuous narrow channels, a knack he could
never get.

They entered one of these channels tunneled by tall pur-
ple loosestrife and cattails. Their heads frazzled and faded,
these latter looked like oversized cotton swabs. Darkness was
lifting as they glided silently along the channels and through
still pools that shone like quicksilver. At their edges floated
pinfeathers plucked from themselves by preening ducks. He
could just see to shoot now and he loaded his gun and stood,

bracing his right leg against the seat, rocking in rhythm to Tony's steady stroke of the pole. Their progress resembled that of the lone gallinule that swam in spurts ahead of them, its head bobbing.

It would be a day early in the season but it would not be opening day. That they passed up. Too many green and greedy gunners then, who opened fire on birds impossibly out of range and scared them off from gunners into whose range they were being decoyed. The bay sounded like warfare then, and sometimes erupted into it, with shots exchanged not far above heads. Now you shared it with fewer, more dedicated, more experienced, and more courteous sportsmen.

They rounded a bend and a pair of mallards flushed, beating the water with their wings in their takeoff. They were thirty yards away when his swing picked up and momentarily blotted out one with the muzzle of the gun. Then the sky reappeared momentarily and in that moment he fired. The boom reverberated around the bay and without pause he swiveled, picked up, at forty yards, the second bird, covered it, swung past, taking a slightly longer lead this time, fired, and followed through on his swing. Whether he had touched either bird he did not know. Or rather, he knew he had, but he had not seen it happen.

"Keep that up," said Tony as Nero swam back with both birds by their necks in his mouth, "and you'll have time on your hands waiting for me to fill my limit."

The shots had disturbed the birds in the area and they took to wing out of range. Without putting up another they reached their blind on the edge of and commanding its own spot of open water. They set out their stool of decoys, concealed the boat, and climbed into the blind. They had built it on weekends in early autumn, boating out on a falling tide with poles for the stilts and boards for the floor and the walls and hemlock boughs to camouflage the whole thing, working when the bay was drained, then boating back when the tide had risen to float them. Just out of gunshot range from one another, other blinds were going up on those weekends.

Come opening day of the season, the bay looked like the site of some primitive tribe of bog dwellers. Yours brought back to you the clubhouse you had built with some playmate as a boy.

They stood back to back and each scanned his section of the gray sky. To the west the mountains loomed loftily, their tops still indistinct, as though the day came up from earth and forced the night to lift. Guns were beginning to sound now, most often automatics emptying their legal limit of three shots, in fire so rapid the echoes, trapped by the low-lying cloud cover, got in one another's way.

"Wood ducks!" Tony hissed. "Wood ducks!"

He too had spotted them, a flock of seven or eight, and had identified them by their speed and by their characteristic bunching and scattering in flight and by their habit, unique to them among ducks, of turning their heads in flight. Both froze, hunching to conceal the white of their faces, not daring to look to the side farther than the rolling of their eyes allowed. This was the prescribed reaction to the appearance of all ducks, but wood ducks were not to be missed. Not because they were the most prized on the plate, for they were not, but because theirs was the plumage most sought after by tiers of trout flies. The five most indispensable patterns required feathers from the cape of the wood duck drake, and the sale of them was illegal. You got your own or you got none—unless, as both were hoping now, you had a father and a godfather to get them for you. For years the breed had been so near extinction that all shooting of them was banned. They had recovered from decimation and come back in numbers enough to permit shooting—limit one per day. Would these wing over now or would they circle and come back, maybe flock in to the decoys?

"They're turning," Tony whispered. "They're circling. They're coming in. Oh, damn it, they've seen us! Now or never!"

This was pass-shooting at tiny targets going fifty miles an hour. The eye had to focus and function with the speed of a camera shutter. He chose a bird out of the flock, tracked it on

its line of flight, overtook and passed it, fired and kept swing-
ing. When he looked back the crumpled bird was tumbling
out of the sky, striking the water with a splash. Tony too had
scored.

These two would not be plucked, they would be skinned
whole. They would make many trout flies; even so, they
would soon be used up. The flytying that Anthony had taken
up as a hobby had become a business. In the beginning he
sold flies to the members of the fishing club. They showed
them to friends and soon he was filling mail orders. Now he
had several part-time employees, boys and girls whom he
had trained and who tied flies as a cottage industry. Never
one to do things by halves, he bred his own gamecocks. He
kept them in coops and incubated the eggs, always in quest of
a strain that would consistently produce feathers with
hackles of the requisite stiffness and of the perfect subtle
shade of dun blue. Toward the undesirable poults he was
unsentimental, businesslike. Lately he had found a use for
them. He fed them to the hawks he had begun to fancy.

Long before they saw them they heard the geese. They
appeared over the mountaintops to the northwest. There
must have been two hundred of them. They grew louder as
the stately beat of their wings brought them overhead. If the
ducks streaked over dipping and banking in formation like
squadrons of fighter planes, these were bombers massed on a
mission navigating a straight and steady course. Big Canada
geese they were, recognizable even at that altitude by their
white throat patch like a clergyman's collar. Tirelessly chanting their command, they were like a column of marching
men in the regimented, plodding steadiness of their pace,
and when one of them got out of line it quickly got back as a
straggler among soldiers closes ranks. For a long time they
stayed in sight before disappearing into the southern sky, and
still for a long time afterwards their honking, more like bay-
ing, could be heard against the wind.

Small flocks, mainly mallards and teal, swooped down only
to flare off. There was gunning now throughout the bay and
the heavy boom of the big long-range magnums of gunners

out on the open water of the river. They decoyed one flock of
five and he singled and missed while Tony doubled. Then a
distant whistle blew.

"Noon in Hudson," said Tony.

A couple of minutes passed and another whistle blew.

"Noon in Catskill," said Tony.

Another couple of minutes passed and another whistle
blew.

"Noon in Germantown," said Tony.

A fourth whistle blew and Tony said, "Noon here."

They stacked their guns, rubbed the backs of their stiff
necks, stretched themselves, and sat down on the bench. A
hot toddy never tasted better than then, and was all the
better for being limited to one—many a hunting friendship
had been ended by a shooting accident in a duckblind. Tony
uncorked the wine and tasted it and said, smacking his lips,
"Why, be this juice the growth of God, who dare blaspheme
the twisted tendril as a snare? A Blessing, we should use it,
should we not? And if a curse—why, then, Who set it there?"
To which he responded with, "I wonder often what the Vint-
ners buy one half so precious as the stuff they sell." In the
hamper there might be a paté, a cold fried chicken, an avo-
cado to share, cheese, fruit tarts with bitter black coffee.
Ducks seen during the lunch break were usually seen too late
and winged away unscathed. Neither minded. They were
there not just to fill their game pockets.

It was in a duckblind that began a practice of theirs. It was
one of the closest of the many ties that attached them to each
other. It came about because of the nature of duck shooting.
Much of the day in the blind is spent doing nothing at all. To
be good, the weather must be bad: gray, misty, fogbound,
with little to interest the eye, distract the mind. The shooting
is best early in the morning and late in the afternoon.
Throughout the long middle of the day the hunter scans the
sky mainly because he has got nothing else to do; only seldom
is he rewarded then by the sight of birds. It was during such a
barren midafternoon stretch on one of their early hunts to-

gether that Tony had said, "You ought to bring along something to read at times like this."

"And yourself?" In those days he believed that Tony had read everything.

"For this I've got something better than a book. I recite poems to myself. I've got a collection in my head and I add new ones to it from time to time. That way I've got something to occupy my mind without taking my eyes off the sky. I do it while I'm driving long distances, when I'm in the dentist's chair, when I'm doing any kind of still-hunting, like this."

So, as they scanned the sky, they passed the time reciting to each other Shakespeare and Milton, Donne and Marvell, Wordsworth, Keats, Tennyson, Browning, Hardy, Yeats—breaking off when birds appeared to wait them out if they came in range to fire. The once-great flights had dwindled. No longer did clouds of them darken the sky or settle upon the river thick as autumnal leaves that strow the brooks in Valambrosa, but on most days they bagged their limit.

The sun would have dropped below the clouds behind the blue Catskills, setting the sky ablaze, the mist would be rising off the water and lights shone from the windows of a north-bound passenger train when they retrieved the decoys, for they would have stayed out late. So, always, would one last lone duck, now hurrying to rejoin its flock for the night. To it he said:

> Whither, midst falling dew,
> While glow the heavens with the last steps of day,
> Far, through their rosy depths, dost thou pursue
> Thy solitary way?
>
> Vainly the fowler's eye
> Might mark thy distant flight to do thee wrong,
> As, darkly painted on the crimson sky,
> Thy figure floats along.

He had not found in the flight of the duck the faith that Bryant had found, that

He who, from zone to zone,
Guides through the boundless sky thy certain flight,
In the long way that I must tread alone,
Will lead my steps aright.

But he had had his little flock then and knew how to find
his way home to them in the dark. Then there had been no
long way that he must tread alone.

*

He was casting better now, straightening line and leader,
laying down the fly with better aim, more softly. The timing
of it was coming back to him. When you had done a thing for
many years you could put it aside and then take it up again,
and seemingly, no matter what had befallen you in the interim, it came back to you. With fly-casting the thing was not
to think about it. It was both subtle and simple and had to be
done unselfconsciously. That was the hardest part for begin-
ners to learn, not to think about it but just do it. Then it was as
easy as a good man made it look, as natural as conveying food
to your mouth. It had nothing to do with size or strength.
Had it had then he would have been better at it than either
Tony or Anthony, both of whom could outperform him any
day. But then Tony was a natural and Anthony a perfection-
ist.

Slowly at first so as not to disturb the pool, then with a
steadily accelerating lift of the rod accompanied by a downward pull with his left hand, he picked the line off the water.
It came back to him showering droplets and went swishing
past his ear. Rod held high, he paused, timing the backcast to
lengthen and straighten itself, to flex the rod. A million casts
had taught him just when to start the rod forward. The line
rolled over in a hairpin loop, straightened, sending the leader
and fly to the fore. He checked it, and the line fell lightly to
the water. In a swirl created by a boulder near the pool's left
bank the fly came to life. It looked more like a minnow than a
minnow did. Through the clear water he could see its feathers pulse as though it were breathing. It looked like a fingerling trout and the slash of crimson along its side like a bleed-

ing wound. Easy prey for a hungry adult trout. *They made of their generation messes.*

The current swept the line slowly toward midstream. When it was straightened to its full length he began his retrieve. He let the fly drift back, retrieved again in short rapid jerks. He began his lift, then felt it stopped by a tug, the throb of a fish, his first in more than a year. Experience told him it was not a big fish but to him it felt big, assisted in its pull by a lifetime, a buried and resurrected lifetime of fish.

It would instinctively make its first turn for freedom upstream toward him. Out of old habit he put his feet together to keep it from going between them. Reeling rapidly to regain the slack line, he saw the fish in its dash past him. It was about a foot long.

Regulated by its drag, the reel yielded line to the fish. The rod, bent in a bow, quivered like a divining rod. The fish leaped, leaped again, then turned and bolted downstream, retaking line. He lightened the drag to compensate for the added pull of the current. The fish stopped, turned, balked, shook its head. To keep the rod from developing a set, a permanent bend, he turned it upside down. The drowning, desperate fish darted past him headed upstream again. He shifted the rod to his left hand and with his right hand reached for his landing net. He drew it to the full length of its retractable chain and dipped it in the water to inflate its bag. He waited while the tired fish floated slowly up from the bottom. The current brought it, spent, tail first to the net. He bent to scoop it up. His reflection in the water, blurred and indistinct at first, sharpened as he neared it. It was as if a corpse, drowned and bleached, was surfacing—his corpse.

*

The storm in the night had passed through like an army on the march and at half past two the distant rumble and the glare of its cannonade was faint and fast fading. The barroom barometer stood at 29.90 and was rising. That should bring fair weather and good fishing. The one reliable rule for when to go fishing, aside from the old saw about going whenever

you could get away, was not to go when the cows were lying
down. Cows lay down when the barometric pressure was
falling, and so did fish. He had read that according to some
researchers mental depression in people followed upon a
lowering of the barometric pressure. If so, then in that, as in
so much else, he was contrary. He had watched the one here
on the wall rise for the past hour as, meanwhile, his own
inner one steadily fell. His weather and the world's weather
seldom accorded anymore, just as the hours he kept were the
opposite of other people's. Fair days, when they were happy,
emphasized that he was not. In gloomy weather he had the
same excuse for his low spirits as everybody else. Now, with
the contrariness that characterized much of his recent behavior, he chose this, always the low point on his chart for the
day, to put himself to the most dreaded of the tests awaiting
him here.

His half-drunk beer had long since gone flat. He went
behind the counter, emptied his mug into the sink and rinsed
the suds from it. He toweled it dry, then, turning to set it on
the shelf, he saw himself in the mirror and the sight was so
startling it was as though he had caught somebody watching
him. He and his reflection stared first wildly, then search-
ingly, at each other.

"Thou comest in questionable shape," he said to it, and it
said the same to him.

Lots of old familiar faces had looked into his now unfamiliar one during these past few hours, with differing expressions of it but with universal shock and disbelief, or with
evident effort to disguise it, and the progress he had made in
getting used to himself had been undone.

All his old acquaintances had said it was the beard that had
kept them from recognizing him. That was his reason for
growing it, to give them that excuse. Or rather, that was one
of his reasons. There were several. One was that he too
needed an excuse for not recognizing himself. Another was
that growing a beard had kept him from having to face himself in the mirror while shaving every morning. Actually, the
beard had grown itself, as hair is said to keep growing on a

corpse in its grave. He had found it there on his resurrection. White as the hair on his head now, it made him look more than ever like somebody brought back from the dead. Like his father's spirit, doomed for a certain term to walk the night.

Some of those old acquaintances of his had actually introduced themselves to him as though to a stranger. To those who had mistaken him for a new member of the club or for a member's new guest the embarrassment immediately afterwards had been acute. But there were those among them who knew him and who seemed to understand that a man who himself had changed almost out of recognition must have undergone something that would give him trouble in recalling their names. They were right. Though in many instances they were people whom he had long known, he had difficulty in recognizing them now. It was because they had changed so little. They were people from a former life. He looked at them with wonder equaling theirs for him. How could they have lived through the same year that he had lived through and been left so unmarked by it? Were these people all Dorian Grays and he the portrait in the attic? Contradictory as it was, while he could not accept the changes in himself he expected others to have changed as he had.

He raised his eyes to the club's motto etched in the glass, then looked again at his reflection. He raised his hand in a gesture of thumbs up and essayed a smile. The hoary old man in the mirror, his face a map of melancholy, stared past him, remote beyond reach.

*

Its walls covered with framed snapshots, the club's sitting room was in effect the family album of a very large family, souvenirs of holidays extending over three quarters of a century. It made the club seem like the ancestral estate of one of those close-knit, fun-loving large clans, all outdoor sportsmen, who come home at every opportunity and who amass photographs of their every get-together. They consti-

tuted a pictorial history of American fly-fishing, recording
the fashions and their changes in outdoor clothing, tackle,
the incursion by women into what was once exclusively a
male domain, the changing concepts of sportsmanship and
conservation, the displacement of the native brook trout by
the hardier and more cunning brown trout imported from
Europe. From one decade to the next rods shrank in size,
waders appeared as the dwindling numbers of fish, caused in
part by growing numbers of fishermen as travel eased, put an
end to leisurely fishing from the bank. Quaint and amusing
and all so long ago and out of date you found the people in
these pictures, never for a moment reflecting that the time
would come when the ones of you would amuse somebody in
the same way.

From before the era of legal daily limits were pictures of
bearded, portly men in plus-fours, tweed jackets and caps,
posing alongside miraculous draughts of fishes. Because of
the long rough train ride through the mountains to Chalfont,
then by wagon and team the fourteen miles from there, no
women were to be seen in these early pictures. Filterless,
they lacked clouds in their skies also. Too long a trip for
weekends then, it was for upwards of two weeks at a time
that the men came. Their creels were the size of packhorse
panniers and their rods the length of lances.

Family likenesses were traceable between the founders
and the square-jawed young men with their hair parted
down the middle, wearing yoke-collared sweaters and long
knotted scarves. Having recently fought the war to end war
and make the world safe for democracy, they now defiantly
displayed bottles of bootleg bathtub gin. Detroit made its
contribution to the look of all our yesterdays with open tour-
ing cars, phaetons, roadsters with rumbleseats, and the inclu-
sion in the party now of women with bobbed and marcelled
hair beneath cloche hats, short skirts with belts below the
waistline.

For men only because of its inaccessibility before, the club
was now turned by paved roads into a place for all the family.
Children began to appear in the pictures and before long

they and their mothers were sporting fishing togs. Black-and-white gave way to Kodachrome, flashbulbs followed the festivities indoors. The club's decor remained unchanged—he was surrounded now by the very objects he saw in the pictures, even by pictures pictured—while young men came home on leave in the uniforms of four wars. The catches of fish dwindled from days of yore but there were still fish to be caught and people kept coming back, finding fun and fellowship here, needing no photographer's injunction to smile, posing with thumbs up. Happy families are all alike, and when they are shown all at the same sport in the same spot the effect might have been monotonous, even wearisome, but in someone who had once been and was no longer one of a happy family himself it was longing they awoke. For him those had been welcome days away from work that made getting back to work all the more welcome. He loved the sport but he had never been a fanatical fisherman. Odd that a man of his outlook should have fathered a son whose intensity in everything he took up was almost manic, but to him it had been important that none of his pastimes become more than that, a pastime. Absorbing, yes, demanding, yes, otherwise no point in pursuing it, but not all-absorbing. The cream on top that enriched the milk of life would have been cloying as a steady diet.

Even so, he had managed to spend a good amount of his time here, as Tony, the shutterbug, who loved every minute of life and wanted mementoes of them all, had recorded. Much of a wall was covered with his snapshots of them in those days. It was like Tony to want to share his good times with everybody and to assume that everybody wanted to share theirs with him. Envying no man his pleasures, he could not imagine any man's envying him his. Just when the two of them had caught the fine catch of fish in the picture he was looking at now he could not remember. It was not all that uncommon, and when good times followed one another with no end to them in sight they were not prized enough to be labeled. Happy days are all alike; every unhappy day is unhappy in its own way.

It was ungrateful of him, but he found it hard now to realize that he had had so many happy days, and it was contrary of him to expect now to see the man in the pictures when he looked into the mirror and to see the man in the mirror when he looked at the pictures. Why was it that the joys we had had were not only no comfort to us later but brought us the sharpest of pains? A matter of tenses. Had had. Past perfect. Present mirth hath present laughter.

He was trying not to dwell upon individual pictures. Too many of them brought back too vividly the time of its taking. It was test enough of his strength to expose himself to their collective effect. Nevertheless, he found himself lingering over each one because he was afraid to let his eye stray toward the section of the wall that he dreaded most of all. Reliving it in these pictures, he could feel his life coming up to the recent past.

One spring they had driven up, as always, on the eve of opening day, went to bed that night as the barometer was falling, and in the morning woke to find a foot of snow on the ground with more still falling fast. It was wet, heavy snow and the club members were wakened as one by the loud crash of a nearby limb breaking and falling from its weight. The clubhouse was cold and dark. Powerlines were down, unreachable by repair crews. Kerosene lamps for this contingency were brought out and in all the fireplaces fires were started.

To listen to, it was as though they were under siege all that day, with tree limbs crackling like rifle fire and mounds of snow falling into the snow with a sound like the impact of artillery. When finally the snow stopped falling during the second night it had deposited over two feet. Then the barometer rose, the temperature plummeted and everything froze solid.

They were snowbound for ten days. They sawed and split firewood, hauled water in buckets from the stream and used the old, disused outhouse, and the men, as shown in this picture of them posing in the snow, all grew beards, his then as black as now it was white. By the fourth day Pauline's fare —she was Eddie's wife, in charge of the clubhouse kitchen—

was growing stale, by the sixth it was giving out. Armed from Eddie's private arsenal and bolstered by Tony's "To hell with the game laws. This is a matter of survival," the men took to the woods. The photograph showed them with their bounty, he with his four-point buck, Tony with his spikehorn, another club member with a mess of squirrels, still another with a heap of rabbits, and Eddie with half a dozen grouse. They ate so well none of them cared if it never thawed.

In contrast to this were summer afternoons when heat waves struck, when the water was low and warm and the fish wary and off their feed, and then it was more fun to swim in the pond, play croquet or badminton on the lawn, drowse in a hammock hung in the shade. Often they were kept indoors by wind and rain. Then they passed the time reading, fussing with tackle, playing games, solving puzzles, and drinking too much, and Tony with his camera had snapped them at all these activities. Such a lot of activity! You could almost hear these pictures, the laughter on the lips, the raillery, the songs, and it deepened the silence of the night, the stillness now of this the scene of all that play, lengthened the distance from those days and from all hope of reunion with those people. These moments caught and mounted along with the memorable fish on the walls brought to mind a multitude of similar ones. They littered his memory like dead leaves from a tree.

He was nearing the end of the wall and in these pictures they were all a little older but still as carefree as always—if anything, more contented than ever. And why not? Their luck had held for so long they had been lulled into a sense of its permanence. With a daughter like Tony's what father would not look self-satisfied? Happy man, how could he know that before another year was out she would leap forty-seven stories to her death? And himself? The big, hearty fellow without a worry in the world or a thought for tomorrow, with the pretty little woman, his loving wife, always at his side?

On reflex he turned aside and in so doing saw another picture. It was not the hot tears in his eyes that distorted it— or maybe it was. He saw the picture of a dead boy of eighteen with a face made livid by trapped blood, with bulging eyes, a swollen, blackened tongue protruding from swollen lips, a twisted and swollen neck stretched and scarified by a rope. What the picture actually showed was a much younger boy holding up a fish and smiling at the camera, but in his father's eyes that final image of him now intruded upon all others from the rest of his son's short life.

*

They had been at sea for a week, sailing out of Gloucester up the coast past Portsmouth, Portland, past Monhegan, and into Penobscot Bay. They had moored at Boothbay Harbor, anchored off Vinalhaven, gone ashore at Castine and Blue Hill. Then back down the coast again. Now landfall. Home port and then home again. For the Thayers it was back to their big haunted house, their incurable pain and their incessant self-questioning, for him it was back to his wife and the troubles between them. Just one last time-honored ceremony before coming in to dock and then it was back to all they had sailed away from.

Now all three were busy pretending that nothing had happened yesterday. Up from the galley came the smell of onions frying. Sails were furled, bags packed, and already dressed for shore, he sat at the wheel, the chart at his feet on the cockpit deck. After yesterday, no more of that navigating from below.

He came chugging in under power, keeping the rocks, the Dry Salvages, to portside, listening to the scream of the gulls and the funereal tolling of the buoy bell. The bell set the cadence for Eliot's lines inspired by this place. At the time he could not recall them exactly, and shortly he was to forget all about them and everything else. It would be several days after finally getting home when he would think of them again and look them up and then find in them an added applicability.

....we come to discover that the moments of agony
.......................are likewise permanent
With such permanence as time has. We appreciate
   this better

In the agony of others, nearly experienced,
Involving ourselves, than in our own.
For our own past is covered by the currents of action,
But the torment of others remains an experience
Unqualified, unworn by subsequent attrition.
People change, and smile: but the agony abides.

For the Thayers this cruise was to have been their coming
out. There was a time to mourn, as both the Bible and the
book of etiquette counseled, and while the time to dance had
not come, the period of mourning prescribed as mentally
healthy and socially acceptable was over. Life must go on,
although sometimes, along with the poet, one forgot just
why. Pris packed her black dresses away with her veil, and
Tony thumbed through the latest issue of *Yachting.*

A cruise without Ben aboard was not a cruise. This one
absolutely depended upon his saying yes to their invitation.
Or rather, upon his and Cathy's saying yes, of course. The
Thayers were perhaps not quite as sorry as they tried ear-
nestly to sound over the phone when he declined for Cathy,
explaining that she was away from home and would not be
back by then. They were coming out but they were still
tender and tentative, and while they always got along with
Cathy, with him they never had to get along. They would sail
the old familiar waters and do the things they used to do
before. That "before" was unfortunate. It pulsated in the
earpiece, waiting to be finished off with a phrase.

The invitation to go on that cruise had come as a godsend
to him. Cathy and he were squabbling again and she had
gone away. She had not left him; things were not that bad;
but she had gone away. He had been batching for several
days, and he was not meant to be a bachelor. Remorseful,
regretting things he had said in heat, yearning to have her
back while at the same time still loyal to his angry mood—in
the midst of all this had come Tony's call. It signaled something that gave him even more pleasure than the relief from
his situation at home. It meant that Tony, dear Tony, his poor

broken friend, had begun to recover at last from his terrible blow.

He brought with him the champagne and his ritual, his penitential offering of a steak for their last meal on board and from the Oyster Bar in Grand Central Terminal the customary quart of fresh bay scallops, for, while they were a reminder that it was from atop the Pan Am Building overlooking the terminal that Christy had leaped, the scallops were a shipboard tradition of theirs of long standing and not to have brought them would have made it seem that all reminders of her were henceforth to be avoided. When they had stowed the gear and the provisions and filled the gas and water tanks they spent their first evening charting their course and planning their anchorages and their moorings and then, full of Veuve Cliquot, went to their bunks and were cradled and rocked by the rhythmical lapping of the harbor swell, lullabied to by the buoy bell. Perhaps in the very volume of their talk—his talk, mainly, for the Thayers seemed content to leave it to him—there had been an uneasy evasion of the topic, but they had gotten through the evening with no allusion to Christy.

Even to his best friend Tony talked of this trouble of his no more than he ever talked of any of his troubles. His was the patrician avoidance of display. To those like Tony it was bad form to spill your insides—the code of the club carried over outside the club. To some of Tony's class it was bad form to have any insides. Tony was not like that. Tony was deep. But his depths were not for public view.

Alone in the cabin that night, lying in his bunk, he assessed the damage to his friends still in evidence a year and more after their calamity. Or rather, the damage to one of them: Tony. It was presumptuous enough of him to try to imagine the father's grief and guilt; the mother's, she in whose body had ripened that one smashed by itself out of all human semblance—at least he had the humility not even to try to imagine that. The outward evidence of damage to Tony was all too ample, and it of course could be no more than a token of the inner ravage. It was to be seen not only in the added

and deepened lines of his face; in the stoop of his shoulders
and the inclination of his head, slight but, in him who had
always carried himself so erect, marked; in the blanching of
his complexion caused by his long confinement indoors, he
who before was always browned by the sun the year round,
and the spread of white strands in his hair—it was even more
noticeable in his manner. Always ebullient, Tony was now
subdued; always decisive, he was now vague; always self-
assured, he was now timorous. He peered at the world with
eyes troubled by some nagging, unanswered question; it
gave him the look of a man whose vision was beginning to
fail. Even with his dearest friend he seemed unsure whether
his company was welcome. There was an air of self-mistrust,
of uneasiness about him—about Tony Thayer, of all people!
Whenever he caught himself smiling, and that was all too
seldom, he corrected himself and put on a sober look; whenever he caught himself looking sober he corrected himself
and smiled. He seemed to feel it would be thought unseemly
for someone who had suffered what he had to evince interest
in life, and again he seemed to fear it would be thought
unseemly to let it be seen that he had lost interest, to let his
suffering show and inflict the burden of it upon others. He
must surely ask himself whether even his friend was not
wondering how much he was to blame for what had happened, in what way he had so wretchedly failed as a father. It
was as if Tony's conception of himself had been shattered and
a new one, strange to him, substituted for it. An analogy
suggested itself. Just days earlier he had heard on the radio an
interview with a famous surgeon. From it he learned of a new
departure in heart transplants. Instead of replacing the patient's own diseased heart with the donor's they now left it in
place alongside the new one. In tandem, the pair shared the
work. For whatever the period of reprieve from death given
him by the operation, the patient had two hearts, neither
very reliable, the one defective, the other susceptible to rejection by its host. Tony's emotional infirmity was now com-
parable to that two-hearted person. His old shattered self
coexisted with a new one alien to him. And all this was evi-

dent in a single evening, an evening, moreover, devoted to the planning of a pleasure cruise. How much more must lie concealed from sight!

Suffering was not ennobling; on the contrary, it was demeaning. Suffering distorted the heart, perverted its impulses. He could not claim to have done very much suffering, maybe not even his proper share, but from his limited experience he knew that much about it, and maybe there were moments now when Tony begrudged him his immunity, when he said to himself, why me, why not you, my friend? He would loathe himself for feeling that but loathing himself would not keep him from feeling it.

Meanwhile, notwithstanding these disquieting thoughts, he was getting drowsy. The rhythmical rocking of the boat, the good food and wine and the regular tolling of the buoy bell, the heady salt air were working their spell on him. Was there not a distortion of the heart in nonsuffering too? Luxuriating in his satiated senses, secure in the blessings of life: that was incompatible with his sorrowing for his friends, but of just such incompatibilities was life composed. He was not unmindful that at home, or rather, gone from home in a pet, he had a wife with whom he was spatting, but in comparison with his friends' his troubles were trifling. For him life was good, and perhaps to excuse himself for the difference between his luck and theirs he felt a moment of resentment—no, he felt a moment of sheer exasperation for the poor, desperate girl, his own goddaughter, who had done this to her parents. How could a young person with everything to look forward to, pretty, privileged, pampered, have done this to them, have been so ungrateful for the life they had given her? In a moment of obliquity both moral and mental he said to himself that her life was not hers to squander so frivolously.

For "frivolously" was how he thought of it. The inviolable sanctity of each human life and the right of no one to take another's in which he believed carried with it for him the inviolable right of a person to end his life when it became unbearable. The choice not to live was as precious as the right to life, and were he yet to suffer unendurable anguish of mind or an incurable, long, excruciatingly painful illness, he believed he had the right to end his life, even a duty to do it and spare his family and friends the sight of his pain, his helplessness and dependency. Those who were ill, alone, who had lived the best years of their allotted span and were nearing the natural end, to them we, at least some of us, were willing to extend the right to choose their own deaths. But like so much else done for their own good, this freedom was one forbidden to the young. Their despairs were no more to be taken seriously than their loves. The suicide of a young person called in doubt the worth of life itself. Was it for this reason that we felt it not to be their right but a childish senselessness and took it as a personal affront? Whatever our reason, we felt there was always hope for the young. With them things were never as bad as they seemed. If only they gave us the chance we could reason with the young, coax them back from the brink, reconcile them. Wasteful: that was how we thought of them. Every moment precious to us as life rushed to its ordained end, we recoiled from their waste of it.

In the early morning light the gray windblown water had looked like hammered lead but by the hour appropriate for the moose juice to appear abovedeck the skies had cleared and in the afternoon they anchored off a rocky pine-peaked shore and rowed the dinghy in and went musselgathering and at the happy hour the Jolly Roger flew from the mast and it was just like old times. Except for the bloody, mangled ghost who now haunted the boat, who foreran its course, its every veer and tack, as though on the prow it had a lifesize figurehead of her. But that went without saying. Her they had with them now always and everywhere, and always would; meanwhile life went on.

It was October and after this last cruise of the year the boat would be hauled out of water and put for the winter in dry-dock. For the past two seasons while the Thayers themselves had not sailed she had been chartered for a week or two weeks at a time to strangers. Indifferently treated, she was now in need of her owners' care. For the first couple of days under sail all hands were busy, when not taking their turns at the wheel, putting things shipshape. While Pris tidied the head and folded and arranged the charts and scrubbed and polished and put things back where they belonged in the galley he tinkered with the engine trying to find the cause of a knock he had not liked the sound of as they left port under power. The captain meanwhile familiarized himself anew with his boat. He had been away from her for a long time; he acted as though he had been away even longer than he had. It was as though he were chartering her. Even after Pris had restored all to its wonted place things still eluded him. Where was the such-and-such kept? he was obliged to ask, until Pris grew impatient with this absentmindedness, impatient or else embarrassed for him, embarrassed by this revelation of the width of the gap in his life. His seamanship had grown rather dull from disuse. He was no longer nearly as sharp as he used to be in trimming his sails to catch the least breath of a breeze.

Pandora was spacious as sailboats go; still they lived closely confined aboard her and soon there were moments when he sensed that Tony now found being constantly companionable wearisome and chafed for privacy, for silence. One of the most engaging of his traits had been his attentiveness. It made you feel that he had cleared his mind of everything else in order to concentrate upon the important matter you had to impart. This stimulated you in your choice of words and made you either thoughtful or else inspired in your silliness. He brought out the best in you, made you more inventive, more entertaining, and raised you in your own esteem. Now a diffuseness in his gaze sometimes revealed that he was only half attending, or attending with effort. Tony had something on his mind now that would not be cleared. His thoughts were elsewhere. It was not drink that caused his distractedness; on the contrary, it was the distractedness that was causing him to drink.

Such observations as this he made of his friend while striving not to seem to be observing him. The last thing he wanted was to make Tony feel that he was being studied, that he was the object of morbid curiosity. Under surveillance must be how the Thayers felt themselves to be now whether they were or not. He could imagine—he was continually beginning observations to himself about Tony with that: *he could imagine,* only to break off and rebuke himself with, No, he could *not* imagine. It was presumptuous of him to think he could imagine the feelings of someone who had undergone Tony's soul-shattering experience.

But there was hardly a waking moment when they were not thrown together like dice in a dice cup and he could not avoid seeing what was to be seen. As on that day off Monhegan when foul weather forced them to ride it out at anchor and kept them battened down and cooped below. Then he had—it was forced upon him—the opportunity to study his friends like creatures in a cage. They bobbed, they yawed; the boat ran the length of the anchor chain one way and then the wind shifted and back it went the other way. The portholes streamed with rain and in the cabin silence thickened like the fog. Such close confinement tried the patience, not to say the tempers, of even the best of friends.

Trying that day to dispel the deepening gloom, to earn his passage by enlivening things a bit, he learned to his chagrin not only that his efforts were unavailing, but that they were unwelcome, wearisome. He longed to say something that would distract his friends' minds. Console them, cheer them. He believed in the power of words to do anything but he could not find the right ones. And he doubted his own sincerity—perhaps that was why he could not find the right words. What masqueraded as a selfless longing to comfort his friends was equally as much a longing to still horrors of his own which the suicide of any young person aroused. However pure or impure his intentions, he failed, and though not a word was said in rebuke he felt nonetheless rebuked for his frivolousness. Without the boat to keep him busy Tony's thoughts drifted to his troubles, and once in those waters, like the boat itself wallowing in a calm, he could not get moving again.

A part of Tony had died with Christy and it was precisely

the part of himself that before he had shared with others. Now, try as he might, regret his failure as he evidently did, he could not be the friend he had been. You could almost read in his face a plea to be forgiven this contraction of himself. Two hearts were not more, they were less than one. The company Tony longed for now with both his flawed hearts was that of his dead daughter. It was she whom he sought with those unfocused eyes, she and the answer to the question as endlessly repetitive as the waves: why?

It was on that day at anchor that something else surfaced too, a thing so unexpected, so unpredictable, so disturbing, and the evidence of it so carefully concealed—from themselves even more than from their friend—that even someone who knew the Thayers as well as he did had difficulty in detecting it, believed it unwillingly, sorrowfully. Rather than drawing more closely together in their time of trouble, as, surely, another couple would have done, the Thayers had drifted apart. The rift between them was not wide, but it was there, and in just one week at sea, in their close confinement, he watched it widen.

He noticed first how little the two of them had to say to each other now. Both let him do the talking. They looked interested but the interest was feigned. They smiled at his little jokes, lame as they were, thin, hesitant, perishable little smiles, and each tried to urge the other into any discussion, but when he fell silent the conversation languished and soon lapsed into silence. It was as though they had just one topic to talk about and they wanted never to hear it spoken of again.

They were far too mannerly with each other for a married couple. The least show of genuine feeling would release a flood of it, they seemed to fear. They seemed weary, if not wary, of each other's company, as though what they reminded each other of was their mutual pain and sorrow. The careful consideration each showed the other had in it a suggestion of self-apology. Both were often absentminded and abstracted and were confused and embarrassed when caught lost in a study.

And another thing from before was missing; what it was he

realized on the fourth day out. On this cruise no snapshots were taken. There was nothing now of which Tony wanted a memento, it seemed.

Far more soothing to the spirit than any words of his was the sun and the serenity and the smooth motion once they weighed anchor and got going with the wind in the sails again. The hiss of the water against the sides of the hull was the very sound of silence. In the vastness all around and overhead there was solace. If you felt belittled by the immensity of it all and your chatter was hushed by humility and you were reminded once again of the impermanence of everything but sea and sky, there was, oddly enough, solace of sorts in that too: in the sense of how much suffering had anteceded yours and now was over, all passion spent, long forgotten—human lives as numerous as the waves and now as anonymous.

Along with this infinity encompassing him, his friends' troubles trivialized his own. He felt ashamed to look them in the face. And—petty, perverse, mean, miserable involuntary muscle that the human heart was!—there were moments when he actually resented them for that. We do not thank those who have put us to shame. Yet to them and to the silence and the spaciousness he owed this—and surely his friends would be glad to know that anything worthwhile could be derived from their misfortune: a sense of his foolishness and a determination to reform. Here in the close presence of inconsolable loss, here vividly reminded of his own paltriness and the brevity at best of life, he knew how blessed he was and how ungrateful he had been. He was ashamed of his own childishness and he felt it was his fault to have allowed Cathy to be as childish as she had been—or rather, as *he* had been. What an unaffordable luxury it was to quarrel with loved ones! The unforgivable sin was to squander your blessings in bickering with the person dearest to you. It was as if he had already made it up with Cathy, and in his happiness and gratitude, from the heights of his fatuity, so soon to be taken from under him, he could have wept tears of pity for his less fortunate friends.

Already the days were shortening. Having anchored early, they began drinking early. The evenings came down chilly and soon they were driven below and battened down the hatch for the night. In an effort to make Tony's drinking seem less immoderate and to disarm Pris's disapproval, he kept up with him drink for drink, dram for dram. This did not deflect Pris's censorious looks nor soften the set of her pursed lips. That cold, silent, tightlipped female disapproval which was the worst of all reproaches, which made a man feel as though he had been shut in a cell, in an isolation ward. Pris kept count of their consumption like a bartender required by law to serve no more to a patron who had had his fill, but unlike the bartender she was not doing the serving. As for herself, never much of a drinker, she was drinking less than ever, and now as Tony drank more and more she drank less and less.

What surprised and saddened him was to see how little sympathy Pris felt for Tony. Her husband's deterioration: who better than she knew what had caused it, and if he sought solace in the bottle who better than she knew the severity of his suffering?

Taking her book to bed with her, Pris retired early to their sleeping quarters forward of the head, leaving the cabin to Tony and him. Always on the side of the underdogs, baseball masochists, they listened on the radio to the last bitter out of the World Series games. Tony replenished their drinks every other inning, anesthesia for their pain, accompanying each with his "Just one more before we have another." Late on one of those nights, as he lay in his bunk pretending to be asleep, Pris made her way through the cabin to go on deck for a breath of air, intending to be overheard as she muttered to herself, "Damned boat smells like a distillery."

Drinking hours on this cruise had been pushed forward as though they sailed into an earlier time zone each day and reset their clocks. The moose juice came up the companionway at midmorning, the Jolly Roger that flew from the mast at the happy hour was run up in midafternoon. Happy hour! With Pris sipping her lone Dubonnet and looking on with the conviviality of a Carry Nation! She was no less annoyed with him now than with Tony, for it was his presence of which Tony was availing himself to drink all the more out of his duty as host.

Yesterday morning Tony had appeared on deck bearing drinks at an hour that caused Pris an even more pointed than usual look at her wristwatch. He was at the wheel, she knitting. He took a sip of his drink and choked, then choked again trying not to let her see that he was choking. It was almost straight Barbancourt rum. He pretended to drink it but when Pris balled up her knitting and went forward to stretch herself on deck he poured it over the side. There had to be one sober man on board, especially with those clouds piling up on the western rim.

He was at the wheel, Pris sunning and napping, Tony below listening to the radio.

"Skipper," he called, "I'm on one hundred and twenty degrees. Right?"

"Steady as you go," Tony called back.

With the coffeegrinder winch he took up on the sheet and trimmed the mainsail and caught the wind, and the boat responded with a shiver and a lunge like a racehorse feeling the crop. She lifted her bow and rose high, laving her sides with foam. She could be as frolicsome as a porpoise, give her a good breeze and someone at the helm to stroke her. She was in her forties but racy still. Keeping her was as costly as keeping a woman and she required just as much pampering. When she was hauled out and dry-docked yearly her decks were holystoned, her mahogany scraped down, varnished, her brightwork polished to gleam like gold. In an age of plastic hulls and aluminum masts she was a curiosity and in dock she drew crowds like a classic car. She was womanly in her lines, svelte in her prow, broadening appropriately down toward the bottom where her works were. Now the shrouds hummed, the windstreamers snapped. Below, Tony was assisting the mezzo-soprano with *Ma che cos' è quest'amore che fa tutti delirar'?* You would have thought he was four sheets to the wind unless you knew him, then you knew that off-key was the only way Tony could sing. He could not help but feel

a puritanical judgment that this was a bit too much jollity in a
man burdened by Tony's memories and regrets. Yet he felt
he had no right to judge him. If Tony could forget for a
moment any of all that he had to forget who was to begrudge
him that?

When he next called out his course they were skimming
along at a good eight knots. Tony's rendition of *Per la scala
dal balcone prest' andiamo via di qua* was interrupted for
"Aye, aye, Mr. Starbuck. Steady as you go." Hardly was this
said when the boat was rammed by something at least as solid
as a whale. Her bow reared high, she rolled to starboard and
from stem to stern a spasm shook her. Joints and sockets
cracked like bones breaking. From below came the crash and
clatter of gear, galley wares. He spun the wheel hard alee and
she came about and the sails emptied and hung slack while
the boat continued to wallow and to shudder as though
convulsing from the blow she had been dealt. Too shaken to
move, he sat gripping the spokes of the wheel. The dinghy
had been thrown from its davits and now, held to the boat by
its painter, bobbed on the water astern. Through his half-
dazed mind, not ready yet to deal with his predicament,
wandered the odd, idle thought that it looked as though it
were just born and still attached by the cord to its mother.

Pris handhauled herself back by the rail and arrived at the
cockpit as Tony came staggering up from below. He seemed
unaware of the gash across his forehead or of the flow from it
filming his eyes and causing him to weep tears of blood. He
looked like the enlightened Oedipus returning on stage. He
was reeling and appeared to be suffering from concussion of
the brain. He touched his brow, then stared with incompre-
hension at his bloody hand.

Leaving Pris to attend to Tony, he dashed below.

The galley floor was littered with pots and pans, canned
goods, the bunks with things from the shelves above them:
books, binoculars, the radio, still emitting Rossini—it must
have been the latter that had struck Tony in its fall. But in the
cabin, in the head, in the forward quarters there was no

water. She had not sprung a leak—not yet. From their locker beneath the bunk he took life jackets and returned on deck.

A wreck, he said to himself as he drew the dinghy alongside and dropped in its oars. That's what we've hit, he said to himself as he took off his sneakers. Lots of them in these waters and we've struck one. Either a new one or an old one that has shifted its lie too recently to be on the chart in the right place. That's what it's got to be.

He lowered the ladder over the side and, not knowing what was under the surface, lowered himself cautiously into the water, thinking that should they have to take to it they would be frozen dead within five minutes. He took a deep breath and submerged to assess the damage, the danger.

He never told the Thayers when he got back on board what he had found below nor did he consult the chart to see whether the reef they had struck was on it. He never had to tell them, he never had to consult the chart. Nor did he have to tell them that had the boat been a modern one its plastic hull would have split at the seam like a nut and gone down with all hands aboard before there was time even to don life jackets. One chartered by a neophyte sailor and his wife and children had done just that this very season in these very waters and—while horrified, helpless spectators watched from shore—sank in seconds.

What Tony had done was shocking, inexcusable—hardly believable. On even the smallest pleasure craft the captain was the captain, the same as on an ocean liner. At sea his word was law. Laxness in carrying out his orders might not be punishable by being put in irons or hanged from the yardarm, but it was the crew's duty, even when they were his close friends, to obey them. A boat was potentially a dangerous place and somebody had to be in command of it. In turn, it was the crew's right to expect their captain to be alert at all times. To his seamanship they entrusted their safety.

A sailor since he could walk, descendant of a long line of sea captains, nobody knew better than Tony that of all derelictions of the captain's duty inattention to the chart was the most egregious. That he could have committed it, thereby putting in jeopardy the lives of his wife and his closest friend, disclosed the depth of his continuing distraction of mind. It also, by its very enormity, silenced any criticism of him. He must have been drinking down below long before bringing up drinks for all. *People smile, but the agony endures.* . . .

He had toweled a tingle of warmth back into his body numbed by the icy water when Pris came from the forward quarters and joined him in the cabin.

"Anything I can do?" he asked.

She had done it all. Had washed Tony's bloody face and bandaged his cut and put him to bed to sleep it off. She shook her head. He was chilled by the look in her eyes of dull, detached, uncaring apathy. She was weary of Tony's suffering. It reminded her of her own.

But life went on and one dutifully reenacted its rituals, reminders though these were of a lost innocence that was now almost an accusation. And so, once inside the harbor, he cut the engine and dropped anchor at their old spot. At the time that inaugurated the custom about to be observed Christy could have been no more than two years old, his own Anthony not yet born.

While the charcoal in the grill grayed with ash they sat in the cockpit having a drink, all acting as though nothing untoward had happened yesterday, their thoughts on what awaited them at home. Surely the Thayers were thinking already of that; he was, and he had a lot less to think about than they. In fact, he was impatient to get home now, for he had resolved on this cruise to have things out with Cathy, settle their trifling dispute, and get them on a better understanding. The troubles of their friends had made him realize how lucky they were, how petty their squabbles. Trout season was over for the year, but he was considering suggesting a second honeymoon at the club. These were to be his last moments of such self-complacency, for meanwhile, at the marina, the superintendent had spotted them at anchor inside the harbor and his helper was even then on his way out in the skiff with orders to go as fast as he could go.

The superintendent had worked at the marina for many

years. He had been there when the Thayers and the Curtises
first cruised together. That was how he knew they would
drop anchor at that spot in the harbor before coming on in to
dock. They had stopped there at the end of their cruise ever
since the first one, for, because of what happened then, it had
become a rite. The superintendent knew the story. How for
their last meal on board Tony had saved a steak and had
stopped there to cook and eat it. Tony's way of cooking a
steak on board the boat was to soak newspapers and lay them
in a pad on the deck of the cockpit and build his charcoal fire
in a grill set on the pad of paper. Seeing this for the first time,
his passenger was dubious, not to say apprehensive.

They had had a drink and were having just one more
before having another when Tony became dissatisfied with
his fire. He went below to the galley and returned with a
paper cup full of alcohol. When he poured the alcohol on the
charcoal it flared and the stream became a fuse leading to the
cup. It was not the first time this had ever happened. Tony
was used to it. But he was not and when Tony set the cup on
the deck to burn itself out he stamped on it. Tony did a back
somersault over the rail, hit the water feet first and sank from
sight. All this had happened in a second.

Tony surfaced with his drowned pipe clenched between
his teeth. He was wearing shorts and when the cup was
stamped his bare legs had been spattered with drops of burning alcohol. Tony's leap into the water had been as instinctive
as was his stamping out the fire. Now patches of hair were
gone from Tony's legs as though moths had been at him.
They dried him off and rubbed him with an unguent. He was
not much hurt. He, Ben, burned more with shame than Tony
did with pain. Over their next drink it turned into comedy.

Now it was one of the many memories that bound them to
each other and, he supplying the steak, it had become a
tradition to round out their cruise with a last meal in this
same spot. It was this spot that the superintendent of the
marina had kept an eye on since the first phone call the day
before yesterday, not much expecting to see the boat until
about now, but watching nevertheless because of the ur-

gency in the woman's voice at the other end of the wire and because of his promise not just to have the call returned as soon as they docked but to do better than that by sending his helper out in the skiff as soon as they came in sight.

It was Tony's alarm that alarmed him. Not for himself, or if so, only as a reflex and only for a moment, but for his friend. Tony's inner battering was blazoned by that bandage on his forehead and the livid bruise surrounding it and by the bleariness of his eyes, alcohol-induced but that was not to dismiss it, for alcohol was only the symptom of a far deeper distress. Poor Tony, how changed he was! Always so cool, so steady, prepared to cope with whatever came—now this timorousness, this dread of life.

Tony offered to come ashore with him. In the way the offer was made there was something hesitant, apprehensive, insincere, a look in the eyes or an undertone to the words that saddened him for his friend as nothing before had done. Once the bravest and most generous of friends, his suffering had turned Tony cowardly and self-protective. He had troubles enough of his own, he could take on no part of anybody else's. He was able no longer to get outside himself, which was the first requirement for friendship as it was for love, and share in another life. He was glad he had declined that offer and insisted that Tony stay aboard the boat. He was glad of that, at least.

"We'll put everything on the back burner until we know what's the matter," said Tony to him as he boarded the skiff.

"Nothing's 'the matter,' " he said as though to a fearful child. "Whatever it is it'll keep until we've eaten and brought the boat in. I'll be right back." Last words of a life then ending. When, ten minutes later, they returned to haunt him, to taste like ashes on his tongue, they would seem to have come from before the Fall.

The number he was given to dial had the same New Jersey area code as the phone in Anthony's dormitory but it was not Anthony's number and that caused him a moment's perplexity, for he knew nobody else in that area. It could not be a call from Cathy, for she had headed west from home; that was all he knew—all she herself had known—about her destination, but that much he knew. So it was not a call from Anthony and yet it must concern him. Those words of Tony's to which he had just condescended so loftily now nagged him: he hoped nothing was the matter.

This while the unknown phone rang once, twice. Later, hunter that he was, he would liken those final moments of his former life while the phone rang to the interval between the firing of the gun and the meeting in air of the shot and the bird on the wing. Later; at the time he could liken what then happened to nothing that had ever happened to him before. This time he was not the hunter, he was the bird on the wing, and the shot that brought him down, that placed a pellet in his every vital part, was the president of Princeton University's informing him, with a heavy heart and with a father's sympathy, that his son Anthony had committed suicide.

*

He could just imagine what a father must feel on being told that his child had died in an accident or been killed in combat or died of a disease. After the shock of it would come the heartbreak, the anguish, the realization of the awful finality, the sense of loss and the loneliness, the unfillable gap left in your life, your unspent pity for the poor child and your regret at not having been there at the end to soothe him, to say good-bye, your own self-pity and your dread of telling his mother, the special sadness of burying a young person and the inadequacy of your friends' condolences: he could imagine all this with a vividness born of longing, for these sufferings, forbidden to him, were what his heart cried out for. He envied the man to whom they were permitted as a dying soldier might envy his neighbor in the next bed merely maimed by the same projectile. His dead son had unfathered him.

He must do his grieving alone and out of sight and with the consciousness that the object of it had repudiated him and all his works, especially one of his works, his own begetting. Within the space of a minute after hanging up the telephone that knowledge descended upon him. For some while after the conclusion of the conversation he sat with the receiver still to his ear. Finally becoming conscious of the humming in his head he lowered the mechanism. He did not at once replace it in its cradle. He stared at it as though he had never seen one before and knew only dimly what it was. Then there was a moment when he could not recall what he had just been told. It was something bad, very bad, but for a moment he was too stunned to recall what it was.

The manner of his son's death had made him a pariah, had put him in quarantine—or rather, it had drafted him into that army which until now, except for thoughts of the Thayers, had existed for him in articles on teenage suicide in newsmagazines in doctors' and dentists' waiting rooms and which he had read only because of his friends: their survivors, their parents, people whom, now that he was one of them, he knew to be the loneliest alive, like the multitude of souls in any one circle of Dante's hell, all condemned to the same torment for the same transgression, each in too much pain to comfort a fellow sufferer, indeed, seeing in fellow sufferers a mirror image of his own pain, his guilt, his shame.

On the wall in the office of the Gloucester marina hung a clock. At 1:21 he was a man who had not known how happy he had been at 1:20. Within that minute he had been cut off from both the living and the dead. To the living, as he knew before he had yet faced a single one of them, he would embody the ultimate affront to life, and to none more so than his fellow survivors. The unknowing look of strangers would be hard enough to bear but the commiseration of friends straining across the unbridgeable gulf that had opened all around him would be intolerable.

As yet his son's death was not real to him but already his responsibility for it was. For something which he was not conscious of having done but to which he confessed his guilt, he had been judged, convicted, and condemned to a life sentence all in a minute. Just one little minute out of the eternity of time—if only the clock could be turned back that one minute! Yet in his heart he knew that that minute was only the last in a long sequence and that he was the one who, without knowing when the alarm was timed to go off, had wound the clock and set it going.

He had just one person to turn to now, his partner in guilt. When he dialed home and was answered not by her but by the tape recording he had left saying that he had gone sailing out of Gloucester and by a message urging him to call the number he had just called, it seemed the final rejection of him. He felt the world had turned from him as from a criminal in olden times when they were branded on the forehead or had a nostril slit or an ear notched so that people knew on sight that you were a criminal and what your crime had been. The last persons on earth who would want to see him now were the dear friends who would understand only too well what he was going through. Nor did he want to see them. Only now did he realize how little he had really felt, how shallow his sympathy had been, how trite and beside the point his efforts to console them when they were enduring what he was enduring now. This bond had not brought them closer, it had sundered them. The sight of a leper was frightening and disgusting to everybody but surely none did it frighten and disgust more than the poor leper whose company was restricted to those like himself.

The clock on the wall, now one minute deeper into the day, told him it was time he began serving his sentence. He went outside and told the boy who had brought him ashore to return to the boat and tell his friends that he had been called away and would be in touch with them sometime later. Looking at his reflection in the eyes of the superintendent of the marina he saw that he was a marked man. For the father of a child who had killed itself the parts mutilated as punishment were private and did not show but the damage was emblazoned on his face and evident in his every gesture. His son had unmanned him.

*

He kept waiting for his mind to break down at any moment. What a breakdown of the mind entailed he had no clear idea but he was amazed that his kept on functioning—amazed and somewhat chagrined. To be able to carry on after such knowledge was callous, even gross. His hardiness seemed to him hardness, his elasticity coarseness of fiber. Actually he was more impaired than he realized at the time.

What happened was that for the rémainder of that devastating day a sort of automatic pilot took over and steered his course for him. Only the operation of some such auxiliary mechanism of the mind could have gotten him from Gloucester to Princeton. A kind of emotional second wind, quickly expended, dangerous to draw upon, but there when desperately needed to complete the course. With this emergency second self behind the wheel of the rented car, he blanked out, as Anthony, when he was very young and subject to carsickness, stretched out in the back seat and slept through long trips. Indeed, there were moments while driving down to Boston when it was strangely as though it was Anthony at the wheel.

He had once suffered a blow on the head that caused concussion of the brain. Afterwards he carried on as usual but for days he felt queer all the time and he experienced periodical blankness of mind. The queerness was caused by the feeling that none of his senses was attuned just right: his vision was slightly blurred, his hearing somewhat muffled—the world seemed to be in retreat from him. Then, like a failure in the house of the electric current when the lights all go out and you are left in the dark, his train of thought would be disrupted in the middle of a task. He would find himself in some place and not know how he had arrived or what he was there to do, like a sleepwalker on waking. The drain upon his damaged brain had been too great and it was protecting itself, blowing its overloaded fuse. So it was responding now. It was not the stretches of confusion and disorientation that were painful, it was the intermittent return of clarity, when he knew where he was and what he was there to do, when through his involuntary, his self-administered anesthesia, his pain asserted itself.

Such a moment came when it was his turn at the ticket window in Logan Airport.

"Yes, sir," said the clerk. "Help you?"

He opened his mouth to speak but to his surprise he could not utter a word. When he tried, his jaw began to tremble and his eyes brimmed with tears. The clerk, used to people who drank themselves senseless to drown their fear of flying, evidently thought he was one of those. He was not drunk but the sensations he was experiencing were those of drunkenness. Not a gradual mellowing but that moment of sudden, sickening poleaxed stupefaction from having drunk much too much far too fast. He excused himself with a wave of the hand, fell out of line, and found himself a seat.

On any day of the week Logan Airport was busy, a crossroads with thousands of people arriving and departing, greeting and taking leave of one another. Boston was a college town, none bigger, and many of these people were students —none of them his, each and every one of them a reminder of his. He saw several families happily reunited as his would never be again.

The stewardesses' smiles were the same for each and every passenger. Bright, commercial smiles that one must accept as part of the fiction that every trip was a pleasure trip. Everybody on this one was bound for the same place: Newark. The flight was a direct one, with no intermediate stops. Some no doubt were going as he was from Newark on to Princeton. They were going home, going back to school, back to work, going on business to one or another of the industrial research centers with which present-day Princeton was ringed. For them this was an unexceptional day, not one to be circled forevermore on their calendars, another day in lives punctuated by change but not brought to a full stop, fundamentally the same as they had been yesterday and as they would be tomorrow (except that none of them could foresee what lay in wait tomorrow, or even yet today; only this morning he had thought he was sailing back to all that he had left on land). There was always, on any flight, not just one laden with compatriots returning home from abroad but any flight, an atmosphere faintly familial, clubby. To him now the one thing that he and the others had in common, their all being bound for the same place, only emphasized their dissimilarity. A person boarding the plane with the intention of hijacking it and diverting all aboard from their expected destination to his private one could not have felt himself more different, more completely alienated from his fellow passengers than he felt. Nor have disguised his inner turmoil with more of a bearing of studied ordinariness.

He had gotten away from nothing while in the air, yet when the plane touched down and he felt the earth with all its attendant duties underfoot again it was as though he had returned from the weightlessness of outer space and resumed the full burden of his bulk. Exhausted now, down to the last gasp of that second wind, having been sailing a boat off the New England coast early that same day, longing to be alone instead of on a bus, mistrustful of himself behind a wheel and with no need of a car for the day ahead of him tomorrow, instead of renting another one he hired a taxi to take him from Newark Airport to Princeton.

"Wake me when we get there," he said to the driver, thereby averting conversation, and then stared open-eyed into the night throughout the forty-mile drive.

If he had escaped detection by his fellow plane passengers it was probably only by pretending to doze through the flight and avoiding conversation with either of his neighbors, and protected by that universal assumption that all trips were pleasure trips. The desk clerk at Princeton's Nassau Inn spotted him instantly as a suspicious character and said all rooms were booked for the night.

"I had to drop everything and leave on the spur of the moment," he said in explanation of his having no luggage.

But there was more to it than that. To the clerk's trained and experienced eye his appearance, his manner betrayed him as being up to no good. That there was something self-condemning and haggard about his look he could feel.

"Sorry, sir," said the clerk.

He was tired, dead tired, he knew of no other, less particular hotel, and he was going to have to expose himself to the world sooner or later. The news would have been in the local papers and Princeton was a small town, dominated by the university.

"My name," he said, looking away as he said it, "is Curtis." It was the first time in his life that he had ever been embarrassed by it.

He allowed several seconds to pass.

"I'm the father—"

"Ooh," he heard the clerk say. The sound escaped him like air from a puncture.

He faced the man.

Now it was the clerk whose face bore an expression of guilt and contrition. The two of them stood facing each other, both trying but both unable to utter another syllable.

*

His last time in Princeton had been when he drove Anthony there for registration. That that was still not two months ago was as contrary to common sense as that the earth was round. There had not been time even for a change of seasons. The leaves on the trees were only beginning to yellow. It was tantalizingly as if the clock had been turned back to that earlier time and what had happened since had not happened. But of course it had happened and this illusion only made it more achingly real.

That last time was all too green in his memory as, on his way to call on the president of the university the following morning, he crossed the campus.

Actually they had arrived the day before registration to give Anthony time to get settled. By prearrangement over the long-distance telephone they had met Anthony's new roommate, Jeremy, that day. Lunch together was all the time needed for them to learn to like Jeremy. How important it was to like your first college roommate nobody knew better than he. He had been reminded often that day of his.

The boys had been assigned ground floor quarters, a bedroom with bunks provided by the university and an un-

furnished sitting room with a fireplace, with stone-mullioned
windows looking out on a quadrangle. They had agreed beforehand that each would contribute two hundred and fifty
dollars—on Anthony's side a lot of trout flies—to buy their
furnishings. How times had changed! And inflation did not
account entirely for the difference. He himself had lost no
time in letting his new roommate, who looked rather well-to-
do, know that fifty dollars was his limit; with a sigh of relief
Tony had said that that was the very sum he had to spend. He
drove Anthony and Jeremy to secondhand shops in and
around the town that day, and he had been both amused and
impressed by their taste, their mutual tact, their thrift. His
last sight of his son had been of him setting off with his
roommate for supper at their eating club.

It had entertained him all the way home that evening to
contrast himself during his first days at Princeton with Anthony. Then as now it was assumed that the grub you were on
graduation from high school had had the summer in which to
have spun its cocoon and that on or about Labor Day you had
emerged with a full set of wings. You were now ready for and
worthy of Princeton, of the society of your classmates and the
efforts on your behalf of your professors and your preceptors.

Each of your first walks across campus to class made your
heart both soar and sink. All this for you—but were you for it?
There was nothing forbidding in themselves about the build-
ings; what was forbidding was your sense of being out of
place among them. Temples of learning into which you entered like an infidel in disguise, faked the responses to the
ritual by taking your cue from the true believers and sometimes failing to take your cue, nodding knowingly at the
professor's allusions and laughing a bar late at his jokes and
being stared at by your classmates who had laughed on time.
His references to books you had not read sent you scurrying
after class to the library, there to be overwhelmed by an
ocean of unread books awaiting you. You and you alone
seemed to have missed some session in school that would
have made college algebra comprehensible. You turned in

disgust against yourself and in anger against the school that had sent you there so unprepared.

An orphan from the age of ten, brought up by grandparents in an atmosphere guaranteed to stifle the mind and to scare it witless on first being exposed to matters intellectual, far from home—in fact, without any home to long for—he had been countrified and callow, shy and self-conscious when he arrived at Princeton, not strongly silent as was the impression everybody had of Anthony. Had it not been his good luck to be assigned Tony Thayer as a roommate he might have fallen into a desperate mood of loneliness and a paralyzing sense of inferiority. Anthony was so much more mature than he had been at that age. More worldly, more resourceful, more independent and self-assured. He was better educated. He had grown up in a bookish home. He was *his* son. It was pleasing to recall that Princeton had soon set to rest his fears of it, even more pleasant the conviction that in Anthony it would arouse none.

Even now—acutely, piercingly now—the beauty of the campus struck him as it always had. It was hard to understand how anybody could be anything but happy here. Yet it was easy to understand how, if you were unhappy, being surrounded by beauty to which you were privileged but unable to respond to would deepen your unhappiness, and the sight of others at home in it would make you feel even more alienated and unworthy of all that was being wasted on you. The very sight of the groundskeepers at their work would make you feel out of place; then, if you were a dutiful child, there would follow a feeling of guilt over the money your being here was costing your parents. There was no end to the number of bypaths leading off the trail of sorrow, and when you were young it was so easy to get lost.

A look of uneasiness crossed the president's face when they were introduced; that was predictable, but it lingered on long enough to be seen as something more than just uneasiness. The man seemed to have been so certain in his expectation of something different that he found the reality disconcerting. This caused him to take quick stock of himself and then he saw what was lacking, what it was that the president had been expecting. A couple, man and wife, father and mother—even if estranged, brought together now. The realization stunned him. In his shock, in the press of duties all requiring urgent attention, in his personal pain and consequent numbness to all else, he had put Cathy out of mind, had set her aside as another of his duties, to be attended to when her turn came. Abashed at his unmindfulness, appalled at the task awaiting him of telling her all that she did not know, unable to believe that she did not know it all, he hardly heard what the president said, hardly knew what he himself replied.

Not that there was much to say. The president expressed his own and the community's shock and sorrow. Still, apparently, not fully recovered from his surprise at there being no Mrs. Curtis present, he said their sympathy went out to him and to—all of his. If there was anything he or his staff could do to facilitate arrangements, please call on them. He offered the use of the university chapel for a memorial service. The cadence of their speech soon signified that the interview had run its obligatory course.

He felt awkward about asking for help or advice. He and his had caused embarrassment and trouble enough. However, "Can you tell me," he asked, his face flushing hotly, "what is expected of me now?" At once he wished he had expressed himself somehow differently. He had not meant to imply that student suicides at Princeton were commonplace enough for there to be a set of rules for their survivors. "I mean, to claim the body must I go to the police?"

The president said he understood there were certain legal formalities. He himself was not familiar with them; however, the head of the university security department, who had been in touch with the local authorities from the start, understood the rules. He was on his way over now. That—the phone rang—would be to announce him.

Everything was being done to smooth his passage. The president turned him over to the security chief. He in turn, in order to spare them a visit to the police department and possibly a wait there, had arranged for an officer to meet them at the undertaker's. This was on one of the streets leading off Nassau and there he drove them, refraining from conversation. It was a lovely day that Anthony was missing.

At the undertaker's the security man and the plainclothes policeman remained upstairs while he was conducted to the basement. A door was opened for him and then the undertaker discreetly withdrew.

The body, illuminated by an overhead light, lay on a table in the center of the room. It was dressed in the familiar jeans and flannel shirt, missing the loafers. It lay face up, or rather, it lay on its back but from the doorway it was the back of the head that was to be seen. It was as though, hearing his father coming, Anthony had turned his face to hide his shame. He approached, went around to the other side, and the curiosity he had not dared acknowledge to himself was amply satisfied. The boy had hanged himself.

His eyes shut of themselves but that did not shut out the sight; on the contrary, in the darkness of his mind the after-image glowed phosphorescent.

At just what moment, or rather during what full five minutes—for it must have taken all of that—during what five carefree minutes of his had it been happening, what idle thing had he been doing even as his son hung threshing in air? The answer to his question came all too promptly. His mind, his horrified but irrepressibly curious mind, like a dog nosing in ordure, brought it to him and laid it at his feet. Out sailing on the smooth and soothing waters of Penobscot Bay, he had been silently dispensing pity to his friends for the suicide of their child.

Back upstairs he signed the papers presented to him by the police officer. Seeing that he was incapable of reading, it was explained to him that with these documents he identified the body as that of Anthony Curtis, age eighteen, son of Benjamin and Catherine Curtis of Blairstown, New Jersey, and as next of kin claimed it and, the death having been violent, neither natural nor accidental, affirmed it to have been a suicide and absolved the Princeton police from the duty of investigating it. The security officer volunteered to drive him wherever he might want to go. He thanked him but said he was familiar with the town and that he would prefer now to be alone.

It was then shortly past ten. He was to come back to the undertaker's at five. He returned to his room at the inn. He hung the Do Not Disturb sign on the doorknob and stretched himself out on the bed. There he stayed until checkout time at two, when he paid his bill and left. Meanwhile, after several tries, he had reached Jeremy on the phone and made a date with him for three. Classes would keep him until then. The world kept turning although your son had dropped out. He walked over to the campus, passing on Nassau Street a troupe of Hare Krishnas in their sandals and saffron robes banging their tambourines and chanting their mindless incantation—people who had found the answers but not the questions.

It came back to him as he strolled along the campus walks, through quads and cloisters, as he rested on benches and watched the odd, skull-faced, black Princeton squirrels at play, a couple of students his son's age flinging a Frisbee, how pleased he had been at Anthony's choice of his father's old school, and this though he had never urged it, never even proposed it. He had not opposed Anthony's decision not to go to college. He had deplored it, for college had meant so much to him, but he had not opposed it. He believed that going to college was the easiest way to begin to acquire an education, the only way for people like himself, but the easiest way was not the best way for everybody. Intellectual though he was, he was by no means bent on his son's becoming one. When Anthony changed his mind and decided to go to college after all, he was glad; when he chose Princeton, it had seemed to his father a mark of approval of him. It was another bond between them. It would give them memories to share.

Motivated: that was today's word. It even appeared on college admissions evaluations. He himself had arrived at Princeton with no motivation beyond wanting to play on the baseball team and to earn the degree needed for getting on in the world. Once Anthony had changed his mind and decided to go to college after all he must surely have been the most highly motivated member of his entering class. He was already looking beyond Princeton, had chosen his professional school, picked a wife, planned a family. How had all that drive and determination and sense of purpose been lost in so short a time?

The same differences between father and son that were matters for pride one moment became matters for reproach the next one, and he was tempted to commit the common parental sin of contrasting his own disadvantages to the advantages he had given his son and to charge his early discouragement to his being spoiled. It was a charge he could never make stick. Anthony had not been spoiled; he had resisted all his parents' efforts to spoil him.

It was unfair of him to expect that to Anthony Princeton would mean as much as it had meant to him. As unfair as it would have been to expect his roommate Jeremy to be to Anthony what Tony Thayer had been to him. The two dormitory rooms that Tony and he had shared were the first home he had ever had to call his own, and he would have loved them even if he had had to share them with someone less agreeable than Tony. Pleased as he was with them, that fact was one he kept from his roommate.

He was obscurely ashamed of being an orphan, as though he were somehow to blame, and, just because he was loath to talk about it, did not yet know that all orphans were more or less ashamed; as we all think when we are young about our shortcomings, he thought his were unique. Tony's affectionate references to his parents, his reading aloud from their letters, made him all the more self-conscious, and by silence and evasion he managed for a while to keep his secret. Then came Thanksgiving.

Tony was going home for the holidays. That he was not doing the same came out one day. This year for the first time he did not have even the elderly grandparents who had taken him in on the death of his parents. He was not sorry for himself. He did not think himself unfortunate. He was looking forward to spending his holidays here alone, having the campus all to himself.

When finally it came out that he had no home to go to, Tony was appalled. You would have thought he had just found his roommate in his swaddling clothes abandoned on the orphanage steps. He did not invite him home with him, he decreed it. They took the spur line train, the time-honored "Dinky," from Princeton to the main line, from there the train to New York, then upriver to Hudson. That visit was his first to Riverside. His experience, that of an orphan of eighteen fresh out of Kansas, attending an Ivy League college on a baseball scholarship, provided him with only one comparison: it had been a movie set come to life. And he had been sharing digs with the heir to all this! Was it owing to Tony's graciousness or to his own backwardness that he had never suspected? Recalling in the midst of all this splendor the shabbiness of their furnishings at school, for which he felt himself responsible, he began an apology. He was silenced by Tony's saying he had thought he liked their rooms. His ingrained class prejudice got a shaking-up on that visit. No one was less nice for not being poor.

It was observing Tony as they studied together in the evenings that first piqued his intellectual curiosity—or more accurately, that opened in that previously unbroken ground the first furrow. He had unquestioningly assumed that after graduation he would go into business, and his evenings were spent grinding away at mathematics and economics texts. Seeing Tony shake with laughter or lay down his book enraptured and gaze off into some scene conjured up by words on a printed page was something he had never before seen anybody do, could not comprehend, could only marvel at. There was something to be envied in such enjoyment, and in Tony's case it was genuine, not affected. Timidly, furtively, afraid of being laughed at, even taunted for his presumption, as Caliban might have stolen a peek into Prospero's book he looked into one of Tony's. His horoscope for that day must have been in all the right conjunctions: his first book was *Don Quixote*.

Like Prospero's, it was magical; unlike Caliban, he actually appreciated something of what he read.

Good books were *good:* it was the most eye-opening lesson of his life. Though unable to ask why nobody had told him, he felt nonetheless that he had been deprived. Somebody should have said that "good" meant just that, not good for you.

He began to wonder whether, to dare hope that, inside his hulk of a body there might be an unsuspected brain. He had learned that not everybody well-to-do was a ne'er-do-well; maybe not every jock was a jerk.

To none of his professors did he owe more of his early education than he did to Tony. The sharing of his enthusiasms was Tony's greatest pleasure. He never put down your enthusiasm for a book you had just discovered for yourself and which he had outgrown, but he always had one to recommend that replaced yours. And in those days, when they had time for everything, Tony was always ready to lay down his book and go outside for play. In their senior year he was batting .299 as the varsity first baseman and, along with Tony, was on the staff of *The Nasssau Lit.*

The tower clock struck three. As he rose from his bench to go and keep his appointment for this hour it was as if the double images of vision which all his life had been fused into a single image by the receptors of his brain had split and separated. With one he saw the two young men that Tony and he had been and with the other saw this very moment, germinating in them even in those early days—another bond between them.

*

With a thoughtfulness and tact that touched him almost to tears, Jeremy had packed all of Anthony's personal possessions, thus sparing him having to handle them. A duffel bag and a cardboard carton sufficed to contain them. Anthony had been one to pare life to its essentials. But lest it seem that he was hurrying his guest's departure by having everything ready to be removed, that he was trying with unseemly haste to exorcise the ghost that now haunted the premises, Jeremy offered him a drink, and lest it seem that he was anxious to get away, he accepted. Over them hung a pall that both were trying to disregard. The boy was on edge despite his efforts, afraid of him, afraid for him, in dread of his questions and painfully ill-at-ease here in the very setting of his sorrow.

While Jeremy brought a bottle from a cabinet and water from the bathroom tap he took in the surroundings in which his son had lived his final weeks and which had been the last his eyes had closed upon—except that they had not closed but had bulged from their sockets. His own eyes strayed upwards against his will and searched for something to attach a noose to. An overhead water pipe was the only possible thing he could discover.

"We kept a bottle, Mr. Curtis," said Jeremy as he poured, "but, please, don't get the idea that we did a lot of drinking. We didn't. We—" He stopped, sensing how superfluous it was now to defend Anthony against his father's suspicions, how any testimony to his good behavior only added to the pain. And how the past tense evoked the present, the future.

"Were you the one who found him?" The drink helped him ask that.

Jeremy nodded and, once started, kept nodding, unable to stop himself, confirming what he still could not accept. Through the boy's eyes, wide with shock, he saw as clearly as through panes the image imprinted on his mind. The stage itself surrounded him; the only property missing was the body. Cut down and removed from the scene, it still hung in place in Jeremy's memory, and would for as long as he lived. As if by a process of mental photography, in the look that passed between them it was copied permanently onto his mind. Unable to sustain their look, Jeremy averted his gaze. His involuntary upward glance lingered momentarily on the water pipe, and the picture was replete.

"I was away," Jeremy said. "My father had an operation and I went to New Haven to be with him. I was away for three days. When I returned . . ."

He let the boy lapse into silence. Actually, to his perplexity, he was curious, even avid for details, but the boy was suffering. No doubt he had already had to recount it to the campus guard, the town police, the coroner, and they were simply people doing their jobs. He let the boy think he was sparing him.

"There was no note?"

"No, sir."

There seemed to be nothing more to say, no reason to prolong this further. He drained his drink preparatory to leaving. He looked at his watch. What then passed through his mind chained him to his chair. As surely as if he were present to see it, he knew that this was the moment when Anthony's body was being consigned to the flames. He had never been inside a crematorium but imagination supplied him with particulars. He saw the body conveyed on rollers, as in a foundry, to a furnace too fiery to be looked into. He saw the hair burst aflame, the eyes whiten and turn opaque like those of a fish in a frying pan. He saw the assaulted skin cleave to the skull and the lips draw back exposing the teeth in a last grisly grin. He saw the flesh shrivel and sear like a roast in an oven and saw the body jerk and writhe as nerves and muscles and sinews contracted spasmodically in the infernal heat, then saw it charred black. In seconds the flesh was consumed away, oxidized; held together at joints momentarily annealed, only the skeleton remained. The bones glowed red then white, a tissue of incandescent ash like the mantle of a lamp. Then all burned out, grayed, decomposed and crumbled into a layer of dust.

"I know what you must be thinking, Mr. Curtis," Jeremy was saying. "Here I was, living with him in these two rooms: in all that time there must have been something, some hint that something was going on in his mind. A person doesn't . . . doesn't do that to himself without giving it some thought, without dropping some clues. Maybe half wanting to give himself away and be stopped from what he's planning. If so, I never saw it. I have sifted my memories—"

Sifted my memories. Arresting phrase! That was going to

be hard to forget. With so many more of them, he would be sifting his memories for a long time to come.

"Maybe there were things I should have noticed. Maybe he was trying to reach me. Maybe I was just too wrapped up in my own concerns. I'll never stop asking myself—"

He wanted to beg him, please, to stop. In trying to exonerate himself from blame or to assume his rightful share of it Jeremy had no notion what pain he was causing to the one who had lived all the boy's life with him, the one who ought to have noticed any warning signs, who had been too wrapped up in his own concerns, who would never stop asking himself . . .

*

He rented a car. In the parking lot below Palmer Square he saw a Salvation Army collection bin. His decision was made on the spot and the duffel bag and carton disposed of. At five o'clock he made his second appearance of the day at the undertaker's.

This time he was shown into the office of the establishment. He took the chair offered him beside the owner's desk. He was presented with his bill and lent a pen to write his check. The undertaker supplied him with the date. He recorded the check on its stub and returned the borrowed pen. The undertaker signified that their business had been transacted by standing up. He stood too. The undertaker picked up and held out to him the package which until then he had not noticed sitting on the desk.

It was a small, square, plain package wrapped as though for sending through the mails. One expected to see a label on it, and in fact, one did. It seemed to read, "Curtis, Anthony." He stared at it and then at the undertaker, uncomprehending. Just what he had expected to be given he could not have said, but this was so far from it that when he took the package in his hands it was still without realizing what it was. He was still further from that realization when he felt its weight, or rather, its lack of weight. Then into his mind flashed an image. The image was that of a newborn baby, its passage-

racked, red and wrinkled little body lying steaming with its
mother's body heat in the snow, then, as in a sequence of
time-lapse photography when a flower is shown to bud, blos-
som, blow, and wither all within the taking of a breath, he
saw that baby shoot up to be a man and that man transmuted
into this little box of nothing in his hands. He looked from it
to the undertaker as though to ask "Can this be all?" The
rapidity of events culminating in this one rushed in upon him
and he stood for some seconds bemused. The day he had
spent in arriving at this moment passed in review through his
mind. It presented itself to him as a series of narrowing cir-
cles as, in being passed by the university authorities to the
town officials, by them to the undertaker and from there to
the crematorium, his son had been progressively detached
from the world and processed into this product, packaged in
this container. His hopes had gone up in smoke and he held
in his hands the ashes.

He thanked the undertaker, who held the door for him,
and, carrying his acquisition before him, walked down the
street to his parked car. With the package on the seat beside
him he drove away from Princeton for what he knew would
be the last time.

*

His involuntary first reaction in Gloucester had been to
phone Cathy. It had been instinctive, like gasping for breath,
and getting no answer had been suffocating. But on reflection he had been grateful that he had failed to reach her and
this kept him from trying again in Princeton. News this har-
rowing was not to be broken over the telephone. It was
unbearable to think of her alone in the house with it until he
came. Even as he listened to the ring he began half to hope
that it would go unanswered. Afterwards he felt that had she
answered he might have hung up without speaking.

But somehow he never doubted that she would be there
waiting for him when he got home, for it did not seem to him
only a short time ago that he had tried and failed to find her
there—it seemed a lifetime—and now he could hardly be-

lieve that she was not. The house—meaning her—had been the oasis for a man parched and perishing of thirst and he had reached it only to find that the well was dry. That everything in the living room was just as he had left it, just as it had always been, enforced its strangeness now that nothing would ever again be the same. A wave of hatred for the house, for its many reminders of a happiness now lost, passed over him. It was the same as ever, but so changed was he that he felt himself a stranger in it, alone and lost.

From a wry, ironical source came a glimmer of hope. He remembered to his shame that when they were last together Cathy and he had been quarreling. The triviality of it under the harsh light of the present made him groan for their childishness even as it cheered him. Impossible as it was to believe, Cathy still did not know what had befallen them and might, poor fool, still be nursing her grudge against him, might be in the house, in her room sulking, aware that he was here and refusing to come down and greet him.

She was not. He returned to the living room, sat his weary body down, found himself staring at the carton containing Anthony's ashes and broke into sobs.

Days dragged by and still Cathy did not come home. Either she was innocently enjoying herself or else she was still sulking at him. Whichever it was, he pitied her with all his heart, for either way she was storing up regrets and self-recriminations with every passing moment.

Reason told him it was better for them both that she was not there just now. The wound would have been reopened with their every word, every look. They would have reminded each other constantly of Anthony. Meanwhile, though the pain remained as sharp as ever, surely he was forming scar tissue. He worked always at home and being together in the house all the time they had always contracted the same illnesses but somehow they usually contrived to do so by turns, thus the one was able to nurse the other; this would be something like that: he would have lived through the first devastation of it and be better able to look after her.

For the time being he busied himself in the garden daylong and drank away the evenings.

On one of those evenings he was struck by the realization that he had put Tony altogether out of mind. This pained him. It also puzzled him. Of all people Tony was the one of whom he should have been reminded most often. How could he have forgotten the dear friend who had suffered the same loss as he? Was it out of consideration? Was that why he was sparing Tony his news? No, he had forgotten his friend. A numbness of spirit had settled upon him, listlessness, self-absorption, apathy, grief, and a shutting out of the world—but Tony? How could he have been unmindful of him? He reckoned it was like Freud's explanation for your forgetting a certain person's name when it should have been the easiest of all names for you to remember: it was your name and you resented sharing it with anybody. What contrary creatures we were! Selfish with our sorrows!

To Tony and to the other people who had to be informed personally he broke his news by letter. It brought home to him how few friends he had. There were times when a man was glad that they were no more numerous than they were. That many fewer to hurt. If this was hard to do what was breaking the news to Cathy going to be like?

The writing of the letters was another milestone making Tony, along with everybody else, seem far away and the time of their association long ago. Between him and his past a gap had opened. His entire life, every event, every scene of it had receded a distance from him. It was like the occasion of first sensing the need for eyeglasses, when the physical world had shrunk and grown hazy. Now, however, it was not space, it was time that had lengthened for him, time which is measured differently for each person on earth, not in calendar units but in losses, life's steady contraction. The sensation was unfamiliar to him but he recognized it at once, it had been delivered to the right address: he felt suddenly old. Old, tired, and lonely. It was a loneliness that nobody, not even Cathy, was going to be able entirely to fill.

The thought of Tony brought with it the memory of what

he had observed on board *Pandora*—the widening rift between Tony and Pris—and this was attended by a pang of
personal misgiving. He had been counting on nothing less
than total oneness between Cathy and him in facing up to
their loss, but suppose that in her shock and horror and self-
defensiveness she disowned that side of Anthony that had
turned against his other half and laid the blame for it at his
father's door? Even just speculating upon such a possibility
filled him with guilt toward her, yet such things had been
known to happen. If only she would come, put an end to the
solitude that bred such disloyal and unworthy suppositions!
She would hardly need to speak. The sight of her face would
be reassurance enough.

On another of those days he borrowed from somewhere
the courage to enter Anthony's room. This room had been
awaiting him when he was born. It was a plain enough room,
yet had he been overcome with homesickness for it? He
himself could have no idea how powerful an emotion homesickness might be. He had thought that Anthony was im-
mune but he knew those first weeks away at college were a
difficult, even a dangerous time. You were suddenly on your
own, expected overnight to be an adult, an expectation that
all the other students seemed up to. What was the matter
with you? You had done well enough in high school but now
you seemed to be the only one in your class who did not
understand the professor. Had Anthony phoned home in his
loneliness and fright and, getting no answer but that recording, in a moment of despair done what he had done?

Within the four walls of this room he was formed. On one
of them the stages of his growth were recorded. Beginning
with the twelfth, they had measured his height on each of his
birthdays. On the last one he had stood exactly six feet tall.
Meanwhile within that strong, straight frame, now reduced
to a handful of cinders, some crookedness was growing. Between which two marks on the wall had it begun, and how
had his father not detected it in time?

He once had a friend who, though twice Anthony's age,
died all too young of brain cancer. Toward the end his entire

brain was involved but originally the section affected was the one in which the names of things are stored. His memory had been getting worse for some time but he got medical attention only after setting out across town one evening to visit his sister and being found hours later wandering lost in the streets, having forgotten his sister's address, her name, his own name, and his address. Surgeons opened his cranium and then just sewed it back up. He was past help. Within weeks he was an anatomy student's cadaver at the medical school to which his body was willed.

To this day he reproached himself with thinking how for years his friend had said what's-his-name and thingumabob, unable to remember their names, and how, out of what he thought was consideration, he had said nothing about it. The tumor was even then pressing on that lobe of the brain, and if only he had said something his friend might still be alive. But he was not a doctor, and even if he had been he could hardly have said "Donald, that habit of yours worries me. You ought to have exploratory brain surgery to see whether you haven't got a tumor. Maybe it's not too late to have it out before it turns malignant." The impossibility of that showed how senseless his self-reproaches were, but he made them nonetheless. Ought he to have seen in Anthony's intensity a threat of suicide and taken him to a psychiatrist? That was just as senseless, and just as insistent, a self-reproach. Death was deaf to all extenuations. That which one had not done was that which one ought to have done.

Had he been less self-concerned, more attentive, had he been sensitive to them, surely there must have been signals, warning signs, distress calls, indirect pleas for help, symptoms, something like his early-dead friend's forgetfulness. What ought he to have noticed that he had been obtuse to? That was not a question that occurred to him now at intervals; it was constant, unrelenting, as involuntary as drawing breath.

The suicide wanted to obliterate himself and what he did was to make himself unforgettable. His last act shed a lurid light upon every memory of him. It drew suspicions upon his most innocent, ordinary, everyday behavior. His every trait must be reexamined for signs of morbidity. Harmless, even endearing little quirks of character were now seen as having been potentially pathological, and one was remiss in not having detected their sinister import in time.

Anthony could not have been more than twelve when his father knocked on his door one afternoon and was told in a weary tone to come in. He found Anthony lying on his bed with his hands clasped behind his head.

"Busy thinking?" he asked. "Hope I'm not interrupting."

"No. I'm not thinking. I'm just lying here."

"It's too nice a day to stay indoors. Up! Let's do something. How about clay pigeon shooting? Perfect day for it."

Anthony did not stir.

"A swim?" he suggested. "Or a walk in the woods?"

"I can't." This was said in a tone of misery.

"Aren't you feeling well?"

"I'm feeling fine, thank you, and I would like very much to shoot clay pigeons or take a swim or go for a walk in the woods with you, but I can't. I've got to stay in. It's my punishment for something I did."

"Oh? Your mother is making you stay in?"

"Mother doesn't know anything about it," said Anthony scornfully. "I'm making myself stay in. All day long."

"What have you done to deserve that?"

Anthony turned his head and gave his father a look of exasperation. "Do *you* want people to know about it when *you've* done something dumb?" he asked.

Anthony's self-punishments spared his father having to recall many times when he had inflicted punishment upon him. There were some and they returned now to repay him tenfold for every lash, but they were blessedly few.

He learned to expect—and to respect—Anthony's days of self-castigation. Now he had to ask himself, was it for some unatonable error that he was punishing himself at the end? Before it had seemed, if a little unusual, perhaps even a little excessive, not alarming, indeed rather amusing and even admirable, probably indicative of a life of high achievement, that impatience with his own imperfection. Did some people hasten their mortality because they could not accept that it was the common lot?

To someone who lived at such a pitch of expectation, someone young and tender, not toughened to disappointment, like Anthony, not much would have been needed to topple him from his high, and when he fell he would fall low. Completely uncompetitive against others, the boy had always been fiercely in competition with himself. Like a lone pole-vaulter, no sooner had he cleared a height than he raised the bar. There had seemed nothing ominous in that at the time, but the way he tested himself against no standards but his own: what was one to make of that in light of what came later? Was it a morbid fear of being bested or was it a Luciferian pride—the feeling that no one was good enough to be worth his contending against? Organized sports he had shunned, yet as did every adolescent American boy he had his basketball hoop over the garage door and spent hours shooting at it. But always alone. Whenever one of his few friends suggested a skirmish he said no. To his father this had been a trifle worrisome; too late, he wondered whether he ought not to have worried more. Yet surely he was not to blame for not having seen in it a clue to what was to come?

Intensity did not cover it—the boy had been compulsive. Whatever he took up it was with passionate involvement and the determination to master it. And once he had, he seemed to hold his own attainment in contempt, as though to say "I've licked that one, what other tests have you got for me?" Should a father have seen in that a tendency to run through life's challenges and exhaust them all too early? He had excelled at whatever he attempted and he envied no boy his abilities. Anthony had his faults but envy was not one of them. He was saved from that by one of his faults. He was too proud ever to envy anybody anything.

For as long as something interested him nothing else did. His absorption in it was single-minded. Such devotion could not really be requited, not by any boyish pursuits. To expect trout fishing or any other pastime to reward in kind devotion that intense was sure to lead to disappointment for anybody but a fanatic. But having run through one interest, Anthony was quick to replace it with another just as absorbing. Who could have read a tendency toward self-destruction in what had seemed instead intense self-exploration? Could the world pall and go flat for a youngster interested, one thing at a time, in so much of it? Apathy, indifference, boredom, lack of curiosity, premature cynicism, those would seem to be attitudes more to be suspected, mistrusted. He spent much of his time alone but that seemed then to suggest a liking for his own company, not a predisposition toward a murderous rejection of it.

People who killed themselves on the doorsill of life were ones to whom life's challenges seemed too great for the effort, weren't they? That certainly did not fit Anthony. He thrived on challenge, sought it out, added to it on his own. Had there been no other, his falconry alone was evidence of that. What did it tell you about a person, himself a *rara avis*, who took up that uncommon sport?

Wild animals had been Anthony's first and most enduring fascination—indeed, it was to study biology preparatory to going into veterinary medicine that had made him suddenly change his mind about going to college. (Did unnatural death turn everything to bitter irony? *Biology*: from the Greek for "the study of life.") Every sort of animal interested him. *(Why should a dog, a horse, a rat have life and thou no breath at all?)* He trusted all, feared none. He liked insects, unlike his allergic father, was attracted to reptiles, was rather contemptuous of people who feared or were repelled by them. Was rather contemptuous of people anyway when compared with animals. Wild animals. He was fairly indifferent to domestic ones, kept no pets, but kept at one time or another a menagerie of the kinds the least responsive to human attentions. That certainly included hawks, and now when Anthony came to mind it was most often with his hawk on his wrist. A hawk required undivided attention, repaid it with nothing. Owning one was like being a partner in a bad marriage.

Anthony's first hawk was one he found wounded—and his comment on that was revelatory of his attitude. He said, and he seemed to mean every word of it, "I'd like to shoot whoever shot this bird."

He kept it in his bathtub, nursed it, and callously fed it the pigeons that had been one of his former fancies. When it was plain to see that the bird would never fly again but would be a dependent cripple he broke its neck with one quick snap. As he had broken his own rather than live on in whatever way it was that he felt himself impaired.

He had been violating the law just by bringing the bird home. Everything possible was done to discourage the would-be falconer. Captive hawks were solitary creatures. They would not mate, would not even consort with one another. They seemed to despise one another for having capitulated to their subjection. So even if it had been legal you could not go to a hawk breeder and buy yourself one. But all traffic in them was against the law. You had to capture your own, an eyas from the nest or a passager, an adult bird. For this you had to have the state's permission and to obtain that you had to have a raptor's license. To qualify for a license you had to pass a lengthy written examination, a field test, and an inspection of your premises for a bird. Pass all these and you might still be rejected unless your examiners were convinced of the sincerity of your interest, because hard as they made it for you to acquire a bird, once you had one you were not only not allowed to sell it, you couldn't even give it away, couldn't even release it back to the wild, without their permission. The bond between the bird and you was more than a marriage, it was a Siamese twinship. Nobody who ever questioned him had doubts about the sincerity of an interest of Anthony's.

The apprentice falconer had to capture his bird under the supervision of a master, and apprenticeship was for two years. And just as in olden times when the keeping of birds of prey was the prerogative of nobility and the species were allotted by patent of birth, with the eagle the sole right of the emperor, the peregrine that of the prince, and so on down to

the lowly merlin for the landless villein, so today's apprentice
was restricted to the red-tailed hawk or the sparrow hawk.

Considering all these deterrents it was not surprising that
in the entire state there were no more than a couple of dozen
falconers. For Anthony this very exclusiveness of the club to
which he aspired to belong was one of its attractions, and all
the obstacles in his path only made him the more determined
to reach its end. What was more, once out of his apprenticeship and licensed to own the goshawk which it was his ambi-
tion to own, to add a difficulty himself. He was intent on
capturing not a nestling but a mature hawk, one already
hunting on its own, or rather, on her own, for it was the
bigger and more predatory female that every falconer
wanted, thus one with a will of her own and all the harder to
man and to train.

Of hawks, as distinct from falcons, the goshawk was the
fiercest and most fearless. It was the only one that would
attack a man, and it did so with little provocation. To venture
within a mile of one's nest was dangerous, to look up into its
tree was almost an invitation to attack. One could knock a
man down, lacerate, even blind him. An eyas was taken from
a goshawk's nest only by a man clad in leather from top to
toe. The enthusiasm with which he told all this was enough to
make one think that the goshawk's misanthropy was something Anthony admired, even shared. Indeed, his disgust
with what had been done by man to spoil the environment
had embittered him toward his own kind and blackened his
view of the future. He was always on the side of the wild.

He was now in correspondence with members around the
country of the zealous, beleaguered little band who called
themselves falconers. Despised by landowners, disowned by
their fellow sportsmen, hampered by bureaucrats in well-
meaning but benighted conservation agencies, they were
like a band of coreligionists, proscribed, dispersed, but still
stubbornly devout, keeping their ancient rites and rituals in a
secret brotherhood with its own antiquated and arcane vo-
cabulary. His father informed Anthony that to the ancient
Egyptians the hawk was a god and they worshiped stone and

painted wooden statues of him. Indeed, he and his pen pals might have been the last remnant of that cult. He was telling Anthony nothing not already known to him. In the rather quizzical look he got for his pains he detected a feeling that being uninitiated he profaned that knowledge.

In the fall of the year, excused from classes, even given field credit for the venture in his biology course, Anthony and one of the master falconers with whom he corresponded backpacked into the Ramapo Mountains, on the eastern fly-way for migrating hawks, and, provisioned for a week's stay, pitched a tent and set a trap for the bird he sought. The trap, a net sprung by pulling a string, was baited with a live pigeon, one of several they took with them in a cage, tethered to a stake.

They built a blind of boughs, dressed themselves in camouflage and daubed their faces with mud, and took turns watching the trap, spelling each other every three hours. On the morning of the fifth day, with Anthony on watch, a hawk from out of nowhere plummeted and struck, instantly killing the pigeon. Anthony pulled the string, the net closed, and he had his goshawk. It was a female, his haggard.

Jesses for her legs and a hood for her head, even a name, were waiting for her, and all of them fit. He called her Jezebel for her inbred and incorrigible faithlessness.

Other hawks were paintings, but the goshawk was a pencil drawing in shades of gray. It gave the impression of being as starkly functional as a bullet, too busy at its one deadly task for ornamentation. Its underside was pale with dark speckles, its back black, its tail gray barred black. Its only touches of color were its red eyes, which gleamed like twin warning lights, its yellow legs, and its gunmetal-blue talons. For swiftness in flight its feathers were shingled as closely as the scales of a fish.

He had observed the manning of the bird. Manning: accustoming it to man, his ways, the sounds and the motions he made. The old falconry manuals taught that the initial step in manning a bird was to exhaust it into submission by depriving it of sleep for three days and nights. Which meant the falconer's depriving himself of the same amount of sleep. One wondered how either the bird or the man survived the ordeal, much less cooperated thereafter in the hunt. But this torture was totally unnecessary; nowadays the bird was starved into submission—or rather, it starved itself.

For forty-eight hours this one ignored the bloody half of a fresh-killed pigeon that she was offered. She would have fed if left to herself but she must be made dependent for her food upon her owner (master she would never have) and associate it with his gloved hand. There and there only would she eat from now on. Evidently she would sooner starve to death.

The indomitable glare she fixed upon all humankind, the cold contemptuous blink with which she dismissed it! In accepting her hood it was not as though she were submitting to restraint but rather as though she were obliging you to remove your offensive self from her sight. She would not abide being looked at herself; your very gaze seemed to sully her, and in her rage she would bate—hurl herself off the wrist and hang by her jesses upside down, furiously beating her wings and screaming. Stock still, the boy waited out these tantrums and set her back in place on the glove. When she was stroked with a feather to soothe her ruffled feelings she accepted the attentions with the thanklessness of an empress for a slave.

Between them it was a contest of wills, yet should he succeed in breaking hers the most he could hope for from her was an admission of dependency. She was a heartless thing, incapable of affection or fealty. A pet she would never be. Was it selflessness or was it slavishness, this devotion to a creature that would never requite you with more than bare toleration? Her unapproachable hauteur, her fierce independence, her contempt for all humankind including himself was just what the boy admired in her, though with that sneer of hers and that blink of her basilisk eyes she seemed to say, "The sight of you wearies me."

On the evening of the third day of her hunger strike, here in this dimly lit room, she was offered the half of yet another freshly killed pigeon. An hour passed, although, arrested in that timeless tableau as boy and bird sat motionless, it seemed to stand still. Both expressionless, they might have been a statue in an Egyptian temple, he representing a priest of the cult of the hawk, his head averted in deference to the god that permitted no human to gaze upon it, the bird the cult's remote and inscrutable idol.

It was only after an hour had passed that the hawk's head began to incline. Slowly, stiffly, as though in violation of her will, by degrees it bent down. There was visible an involuntary working of her throat, the pangs of hunger which not even the proudest and most indomitable will could deny.

Her table manners were a surprise. Far from being the ravenous harpy he had expected, she was downright dainty. She mantled, that is, spread her wings to conceal her eating. She plucked at the pigeon, tore off small bits, was satisfied with a morsel of the breast. Or maybe this was not daintiness but loyalty to herself, a way of saying, "I may be in your debt but it's not for much, so don't expect any thanks."

Now Anthony went in for falconry as he did for everything, with unstinting energy, and in this sport there was the added incentive of its having a long history and an extensive literature. The tradition and the lore of falconry were a full-time study, sufficient to occupy a person for a lifetime. The demands of the bird for constant exercise, for regular hunting lest she forget her training, tied Anthony to her. She even had to be weighed regularly to determine the state of her health and to ration her diet. When he returned to school she went with him. One of the school's employees kept her in a coop at his house.

Your troubles were not over once you were licensed and had your hawk and she was manned. In areas suitable for flying hawks you seldom encountered the enlightened attitude that tolerated them and favored their protection. That was found among birdlovers, but they were no friends of falconers; they opposed trapping and robbing nests to capture birds. Farmers and hunters alike hated birds of prey, the one seeing in them a menace to his poultry, the other a rapacious destroyer of the game he himself sought, and both looked upon the person who favored them as peculiar, not to say perverted, one who had betrayed his race by allying himself with one of its blood enemies. They routinely flouted the law and shot hawks and sincerely believed they were doing both nature and man a service. Most who did so would have been surprised, even mystified, but still unmoved to learn that the one he had just killed embodied countless hours of training by someone who doted upon it.

These obstacles and attitudes Anthony seemed not only not to mind, he seemed positively to thrive on them. They seemed to strengthen the bond between the bird, protected by law but outlawed by custom, and him. He soared above the contemptible common prejudice as the hawk soared in her solitary flight. He worried only that he risked her life each time he flew her. Ought his father to have worried over his identification with this predatory pariah of a bird? Princeton University's admissions officer didn't. Anthony's *Falconer's Journal* had been instrumental in gaining him admission.

Anthony found in the hawk a creature like himself in this: neither could endure failure. All hawks, not just his, were the same in their self-demands: nothing short of perfection in their every performance. Should Jezebel miss her mark two times running in a day she had to be hooded and taken home, and she was a disgruntled and bedraggled looking thing then. No pride in her pose, no fire in her eye. A most dejected and droopy fowl she was, more like a wet hen than a hawk. To have flown her for a third time on such a day would have been to risk having her fly away and not come back for shame. The implication was that she would go off and hide herself and die in disgrace. Not disgrace in men's eyes—disgrace in her own eyes. So it was with the boy; for the world's he cared nothing, it was his own disapproval he could not endure.

Jezebel's failures, never many, grew still more infrequent the longer Anthony flew her. Nature had shaped her with a singleness of purpose like that of a knife and all she needed was sharpening. She communicated to him, first by a downward stiffening of her wings, then by a hunching of her shoulders, when she was "in yarak"—that is, when the urge to kill was upon her. A pure bloodlust this was, for she never ate her kill; she was rewarded for it with a portion of a pigeon or the heart of a chicken. Sometimes, when he was home from school, Anthony used his father's old English setter to find birds for her. When her kill was made out of sight but within hearing they could follow it by the sound of her bells. While she hovered in flight they tinkled in the breeze but when she was hurtling toward her mark they rang like an alarm and when she struck, talons extended, they crashed like a cymbal. Then she tumbled earthward with the grouse or the duck—often as big as she, or bigger—in her grasp.

Images in the pristine colors of Persian miniatures, books of hours, medieval tapestries—lords and ladies of the court, hooded and tasseled falcons on their gauntleted wrists, lean greyhounds on leashes, and a recumbent unicorn in jewellike flower gardens amid trees laden with imperishable fruit—a modern-day American boy in blue jeans on a windy hill about to launch the hawk on his wrist could conjure up all that, such was the lore of that princely pursuit brought back from Byzantium by the crusaders, and since then so fallen into neglect as to be an anachronism recalling the days of Roland and the Knights of the Round Table.

Jezebel's glove was stained and stiffened now with the blood of many a pigeon and pullet. That left arm of Anthony's belonged to the bird as a mother's belongs to her baby. And when they were separated, he fixedly tracking her as she glided and hovered overhead, it was as though they were in communication on a wavelength all their own. The thermals she rode in her aerial acrobatics he seemed to ride with her and when the flutter of her wings as she hung on air signaled to him that she had sighted prey he tensed visibly. Then down she dropped the more closely to spy her quarry, gathered herself together, compacted her wings against her body, and aimed herself earthward like a bomb.

They would find her by following the tinkle of her bell. Find her perched upon her kill, clutching it in her claws, imperious as an eagle on a Roman standard. He did not wonder at her, for she was only doing what she was born to do, but he could not help wondering a bit at a son of his who had entered into such an odd alliance. Until Anthony changed his mind and decided to go to college after all they were inseparable.

It was far too late to apply for admission to college that year and it was madness to apply to only one, any one, especially the one he chose, but his prep school record and his interview and his paper on falconry opened the doors of Princeton to him.

He tidied up his affairs at home. He sold his flytying business to one of his employees. There would be neither time nor a place at Princeton for the hawk. He would not give her to another falconer. She would have adopted a new owner shamelessly. He applied for and got permission from the state conservation agency to return her to the wild. She would quickly learn to hunt for herself again, to live on her prey.

He wanted to release her near the spot where she had been trapped. They drove together with her into the mountains. With them went Anthony's newest interest, Jezebel's replacement, Alice Clayton.

Anthony removed the hawk's hood and she blinked her languid, indifferent blink, like the rolling of the eyes of a malevolent doll. Then for the first time since her capture her bells and her jesses were removed. She did not bolt for freedom but sat on on the gauntlet kneading it with her talons, and he wondered whether this unwonted show of unforced attachment would cause the boy to reconsider his resolve. Not for a moment. He raised his arm high and the bird took flight.

Anthony watched the hawk climb and his father watched him, remembering the ancient, almost universal superstition of the human soul being a bird that soars heavenward when released from the body by death. Anthony was letting go a part of himself, perhaps of a self. The bird had been practically an appendage to him. But that left arm of his was his now. He could take on his new life with both hands, with both fists if need be. He was a boy no more. The release of the

bird marked the end of his boyhood. It was he who was free.
He was off to college and a career and how could his father
doubt that this next stage in his son's life would be anything
but interesting and rewarding, maturing?

> Turning and turning in the widening gyre
> The falcon cannot hear the falconer;

he recited to himself as they turned to go to the car, the bird a
diminishing speck in the vast, unclouded sky.

Now the verse completed itself:
> Things fall apart; the center cannot hold;
> Mere anarchy is loosed upon the world,
> The blood-dimmed tide is loosed, and everywhere
> The ceremony of innocence is drowned.

*

He ended his night's vigil when, at half past four, he
switched off the barroom lights and felt his way along the
wall, through the door and to the stairway newel post. He
climbed the stairs and crept down the hall. Behind the bedroom doors the same untroubled snores droned on. He had
come to feel that he belonged to another, nocturnal species,
not to his own.

He dressed in his newly bought pants and shirt and socks
and, carrying his shoes, descended the stairs. He stepped out
on the porch. All was still. The creatures of the night had
ceased their prowls and those of the day had not yet begun
theirs. Above the ground a low-lying luminosity, like the
crack of light at the bottom of a curtain, gave presentiment of
day. A task awaited him there in the tackle shed, and with no
one to observe, now was the time to get it done.

In the tackle shed he found a profound change, here in this
bastion of backwardness where change was so stubbornly
resisted. On the door of the locker which for four generations
had borne the name *Thayer* there was a new name. This
could only mean that Pris had let her membership lapse, had

even taken the step of canceling it, for unless otherwise in-structed, Eddie would have kept it active pending her re-turn, as he had done with his. Often a widow kept it up, and not just in trust for an underage son but for herself, for this was no stag club. Wives and children were welcome and among them were some of the club's most ardent anglers. It was here that he had taught both Cathy and Anthony to fish, she when they were courting, he beginning when he was just ten years old. Several widows and widowers had found them-selves new husbands and wives among their fellow club members. Pris had been a keen fisherman, but now she had decided to drop out, not revisit this scene of so much lost happiness. Ought he not to take warning from her, turn back now? He supposed he would never see Pris again. Having all they had in common, it would be too painful for them both.

Of the gear now to be removed from the Curtis family locker there was not much that had been Anthony's. The little he had accumulated in his life attested not just to the shortness of it: he had always traveled light and had had little to leave behind him. It seemed now as though he had wanted few mementoes of himself. He had been a hard child to give presents to, not because he had everything but because he wanted nothing. He liked to make do. If he had been vain of anything it was of doing a job with whatever tools were at hand; indeed, there had been something of the showoff in his doing better with less. When he had exhausted an interest he rid himself of the reminders of it. A pair of blue jeans had been his wardrobe. His room at home, like his dormitory room, when it had had to be cleared out, was as bare as a cell. Here now was his one fishing rod, a cheap thing of fiberglass, with which, nonetheless, he could outcast men using the best bamboo ones, his much-patched boots, and his old vest con-taining, to judge by its weight, the minimal tackle. Even to someone not put off by their previous ownership these things would be worth little or nothing. To Anthony they had been basic equipment, of no sentimental value. In handling them now why could his father not remember and take comfort in that?

There was a locker in the tackle shed marked "Lost and Found." In it were put not just things found but things outgrown, replaced, perhaps—this struck him now for the first time—things that had outlasted their owners, there for anybody to take who had a use for them. There he discarded Anthony's few pieces of tackle.

Cathy's were not so easily disposed of. Her rod was a reminder of her that he would have to keep. A powerful reminder it was, for it was to please him, to be with him, that she had taken up fishing. A gift from him to her, the rod was the work of a man whose name was to fishing rods what Stradivarius was to violins. He had retired from business some years earlier and at first he refused to make a rod for Cathy. It was the mention of Tony Thayer's name that made him reconsider. Even then he set another condition. There being no more of them, his rods had become collector's items. This annoyed the man. He considered himself a practical craftsman, not a maker of whatnots.

To Cathy he said, "So you want one of my poles. Why?"

"Because my dear, devoted husband wants me to have the best."

"Mmh. But what are you going to do with it?"

"Fish with it," she said. "What else?"

"Catch fish with it," her husband corrected her.

"Catch fish with it," she said.

"Good," said the old man. "That's what it's for."

The man never signed his rods, a mark not of modesty but of pride. Like the best London tailors, who never sewed a label into their jackets, he expected the quality of his work to identify it as his and nobody else's. On the butt of this rod, near the cork handle, was written in tiny, perfect copperplate script, "Made for Catherine Curtis." Coat upon coat of hand-rubbed varnish gave the golden cane a gleam like amber. Like its owner, the rod was short, delicate, but with plenty of backbone.

He returned the rod to its case and put it with her vest and the double-billed Scottish cap she had bought at Kelly's on their last trip. The trout fly in the band of the cap—a Queen

of the Waters it was—he had stuck there. He doubted that
Cathy would ever fish again. He had introduced her to it and
she associated it with him. With him and with Anthony, with
Tony—with everything that she longed now to forget. But he
would have to keep her tackle just in case she should ever
want it, in case he ever heard from her again.

A pair of smallish, chest-high, khaki-colored fishing waders
would not seem an article of clothing to arouse a man's
desires. What woman could be attractive in those clumsy
things? His could. In theirs, most of the club women waddled
like pachyderms, and in a ready-made pair little Cathy would
have looked comical, but these of hers he had had custom-
tailored, and in them she had been a mermaid, as alluring as
in her frilliest frock. Out of them she had been that much
more alluring and he remembered a summer afternoon
when, impelled by an urge more elemental, he quit fishing
early and found her in her section of the stream and she read
his thoughts in his face and waded ashore to him and he
helped her out of her waders and hung them from a limb and
they combined the rest of their clothing to make themselves
a bed on the bank. That day they fished no further.

He wished he had not made that play on Dante's *Quel'
giorno più non vi leggemmo avante.* It brought to mind the
lines preceding it:

> *Nessun' maggior' dolore
> Che ricordarsi del tempo felice
> Nella miseria.*

> No grief surpasses this:
> In the midst of misery to remember bliss.

*

The sun was high overhead as he rounded the bend in the
stream from which he could see to the end of his section of it.
So often had it happened in the past that, against all reason,
he half expected to see Tony working his way toward the
boundary line and the rendezvous with him.

They had always chosen adjoining sections of the stream

and, one of them fishing up from the bottom of his section
and the other one fishing down from the top of his, met
midway for lunch together. When they came in sight of each
other both went on fishing out their sections but he always
did so idly for it was more enjoyable as well as more instruc-
tive to watch Tony. The head start he had gotten by being
born of a long line of ardent outdoorsmen could not alone
account for Tony's mastery of a fly rod or his prowess with a
gun. With either he was a pattern of grace and a study in total
concentration of mind and body. Even in dying Tony had
shown dispatch, originality, style.

If he was fishing downstream, with the wet fly, fishing
blind, that is, fishing the water and not to rising fish, continually casting the same length of line and covering the water by
his progress through it, Tony's wading was as negligent as a
stroll down his garden path. He never seemed to feel his way
with his feet, never faltered or stumbled or slipped and lost
his balance even though the stream bed was strewn with
rocks and they were moss-grown and so slippery the club's
hoariest joke was that Eddie spent his day off coating them
with axle grease.

But it was when Tony was fishing upstream, fishing the dry
fly, that he liked best to watch him. Dry-fly fishing demanded
greater delicacy of presentation, more accurate casting,
closer attention to the currents if the lure was to float with
naturalness and not with a telltale drag. When no fish was
visibly on the feed Tony fished the water, but what he liked
best was the challenge of fishing to a fish rising to a hatch of
flies; he liked to match the natural insect with his artificial
one, stalk his quarry with the stealth of a hunter, lengthening
his line with false casts that hovered above the water just to
the side of the fish's lie, then when it was exactly the right
length drop it upon the water as softly as if it had just that
instant hatched and surfaced there, await the fish's cautious
rise, then strike. No obstacle could ever keep him from making a cast because he knew a trick cast to get around it with.
He was as dextrous with his left hand as with his right and his
casting range was whatever it took. In his hands a fly rod had

been a conductor's baton, a magician's wand: trout sang his tune in chorus, he could conjure them out of nowhere. Whenever, between him and the position he considered best to cast to a fish from, there was water too deep to wade, he swam it. No waders for Tony, except in the iciest early-season water.

They would have left bottles of beer to chill in the stream and their lunch in a hamper in a tree out of the reach of animals. In the hamper would be a thermos of martinis to drink while drying out. They always had just one more before having another, ever since Tony had first proposed that they do.

Today he would have just his one. That was more than he was used to having in midday now. He was looking forward to it. He was wet and cold from the waist down, hot and wet with sweat from there up, tired from lack of sleep, and muscles long unused ached from inching his way among the rocks on the bottom. He hauled himself up the bank, leaned his rod against a tree, and got out of his vest and his creel harness. He knew this spot of old: it was here that Tony and he had met for lunch the last time they fished together, yet as he stood to let the water drain from him he took his bearings. Do I stand here, he asked himself, not only with the sense of present pleasure, but with pleasing thoughts that in this moment there is life and food for future years? He listened to the woods and the water for an answer. None was forthcoming. He had learned to look on nature not as in the hour of thoughtless youth, but hearing oftentimes the still, sad music of humanity.

He was not succeeding in what he was here now to try to do. The reason for that was that he was not here and the time was not now. A new beginning, a fresh start, an object in living was what he sought and his dead life kept reasserting itself. For all the outward change in him he was the same self still. He was like that old oak there. Last of trees to leaf out, soon now it would, and this year's would be like those of all the others. He was like it in this too: his roots went deep and fixed him in one spot.

He had sweated off the insect repellent yet again. After spraying himself afresh he sat in the shade of the tree with his legs stretched out in the sun to dry. His martini cooled him where he was hot and then warmed him where he was chilled.

He felt hungry. He had all but forgotten what it was like to feel hungry but he was hungry now and it felt good. He sipped his drink slowly for he wanted to savor his hunger. It was better that he do everything slowly. He was still in training and must guard against rushing his sensations. They got out of hand when he tried to deal with too many at a time. Having to relearn everything took concentration. Lunch would be leisurely. His stretch of water required resting before he waded back through it, and so did he. And anyhow, the middle of the day was an unproductive time for fishing.

In the old days Tony and he would have reported to each other their observations of the morning now. They would have told of fish hooked and fish lost, of changes in the course of the stream, perhaps of spying an otter or a beaver—it was a pileated woodpecker that Tony had been excited by their last time here together. Tony was keenly observant, boyishly inquisitive, and had no patience with anybody who was not. If one could inherit traits from a godparent then it was from Tony that Anthony had gotten his passionate love of nature, and that impatience with—in his case contempt for—clods who lacked it. To live in this world without wondering what the things in it were and how they lived was not to live. Tony knew wildflowers and weeds, trees, birds and birds' eggs, minerals, the constellations of the stars.

They would be exchanging sections for the afternoon, so at lunch they always told each other what to expect to encounter. Both knew the stream so well that all they had to do was to name a bend or a rock or a tree. Each would have told which flies had been successful for him and which had not, and if one or the other had risen a really big fish he told just where to find it and how best to approach its lie. Of one thing there would have been no mention. Possibly one or the other of them would have published something lately, and though he could be sure the other had read it, yet their talk was never about that. They knew each other too well to talk shop. That they went on being friends testified to their mutual respect, for neither of them could have been friends with a writer whose writing he did not respect, yet praise to the face from the other would have embarrassed either of them.

He leaned his back against the tree and took from his wallet the unopened letter given to him by Eddie last evening at the club. It could not hurt him now. Not again. He had not opened the letter earlier because he had already read it a year ago—or rather, a copy of it. He was sure it was the same, for this one too was postmarked Hudson and dated the same day as the one he had received. No doubt Pris had been more confident of his receiving this one than the other one, for he came here more often than he went to New York. It had fallen out the other way. To make sure it was the same and contained no information not known to him, he opened the letter. He had been right: this was the original of which he had read the copy. Yet he had been wrong: even now it hurt. This one was a reminder of all that the first one had led to:

Dear Ben,

I have tried calling and writing but I got a recording saying that your phone had been disconnected and my letter was returned to me so I am writing you there. Forgive me for adding to your sorrows, my poor Ben, but I must tell you that funeral services for Tony were held today. Actually he died three months ago, in an iceboating accident, but the body could not be recovered until the river thawed. I could not bring myself to tell you at the time, knowing so well what you were going through.

Here in this spot, with its memories, holding in hand this letter and recalling its duplicate, which had also reached him late and which had also been addressed not to his home but to his and Tony's other club, reliving what reading that one had done to him, his identification with Tony Thayer throughout all their adult years made them seem to him like twins. How their lives had paralleled and mirrored each other! The same pastimes and pleasures, interests and outlooks, the same devastating misfortune, and very nearly the same end. For he had not been misled for a moment by Pris's word "accident." The three-time iceboating champion of the United States the sport's first fatality? He needed nobody to tell him what had happened. As plainly as if he had been there lying prone beside him on the passenger's tray, separated from him by nothing but the beam which was the boat's body, he saw Tony catch the wind in his sail and set his tiller and point his prow toward where he knew the ice was thin. He could feel in his face the sting of the icy spray, feel the rib-jolting bumps, the frigid air that seared the lungs. It would have been exhilarating. A last lusty lover's embrace with the ice and then the plunge into instant insensibility. He longed to have been there.

And so, running for his life, running from his haunted house in Stone Ridge to escape the deadly urgings of its resident spirit, he had run into another, realer, far more deadly one at their old New York rendezvous, the Princeton Club. This one with a motive for what he had done and the motive the same as his own. This one his alter ego, the model for much of what he was.

He tore the letter in pieces and sprinkled them on the water. Like petals from an expiring rose they fell. Just downstream a fingerling trout nosed one of the scraps and then swirled away. Some soon sank, others were soon lost in the wavelets and the froth. He watched the last one float out of sight. Then in the distance he spied a fisherman working his way toward him through the section that would once have been Tony's. It seemed to be his still, by rights. Unreasonable as it was, and perhaps all the more because it was so unreasonable, he felt a moment's enmity toward the man, whoever he might be, for not being his dead friend. However, he would have to be cordial. The man waved to him and waded on upstream.

"Saw on the sheet that you had put yourself in Section

Seven for today," said Ken Howard as he clambered up the bank.

Ken loosened his bootstraps and turned his boot tops down to his knees. He slipped out of his vest and detached his creel from its harness. He knelt, unlatched the lid of his creel, and turned it upside down. Out of it slid a brown trout fully a foot and a half long. It was only a short time out of its element. Beneath its lacquerlike coat of clear mucus its undimmed colors still shimmered, iridescent.

He gave a whistle of appreciation.

With a clasp knife Ken slit the fish from vent to gills. He stripped out the innards and ran his thumbnail along the exposed spine. At the stream's edge he sloshed the fish in the water to rinse out its cavity. He then cut open the fish's stomach and studied its contents.

"Cress bugs and caddis nymphs," he observed. "He fell for a grannom fly."

Ken produced a pocket flask. He uncapped it and raised it in a toast. "To a fine fish," he said.

With his martini he responded, "To a fine fisherman."

"To the memory of the fine boy who tied the fly that fooled the fish," said Ken.

It was like lancing a long-festering sore or pulling a rotten tooth: a shock, a moment's sharp pain, and then relief. He was touched to tears. He said—when he was again able to speak—"Thank you for that. Most people think they're doing you a favor not to mention him. It gets to seem as though you never had a son."

*

He remembered how, when they went into seclusion afterwards, silence settled upon the house and with the passage of time spread like an insidious growth. Their living area contracted and outlying rooms died as do the extremities of the body from lack of circulation. The stormwindows were lowered, shutting out the sounds of the world, sealing in the silence, and the shades were drawn in the disused rooms. Routine preparations for the change of seasons, the onset of

hibernation, but this year fraught with more than usual melancholy. It was reminiscent of an experience he once had of
staying on in a summer place after the season was over, with
the pipes drained, the utilities disconnected, the windows
boarded up and the games all stored away, the parties, the
outings, the laughter all gone like the leaves from the trees.

The lawns browned and the flowers in their beds faded,
drooped, and withered. The last of the songbirds left and
their feeder went unfrequented, unreplenished. The days
passed unmarked, uncounted. But they passed, and wintry
winds now wailed over the stricken landscape, the expiring
year. The house stood out from the barren scene as stark as a
letter edged in black. The days shortened, darkened. Cara-
vans of geese departed, uttering their plaintive good-byes. In
the darkness and stillness of a November night the first snow
of the season fell and over the world blackened by frost a
winding sheet was drawn.

The postman drove by without stopping or stopped to
leave bills, mail-order catalogues. The sound of the television
set, the time or two it was switched on, was incongruous,
obtrusive. Daily he listened to the phone to test whether it
was working. The hum, like the uninterrupted drone of an
indifferent universe, told him it was, but it never rang: a
lifeline gone dead. He had demanded much of people, setting standards that few could measure up to, and thus his
circle of friends had always been small. There were not many
who might have condoled with him now. Of those few, few
did. The world receded further and further, as though they
were alone in a boat drifting out to sea, or in a submarine
sinking deeper daily as its support systems ran down.

However, the delivery man kept the tank of the furnace
filled, the electric-meter reader stopped on his rounds. The
services were being supplied; it was the moral support sys-
tem that was failing him. There, too, lifesavers were tossed to
him, but they were not his fit. To the door one bleak day
came a brace of painfully couth young Mormon missionaries,
plainly not the fruits of the old-time religion but of modern-
day monogamy, and on another day equally dismal a trio of

Seventh-Day Adventists who, when he said he was too busy
just then for a talk with them, tried to make an appointment.
The message they had for him was an urgent one, direct from
On High, and concerned the imminent end of the world and
his eternal salvation. The Bible Belt had extended northward
of the Mason-Dixon line just as had the range of the buzzard
following farm mechanization and the consequent dearth of
dead workhorses down there.

He had believed that by bringing up his child in a household free of religion he was giving him an advantage. He still
believed that. But maybe he had denied his child the thing
that might have saved him. Maybe what had once restrained
people from laying violent hands upon themselves might
have restrained Anthony: the belief that in so doing they
were destroying the image of God, in which they were created. People killed themselves in greater numbers nowadays
than ever before; was that because they had ceased by and
large to believe in God or was it simply because there were so
many more of them? Could it be that the two things were
one and the same: the greater the number of people the
greater the number of opportunities to doubt that God
looked like that?

The time had been like the time he lost his address book.
He had had the book for years but not until he lost it did he
realize how dependent he was upon it. Without it he was cut
off from all but the very few people whom he was so closely
in touch with that he knew by heart their addresses and
telephone numbers. Not hearing from him, some people decided he had dropped them and took offense. Some he had
not heard from for years afterwards, some he never did hear
from again. He had considered placing an ad in the paper
explaining his predicament. It was like that now only in re-
verse: his friends had lost his address and telephone number.
No, rather it was as if his telephone had been disconnected
and his mail all returned to the senders marked "Address
Unknown," for not even those who knew them by heart
called now or wrote.

He knew how they explained to themselves their silence,

their avoidance of him. They called their evasion tactfulness, their self-protection they called consideration of his feelings, respect for his wish to be left alone, allowed to forget. They were sparing him embarrassment, explanation, apology. And he acquiesced. He called none of them to ask, "Where are you now that I need you?" He acquiesced in that universal human conspiracy which consigned the suicide to a double death by denying him the one he had chosen, which put beyond the pale the poor lost soul who had already put himself there, and forbade his survivors to grieve openly for him as was the right of others more acceptably bereft.

What friends he did have were tried and loyal friends. Had any other misfortune but this one befallen him they would have rallied unsummoned to his side. They were enlightened, broad-minded, kindhearted people. None of them was so backward as to believe in sin and damnation, none so pharisaical as to deny the suicide any resemblance to themselves. The barbarity of past ages in forbidding him burial among the righteous, in driving a stake through his heart and burying him at a public crossroads or leaving him unburied for carrion would have horrified them. They were humane people, civilized people; they buried the suicide double deep in silence. In short, they were people like himself, that was why he had chosen them as friends. Yes, people like himself, and hadn't he, when forced to utter it, always whispered that word *suicide* so as not to mortify further the survivors of it? Hadn't he suppressed all mention of the dead one's name? Hadn't he felt the suicide of any young person to be an insult to life, something which rendered absurd our own lifelong efforts not to die? Had he not taken it as a personal insult, a personal threat? Now he was the embodiment of that insult, that threat, one felt, to judge by the way they avoided him, by every parent—all but him. He, to whom it had happened, had never considered the possibility. Upon the unwary falls the blow.

Not even a case as close to him as Christy's had alerted him. In the very way he put that to himself was to be found the source of his unwariness, his self-complacency: Christy's *case*.

A person who was a case was not like you and yours. Cases were curiosities, anomalies, aberrations. Those without names but only initials, classified by types like the inferior phyla, were buried in medical textbooks; notorious ones gave a synthetic shudder to tourists in waxworks museums. Only now, now that parents looked at him as though he might be contagious, did he understand Tony's avoidance of him after Christy's death. And maybe exposure to Christy had shown Anthony the way. Maybe one reason for Tony's silence now was his sense of responsibility. Maybe the parent was the carrier. Maybe there was no maybe about it.

Blood of his blood and flesh of his flesh had asked itself the inadmissible question, was life worth living, and had arrived at the inadmissible answer. Did the frail fiction of life depend upon never asking that? People now seemed to see in him a reproach for the frivolity of their ways and their vanity in carrying on. If he tried with a forced smile to allay their fears of him they recoiled. They wondered how, after what he had gone through, he had the insensitivity, the effrontery, the bad taste to go on drawing breath. If, with our aging bodies, our dulling perceptions, our diminished appetites and our unsatisfactory performances, we were ashamed of outliving any young person, how much more shameful it was to have survived the one who was to have been your continuity, the nearest thing you would ever have to a reincarnation!

He was conscious of having become a public figure, one to be pointed out, whispered about, moralized upon. A dread distinction had been conferred upon him. He had endured what all men feared and thus had spared them having to endure it. He had paid the price that all obscurely felt they owed. They did not necessarily thank him for this and certainly they did not seek the pleasure of his company. When at the end the old blind Oedipus showed up at the sacred grove he himself had become sacred; what all men feared doing he had done; but though he was pitied he was unwanted; he was a sacred monster. So it was with him now. No one liked to be reminded of the dark disasters of life.

Oh, if he was shunned wherever he was known, he was

considerately shunned. The silence in which he was wrapped was nothing if not kindly. In the village, whenever he went there on an errand, shopkeepers and service attendants handled him with kid gloves—if not with tongs. Acquaintances spied him from afar and veered aside or passed by deep in conversation so as to avoid an encounter that would prove awkward and painful to him. Forcibly contained, his grief would sometimes rise in his throat as sour as gorge, as bitter as bile, and as hard to hold down. In fantasy he saw himself crying out in the street, "Have pity on me, people! My son is dead! Comfort me! Comfort me if you can." Reason, restraint, decorum would regain control and he would swallow his grief, and it was as hard to get down again as gorge.

The world could not decide what it wanted of him. It was permissible to survive certain calamities but there were some that ought to have killed you. If you were too grossly insensitive to perish politely then you might at least seclude yourself. These things were managed better back in the days when convents to retreat to were there for women with the decency to realize that nobody wanted to see them anymore and when men, having said all the wrong things, might tie their tongues by becoming Trappist monks as their apology to the world.

But underlying all these was a far simpler and more comprehensive explanation for his friends' silence and avoidance of him. He had only to look into himself to discover it. He could put himself in their place. He could picture someone even now, bothered by his conscience, the neglect of his duty, poised to dial the digits of the Curtises' telephone number or, with pen in hand, to write a long overdue letter. Had he himself not done that, stiff with dread, irritated in advance by his conventional phrases, his vanity stung by the realization of his unoriginality? Then the very fact that he was long overdue made it seem that he was now too late. Inexcusable behavior provided the excuse for more of the same. And he could see that person put down the phone, cap his pen. Discouraged from trying by his foredoomed failure, able all too easily to put himself in the Curtises' place and feel the

incommensurateness of words to wounds, he chose continued silence, comforting himself with the thought, what could
anyone say? Our inability to reach and succor one another we
could live with so long as we could turn it off with an old saw,
so long as we did not put it to the test. Else it brought home to
us the irremediable isolation in which we were each born to
live and to die.

What did he expect? For that matter, what did he want?
Would he not have found any words of comfort not only lame
but a mockery of his misery? Could he be cheered? Did he
wish to be? He believed in the power of words to do anything, though he knew how hard it was even for him, or
rather, especially for him, the tools of whose trade they were,
ever to find the right ones. Did he want now to expose to his
friends their inability to do so, to watch them squirm with
discomfort, to reveal to them their inadequacy to feel for him
as deeply as he deserved? Did he expect his misfortune to
make poets of everybody, or if not, to shame them for not
being eloquent with commiseration? Had suffering made
him selfish? Cruel? Could he not realize that the cowardice
that kept people from him now was mankind's common condition, that it was not aversion to him or self-protectiveness
but simply the recognition that their tongue-tied sympathy
would be no more consolation than that of mutes hired to
mourn at a funeral? Their avoidance of him must have
pained them too. Did he long for further evidence of human
helplessness, of life's ineluctable loneliness?

Not for him the therapy groups he read about now of
parents of youthful suicides seeking and, so they said, finding
relief through talking about their dead children and listening
to others talk about theirs. He hoped they did find relief, but
that was not for him. He shuddered to imagine searching for
clues in his boy's upbringing in discussions with strangers or
spying on the unwanted lives of their poor offspring. It
seemed a desecration of the dead, as ghoulish as grave robbing, and an invasion of the privacy of souls whose consuming desire had been for oblivion. Not for Cathy either, though
hers was a different reason. She wanted no more than knew it

already to know that she had mothered a suicide; she wanted nothing to do with others like herself. Hers was a common enough reaction, he supposed; still it saddened him. He expected something different from his wife than a common reaction.

Personal to you, unshareable, singular as your calamity was, you found that there was nothing singular about it; on the contrary, you were, in fact, a part of one of today's most widespread problems. There had been epidemics of youthful suicide at various times in history, fads for it, but as with so many of mankind's miseries, our age outdid them all. Of today's youth it was the number two killer, second only to highway accidents. Such a scourge had it become that there were international conferences on it. There was a library of books, there were television programs, dial-a-phone emergency counseling services. You could hardly pick up a magazine or a newspaper supplement without finding in it an article on the subject. It was like that other scourge, cancer: when it touched close to you was when you became really conscious of its incidence.

Was it then some malaise of the times, a worldwide wave of *taedium vitae*, an attrition of the life urge of the race, something quite impersonal, without individual motive or explanation, simply an all too common fatal germ that your child had caught?

God knew, these were hard times in which to be young and hopeful. Faiths were bankrupt and causes corrupted. The word *progress* had become an obscenity. Life was longer now that there was hardly anything worth living for. You could go anywhere you wanted to go now that there was nowhere left to want to go to. A dollar bought you twenty-five cents' worth and whatever you spent it on didn't work, fell apart, looked like hell. There was no such thing as craftsmanship anymore. We had polluted ourselves to the brink of extinction. We were up to our asses in our own filth, and the moral, political, and cultural climate we had created would make a buzzard puke. There was little game left to hunt, few fish to catch. Every species was endangered except the cockroach and the rat. Nothing you ate had any taste. Nothing was any fun anymore. The movies were meant to be entertaining, now they were either depressing or dirty, or both. Music used to have the power to soothe the savage breast, now it was meant to turn you into a howling savage. The idiot box had put an end to the magazines worth reading. Painting and sculpture —well, if you were not insulted then you had missed the point. Instead of trying to look their best, the young people made themselves as ugly as they could so as to outrage their elders. Your life was not worth a nickel on the streets of any city in the country. The third-rate ruled the world. In every country on earth, whichever party was in power, it was the mediocrities who were on top of the dungheap. Technology had turned against its masters. Erect skyscrapers to alleviate crowding, build bridges to span rivers, and people threw themselves off them. Invent drugs to ease pain and cure the curse of insomnia, and people took overdoses of them. We thought these blessings were being misused—were we mistaken? Was killing yourself with them one of their uses? The generation gap, the credibility gap, wars nobody could win or end, drab surroundings, shoddy products, dreary lives— was it any wonder so many people stayed stoned out of their minds on drink and drugs? How else could you get through a day of it?

He had heard Anthony himself in that very vein, but of course one never took to heart anything a young person said. Everybody griped about those things and then, like Miniver Cheevy, born too late, called it fate, and kept on drinking. Nobody killed himself for the sake of them. Or did some?

He did not want to be a part of a problem. He did not want to be a statistic. He did not want to be another case. To be truthful with himself, he was resentful that he must share his plight, resentful that his case, if it must be, was not the only one of its kind, or at least resentful of continual reminders that it was not. To know that he was one of many did not dilute his pain; it did not enter into solution, it was not soluble, especially not in other people's tears. Folk wisdom to the contrary notwithstanding, misery did not seek company, it

shunned it. In nothing were we more selfish than in our
suffering. "You don't know what I am enduring!" How often
we said that to the world, and how it dismayed and irritated
us to have somebody reply that he knew very well, he had
suffered the same thing himself before us. We could not allow
that our lonely, steep, and stony path was actually a well-
worn one. We wanted all the world's pity to ourselves, not
just our share as one of a multitude. Suffering, like everything
else, was devaluated by being mass-multiplied. In a fellow
sufferer one saw oneself not just mirrored but mocked. Had
God chosen to silence Job's complaints by showing him a
horde of others like himself, that would have broken his spirit
once and for all and have destroyed his faith. That would
have belittled and cheapened his sufferings, and the one
thing that sustained the poor wretch was the sense of his
distinction in being the particular object of God's displea-
sure.

Through reflection and self-examination he grew philo-
sophical and forbearing toward the world's avoidance of him.
But with the passing of each day of unrelieved silence Cathy
grew more embittered and resentful. To her their friends'
unfeeling consideration was unforgivable. For she interpreted it to mean that she was being left to hide her shame
and disgrace in seclusion. He gave up trying to explain or
excuse them. She wanted to hear none of that.

"Well, love," he said, "we've still got each other."

He got that said only by choosing a tone that totally misrep-
resented his true feeling. Thus it came out sounding rather
rueful, perhaps even rather wry, when actually his whole
heart and soul were in it. What he had meant to convey was
that they were now all the world to each other. But without
some trace of self-irony, some slight, modest disclaimer, how
did one offer oneself as all the world to another person? What
he had succeeded in intimating was that they had nothing
now except each other and must make do as best they could
with that cold comfort. The time for actions, not words, had
come. He held out his arms for her to come home to. His

warmth went cold as she flinched, shook her head, then turned from him with a shudder she could not suppress.

*

Ken Howard said, after swallowing—as offhand as that— "How did he do it?"

To speak of this for the first time, too, was both a shock and a relief. "He hanged himself," he said.

"That'll do it," said Ken. "Every time."

Ken's breeziness was not offensive to him; on the contrary, he found it tonic. "He meant business," he said. It sounded like tough-guy talk. It sounded almost as though he were boasting of his son's deed. He was not. He was simply saying something he had needed for a long time to say and saying it somewhat assertively because his listener was not the person meant to hear it. Hardly more than a stranger to him, this man had asked the question he had waited for the boy's mother to ask. He had waited, first in dread that she would ask it, then in relief, and finally in resentment that she did not.

Cathy decided that Anthony's death was unintentional, an accident, and nothing, she said, could make her change her mind. This was almost the first thing she said, although it was several days after she had emerged from the seclusion into which she had withdrawn on being told the news. It was hardly what he had been expecting to hear her say. But then neither was he expecting her to look or to act or to bear herself as she did.

It was late at night on the fifth day after he got home from Princeton that Cathy finally returned. Finding the lights of the house off and thinking him to be asleep, perhaps not wanting to see him anyway, she let herself in and went quietly to bed. He allowed her this last night's untroubled sleep. He would tell her in the morning. It was impossible for him to believe that she had returned still loyal to the mood in which she had left, but as he had continually to remind himself, she did not know what he knew, and in case she was ready to resume hostilities where they had left off, he re-

solved to break his news to her the first thing, before she had
time to say something she would regret, for it was unthink-
able now that there ever be another cross word between
them. Besides, clean wounds healed quickest. So Cathy slept
that night while he did not.

As he waited the next morning for her to come downstairs
he warned himself what to expect, or rather, what not to
expect. He must not expect her to throw herself into his arms
for comfort and consolation. From such news, and from the
bearer of it, no matter who, her first reaction would be to
recoil in horror. That was what he must expect and not be
hurt by it. He must not take it personally.

It was just what happened, and as he was expecting her to
throw herself into his arms to be comforted and consoled, he
took it personally and was hurt by it.

Cathy fled to her room and there she stayed. From behind
her closed door there came no sound. The day passed and the
night, a second day came and passed and a second night. She
was taking it even harder than he had feared. He could
occupy himself, distract himself, with nothing. Those were
agonizing days for him as he pictured Cathy wrestling alone
with her anguish, longing to comfort her, fearing for her
health of mind tormented as she was by a grief so great she
wanted no one, not even him, to see her. People differed in
their reactions. His had been to long for her, but some must
lick their wounds alone. He must be patient now, wait it out,
hold himself in readiness for the time when she would want
him. He respected her wish for privacy, but the longer it
lasted the more his anxiety mounted. Solitary grieving, like
solitary drinking, led to immoderation. He reminded himself
that he had had his time alone with the knowledge—in his
case not by choice but perforce, yet maybe it was better that
way, better that she had not been in the house. The sight of
her would have melted him. Yet with terrible irony he likened those days when he paced the floors to those of an
expectant father during his wife's protracted labor. In sorrow
shalt thou bring forth children—in what greater sorrow give
them up before their time! His anxiety over Cathy while she

remained shut in her room bred a thousand contingencies. He was prepared for everything but for what eventuated.

He had said to himself, "Three whole days she has been in there!" When on the morning of the fourth day she reappeared downstairs he had to ask himself, "Was it only three?"

There was no trace of redness in her eyes, no tremor in her lips, no pucker in her chin. Although it had seemed an eternity while he waited it out, now it seemed miraculous that she could have attained this self-composure in so short a time. Disheveled, distraught, haggard, hysterical—no, she was none of the things he had been dreading. Her tears had all been shed, and shed some time ago. How deeply stricken she was showed in her lusterless eyes, in the labor of her breathing, in the frequent involuntary shake of her head as her mind spasmed with memories and regrets; but the set of her shoulders, the thrust of her jaw proclaimed her refusal to feel the shame and the disgrace she was expected to feel. It was an astonishing feat of courage, of strength of will. She seemed to have passed her days in seclusion allotting one to the question, must it be? another to the answer, yes, it must, and the third to the resolution, then so be it. What was more, she seemed to suppose that he, who had lived longer than she had with their new situation, had faced up to it and arrived at the same mood of resignation.

He had now had an opportunity to observe the reaction of four people to the suicide of their child. Pris had been numbed by it. Tony had been crushed. Cathy refused to accept it. The one whose reaction he could not label was his own. From which he deduced the obvious: that he knew himself better than he did the other three, and that he was fatuous in thinking their reactions any more definable than his. Surely from the little we were able in a lifetime to learn about ourselves one lesson to be drawn was that about others we knew nothing at all.

Cathy's days in the fiery furnace had not melted her, they had tempered her. Whatever may have been the stages she had passed through, the woman who emerged was, as far as the world was ever to be allowed to see, one unbroken, one who would not look back. He was glad of it, he was overjoyed, but prepared as he was for the worst, he hardly knew what to make of the best. She had no need of him, or if she did she would not admit it. The strong arm he had readied to steady her with, the shoulder for her to cry upon, would not be wanted. The answers to her questions that he had painfully prepared would not be wanted. The grisly details of an event she was determined to put behind her she did not want to hear. The world could keep its pity, and pity, like charity, began at home. His was the first pity she could do without.

He admired, he envied her bravery, and all the more as she mistakenly credited him with the same, supposed that she was only catching up with him. True, he had lived with it longer than she had. But her strength and resilience shamed him for his weakness and dependency. He could have used some support from her. So much the smaller of the two of them, she was that much the stronger. A stubborn, defiant refusal to accept it, or to accept responsibility and shame for it: that was Cathy's reaction, and he was sure it was the right, the reasonable, the healthy-minded reaction. And yet, how different from his own! No dread, no premonition of such a possibility had ever darkened his mind, yet what did it say about his sense of responsibility that he had so readily, so unquestioningly accepted the event? His easy acquiescence seemed to accuse him of a kind of complicity.

She was averse to talking about the matter and as he could talk about nothing else they soon talked about nothing at all. They saw nobody, yet they were never alone; with them at all times was Anthony. By absenting himself from them forever he had made himself their constant companion. He had his place at the table and in front of the fire in the evenings. Let either of them speak, his shadow fell between them and they sat in heavy, apathetic silence. Each reminded the other of him and of nothing else of all that was between them. They were like a pair of animals yoked together and with blinders to prevent their seeing outside the row they trod, and holding the reins and the whip was Anthony.

But oppressive as it was, the silence between them was

preferable to the dread that came whenever she cleared her throat to speak: she was now about to ask him how Anthony had done it. She had worked up the courage to ask. Each evening that passed sparing him that was a reprieve. There was no nice way of killing yourself but there were degrees of ugliness, of violence to the body, the duration of the agony, the disfigurement. *Shot? so quick, so clean an ending?* Let her think it had been that. Or, since sleeping pills had made it all so easy and tidy they had just about replaced other methods, she probably assumed it was that, perhaps even felt she had a parent's right to assume it. That was the thoughtful, the considerate, the civilized way. It did not pain or inconvenience the survivors any more than was unavoidable. You were found already stretched out in bed looking as though you were just asleep. No gore. Whoever found you had the minimum fright and bother. Just to name the way Anthony had chosen to die would produce an image to sear his mother's soul.

And he? Would he have been any happier now if what he had been shown in that basement in Princeton was a body outwardly unmarked? Had the boy chosen a different way to die would he be any the less dead? The answer to that last question was obvious, the one to the other more complicated.

Unlike Cathy, he had wanted to know the details. Maybe that was morbid curiosity, but he had wanted to know. No doubt about it, it was morbid, because his reason for wanting to know was so that he might, as nearly as he could in imagination, experience the death of his child. Flesh of his flesh that was, and it was imperative that he know what throes it had undergone in destroying itself. That might be morbid, but was there not something unnatural in the boy's mother's incuriosity about the details?

"It was an accident," she said. Out of their strained silence on the subject it came like a shot, and it was so wide of the mark it left him speechless. "That's what I believe and always will. I mean it was—how shall I say?—a stunt that went

wrong. He meant to be found in time and saved. He wanted
to throw a scare into somebody. And I know who."

He would consider that last remark later; for now, he was
too distressed by her first statement. It placed before him
more vividly than ever, as evidence to the contrary, that
twisted neck, the swollen, livid face, the bulging eyes, the
protruding tongue. He set down the drink in his hand before
he should spill it and turned away to hide from her his agitation. He felt himself choking, strangling. He could not swallow his mouthful. He pictured the boy in those last lonely
hours, his world now reduced to that dormitory room and
peopled solely by a self he was determined to rid the world
of. It seemed a bitter belittlement of that terrible desperation to suppose it was some sort of bad joke, a stunt that had
gone wrong, a mere accident. Deplorable, misguided, rash,
juvenile though it might be, his taking his life had been the
supreme act of his life, and it seemed his right to have his
seriousness acknowledged. Surely his aim had not been just
to hurt his mother, but just as surely she was denying herself
something in rejecting the full measure of her hurt, of the
deprivation she had coming to her, in denying him his agony,
his dignity. It was hard to grieve properly for a poor joker
who had not meant to kill himself but had bumbled into it.

It was not the evasion of her responsibility—if any—that he
objected to. He could have understood and forgiven that. But
to insist upon its having been unintentional without asking
how it had been done was to deprive the boy of the death he
had so determinedly desired and so painstakingly planned
and executed. Until those whom he had left behind granted
him that death he would be an unquiet ghost, forever strangling in that noose with which he had tried to end his pain.
Surely for those left the hope of curing their pain began with
the full admission of it.

Thus he began to resent her incuriosity, her comfortable
assumption that it had been done somehow painlessly,
quickly, cleanly, decorously, perhaps with an overdose of
sleeping pills from which there was a chance of being wakened as though from a nightmare, maybe scolded a bit for

having given everybody a scare, but then soothed and made to realize that it was all a bad dream. Did he resent also the fact that now he could never tell her otherwise? Was he resentful that by her indifference she forced him to live alone with that vision? No, for sharing the picture imprinted on his mind with anybody would not attenuate or diminish its frightfulness. Like a painting, it could be reproduced, distributed in large editions, and the original would remain the original in all its vividness. Yet being the one witness to the body gave him something of a sense of having been his son's co-conspirator in his death.

He wanted not to think about this, he wanted to think about anything other than this, and he could think of nothing else. He wanted not to generalize, not to categorize, not lose his son in abstractions, not let him become a case, a statistic, another in that vast army of teenage suicides. Yet the image of that body suspended in his thoughts (how long had it hung from that ceiling before being found and cut down?) forced him to wonder whether in all cases the method contained a message. Anthony might have been as dead one way as another, but he had chosen a certain way and not an easy one. His way certainly spoke of premeditation. So elaborate a means suggested that he had plotted long, or if not long then intently, against his life. There had been nothing impulsive about it. That side of him that had turned against himself had stalked its prey and it was the deadliest of enemies, for it knew its victim's ways, could foresee and forestall its shifts and dodges. Had there been some sort of perverse thrill in forcing that intended victim to witness all those extensive preparations for his execution? In making him an accomplice in the purchase of the rope, in checking the clock to see that everything was proceeding on schedule? (How did he know that to make it slip a hangman's noose was always lubricated with soap? How did Anthony know it? How did he know that Anthony knew it?) Was such a grisly death chosen so that the victim's unanswered cry for help would reverberate all the louder, all the longer in the memory of those who might have come to his rescue? When poor Tony was summoned to the

New York City morgue to identify and claim as his what was
left of Christy was there an old incident from out of her
childhood which came to his mind and made him say, "When
you climbed to the top of that tall building, my dear, dead
daughter, were you repeating the time you climbed to the
top of the apple tree to sulk over your hurt feelings? I coaxed
you down from the tree, I lifted you down from the limb, but
you went beyond Daddy's reach and his reasoning when you
climbed to the top of the building, didn't you?" What was
Anthony demonstrating to the world by the way he had
chosen to leave it? And wasn't it pity added to pity that the
message had reached so very few in the world? What was it
meant to convey to the only one of his parents whom it had
reached?

One slit his throat, another put the muzzle of a gun in his
mouth: different temperaments, different approaches to the
same end. Yes, the how of it was important. To misapply a
philosopher of popular culture, the medium was the message. A suicide, he was coming to see, was a work of art. It was
a corruption of his mind that he could think so, for it was the
very opposite of a work of art; it was destructive, not creative,
and yet it was art, inverse, devilish art, and there were different media at your disposal. Or perhaps there was a hierarchy
of genres as there was once in painting, with the historical at
the top, the sacred, the allegorical and so on down to still life
—nature morte—at the bottom. Or it was like music. Why
was one person drawn to the viola and another to the violin?
What made one person choose to hang himself and another
to jump off a building? Was the spurning of easy outs and the
choice instead of an elaborate and gruesome mode of self-
destruction a test of the sincerity of your intentions, the gen-
uineness of your resolve, of your nerve? Was it meant to leave
no comforting doubts in your survivors' minds that you had
known what you were doing, that you meant business? Or, by
making death a weary lot of trouble to go to, gory and nasty
and as painful as possible, were you trying to face it at its
worst and face it down, or giving it full rein to terrify you
from it? Was each additional floor that lonely little Christy

climbed that afternoon meant to give her another chance to reprieve herself as well as another dare to mount still higher and plunge still farther? Such stark methods must appeal to those who had turned against themselves with pitiless savagery, not just to those weary of the diuturnity of life but to passionate haters of it, disappointed beyond reconciliation. Or else to those determined to horrify the world that had rejected or disillusioned them and show its self-contented citizens a different estimation of the unexamined existence they clung to.

They had not gone gentle into that good night, those two, but had it been, until too late, a game, a kind of game played with—against—yourself, like a game of chicken in which you were the driver of both the cars? An adolescent flirting with death and with the assurance only an adolescent could have of his ability to win?

Had his Anthony said to himself, "Really, I'm just exploring this. Just curious. I'm not really going through with it. I'm just testing the water"? In going to the hardware store, buying the rope and paying for it and getting his change from the salesclerk (who doubtless concluded the transaction with "Have a nice day") did he say to his reflection in the show windows, "See? The fact that I can do all this so coolly shows I'm not crazy, that I'm not really going to do it. I'm testing myself, seeing what my powers of resistance are. A time will come in all this when I will have gone as far as I need to go in order to prove myself. At that point it will become real— until then it's just a game, just make believe. When I say to myself, now all I have to do is kick the chair out from under me, then I won't do it because I will have proved to myself that I could go all the way. Then I will have called death's bluff, and my own"?

Then suppose that at the last moment the suspense and tension built up so that you did it just to escape from that. You didn't want to do it. Even then, at the very last of last moments, you still wished to be saved from yourself. But nobody came. Your father did not come—in itself a reason to do it. You did it because you could not stand not to do it. You had worked yourself up to this pitch and had left yourself only one out.

Had there been a sense of excitement and challenge in it? Forbidden games played behind parents' and teachers' backs, played for the highest of stakes? Did it make you seem more mature? If maturity was age and age was proximity to death, what better way to steal the march, overtake and outstrip your elders, get there before they did and repay them for what the poet called the ignominy of childhood? The secrecy, the danger, even a sense of complicity, of conspiracy between your two selves, the plotter and his prey, in league against an unsuspecting world. Did it make you seem more interesting to yourself and give you a feeling of superiority over those who assumed on face evidence that you were content with the same safe existence as theirs, or, in the case of a youngster with his way still to make in the world, that you would go through the mill and make the same compromises they had made in order to achieve their dreary, dull security? The sense that *you* were destroying *them? Good creatures, do you love your lives? Here is a knife like other knives—I need but stick it in my heart and all you folk will die.*

He drew up short, having already traveled further down this path than he ever expected to get, suddenly fearful of proceeding, daunted not by its difficulty—that was what he had anticipated—not by its strangeness, but by its menacing ease, its frightening familiarity. He had begun in dismay at the utter hopelessness of finding a motive for his son's doing what he had done; he was dismayed now to discover the fertility of his mind in finding them. It hardly seemed to be his mind, so unexplored a side to it this was. Searching for the one, he had found a multiplicity of motives, all plausible, all sufficient; a bit further on and he might find what he was looking for, what he was suddenly not at all sure he wanted to find: the right one. Could it be that not to know, painful and tormenting as that was, was better than to know? Doubts were dreadful but was certainty worse? And was the answer not only not complex but hideously, horribly simple, mockingly apparent? He had thought he was entering a maze, an issueless maze; now he felt himself being lured on with the promise that there was an issue. It was obvious—that was the reason so many failed to see it. To find it he had only to open his eyes, only to look into himself. He was searching for the motive? Suppose he found there was none? Suppose he found that none was needed. There came to him, too quick for him to escape it altogether, an intimation that the answer to his question, "Why?" might prove to be a question: *Why not?*

That was not to be dwelt upon; besides, if it was for anybody it was not for the young, it was for those who had run out of reasons for why life must go on. For example, parents of a child who had committed suicide. As for Anthony, in his case questions found no answers, they only raised more questions, and he wondered whether that had been a part of the boy's motive. He heard him say—actually heard him—his ghost—say, "I'm realer to you now than I ever was alive, aren't I? I've gotten your attention, your full attention, at last. You realize now that I was somebody you never knew and you will speculate endlessly on what he was really like, that stranger whom you brought into the world and, because of that, presumed that you understood. *Why?* you will ask yourself with your every breath, with every beat of your heart: *why? why?* And for all your conjecturing I shall remain a puzzle. You cannot put your questions to the one person who might resolve them, for I have taken all the answers with me. By one action I have overturned all your perceptions, all your presumptions about me, and wrapped myself in impenetrable mystery."

The ghost faded. He would have called it back and begged it to torment him further rather than leave the void it left: this thought: was it the height of fatuity to suppose that he had figured at all in his son's last thoughts on earth? Better to live with the certainty that Anthony's sole motive was retaliation for his father's lifelong neglect and misunderstanding of him than to know that he had come in the end to such an

extremity: a solitude so desolate that his father no longer
existed for him.

*

"With me it's not idle curiosity," said Ken Howard, "because when I was fourteen years old my father killed himself." Even now, all these years later, and even confessing it
to a kindred soul, it still brought a flush of embarrassment to
the man's face. "I was the one who found the body. My father
had gone to some pains to get himself ready for what he was
about to do. Knowing that his dead body would soon be
handled by strangers he had followed my mother's advice to
me whenever I was going anywhere, to be well dressed and
wear clean underclothes in case I had an accident and was
taken to the hospital or was killed: then I would not disgrace
us by being unpresentable. My father had bathed and shaved
and had put on his best suit. He had tied on a necktie. Then
he had swallowed lye. The tumbler he had drunk from and
the can with the red skull and crossbones and the spoon he
had stirred it with sat on the bedstand. He had drunk it and
had stretched himself out on the bed to wait.

"He had nicked his chin in shaving, and he had treated the
cut with a styptic pencil. A thin red line of dried blood
showed through the white coat of alum. He was about to kill
himself and yet he had treated his little cut. I wondered
whether he had said 'Ouch' and whether he had winced at
the sting of the styptic pencil. All his little efforts to be neat,
to make as little trouble as possible, made me feel he had
been ashamed and apologetic for what he was doing, and that
made me feel ashamed for him, and people's silence about
him afterwards made me feel they were trying to spare me
my shame. When they do it to themselves you not only lose
them, it is as you say, as though you never had them."

The last person who wanted to hear this, he was the one
chosen to listen. So it always was. Wakes were the time when
conversation turned inevitably to and lingered upon the subject which all were there to forget. Speak not of rope in the
hanged man's house, went an old proverb, yet always in the

hanged man's house rope got mentioned sooner or later. It had in his house. He himself, that last time on board *Pandora*, had spoken of once being so desperate over something he was ready to jump off a bridge—and then wished there had been one handy. Now he knew as though he had already heard it said what was coming next. He had already heard it. He had said it to himself times out of number.

"To all outward appearances my father was a contented man, one with everything to live for. He was just forty years old. He was a successful lawyer and was being mentioned for a judgeship. He was a loving husband to my mother and a devoted father to me. He was in good health and his finances were in order. He was a man with no secrets in his life. What made him do it no one ever knew. To this day I have never stopped wondering."

*

Why? Why?

In every sound he heard that question asked.

Clocks ticked it. Winds moaned it. Sirens wailed it. Crows cawed it. Wheels clicked it. Dogs in the night howled it. The blood in his veins pulsed it. Why?

Waves on the beach pounded it. Gulls screamed it. Leaves on the trees whispered it. Rain on the roof drummed it. Why? Why?

Bells tolled it. Trains shrieked it. Flames hissed it. Silence thundered it. Why?

Not only did he hear it all the time, he saw it everywhere. Each block of pavement underfoot, each square of patterned wallpaper repeated it. It was woven into the carpet, it was every word on every page. Why? Why? Why?

Asked that question by every sight and sound, at every turn, his existence narrowed to a single purpose as the rays of the sun are gathered by a lens and focused upon one burning spot. To answer it he must try to get to know the son he had thought he knew.

There came over him a sense that the life he was leading was not his. That his body had lived on after he himself had

died and had been occupied by someone else as the shells of
snails survived to house the next generation. A spirit had
dispossessed him and its name was Anthony. Some people
when they died left debts to be discharged by their survivors;
it was life itself that Anthony had defaulted on. His father was
left to live out the balance of that unfinished life. That was his
son's legacy to him. Life: we could not get enough of it, yet to
be burdened with an unwanted life made one's own a burden.

He longed to talk about him with the boy's mother but she
found the subject too painful, too distasteful. She appeared to
have concluded that the person who had done this thing to
her was not her child; he had disowned her. His act had been
a declaration to the world that his mother had failed him.
How had she failed him? He was not required to show proof.
It was an unjust punishment and it was impossible for her to
defend herself. She saw what Anthony had done as an act of
childish impulsiveness. Her belief that a girl was the direct
cause of it made it all the more juvenile. She said bitterly,
"He might have thought of us."

Maybe hers was the right, the healthy-minded reaction: to
reject whoever had rejected you. It was not for him to fault
her. But for his part he saw it not as a childish act of
Anthony's but rather as a pitifully premature agedness and
disillusionment with life, however it had come about, and he
chose to credit the boy with some understanding of how
deeply he was about to hurt his parents and thus with an
unhappiness too deep for that to deter him.

As for Cathy's dismissal of what she called calf love, he
could only wonder at the shortness of her memory or else
suspect the hardness of her heart when young. At sixteen he
would have died for Louise Avery, at seventeen for Mary
Ellen Edmonds, at eighteen for Elizabeth Gibbons, and the
wonder was that he hadn't because for all they cared he
might have. To some it might seem to trivialize his present
suffering to say that nothing until now had so broken his
heart as the indifference of those shallow, flighty girls of long
ago, but not to him. There were greater pains in life than

unrequited young love, but not at that age, and if that had contributed to Anthony's unhappiness, to a feeling of being unwanted by all the world, then he could feel for him, especially as the love of his own life seemed to be dying now before his eyes.

With Anthony's first girl, during his last summer, it had been as with all his interests. Until then he had had no time for girls; now he had no time for anything but Alice Clayton.

Jogging—another solitary, grueling self-test of endurance —was Anthony's consuming craze that summer. Finished with school, tired of textbooks and the tyranny of teachers, of the indignity of never having been anything but a schoolboy, he had decided against college, was thinking of a year out west as a ranch hand or as a lumberjack or as a firefighter with the forestry service, and he was getting himself in shape. It looked instead as though he was destroying himself when he came in from a five-mile sprint drenched with sweat and heaving for wind. It was while jogging on a country road in training for one of those all-male work gang, footloose and unfettered bachelor jobs that he met Alice, she riding her horse.

With any interest of Anthony's it was always as though he were its discoverer, the first ever upon the scene, the holder of the patent. So it was now with Alice. She was the Eve to his Adam and all the world was suddenly Eden, fresh from its creator's hand. He was like his father, a one-woman man, unlike him in seeming to have found his on his first try. He soon brought her home to be presented to his parents. Their reactions to one another he studied as closely as though judging how they were going to get along as in-laws. It took him aback that to his parents Alice was something the likes of which, at least, they had seen before. A nice specimen, very nice, but not a new species. Anthony was an illustration of the truth that there is something in us which resents the discovery, made always just when the first full flush of our novelty is upon us, that others before us have felt, or claim to have felt, our own self-same inimitable emotions, that the world was here ere our coming and there is nothing new under the sun.

We are deflated and diminished by any discovery of our conformity to pattern, and perhaps for some, all aflame with youth and expectation, learning that the world was so old and shopworn and they themselves so unoriginal was too disillusioning, too dispiriting for them to want to carry on. In Anthony this craving for singularity, this irritation with and disavowal of resemblances between himself and the rest of the world, was pronounced. It made him consistently contrary, determinedly different, odd and crotchety in small ways. He worked on holidays, he took his walks in the rain, he went without a winter overcoat, he lived on a diet all his own. Small idiosyncrasies, merely amusing before, but now, indicative of what major maladjustment? Had the end come when he discovered his likeness to humankind in one particular above all, and had he declared his difference in the only way possible, by not awaiting the common fate but by anticipating and thus forestalling it, taking matters into his own hands and making himself master of his? Or was it the other way around? Had his refusal to have his like been all along because of the inadmissibility of that most basic of bonds? No young man believes that he shall ever die. True, but he had better learn better if he wants to become an old man. The mark of maturity was the acceptance of that one ineluctable fact of life. That was the one touch of nature that made the whole world kin. But suppose you could not accept it? Could not? That touch of nature was the one you refused to acknowledge in yourself. A world of kin swamped your precious individuality. Then your only out might be like that of people who threw themselves from a height to put a stop to their terror of doing so.

Never suspecting that it would be the last, he had followed with pleasure the course of his son's first love. Not because through it he was reliving his own. Very different, sweetly different from his own it was, and his gratitude to Alice for that difference grew by the day. At Anthony's age his father had been luckless in love but he had been incorrigible, burned again and again and still as susceptible as a moth to flame. A heart that had been broken almost beyond repair

was barely beating again when he offered it all eager and
palpitant and guileless and humble to yet another little flirt
for her to play with like a yo-yo and then toss indifferently
aside. To him, people who laughed at young love were unfeeling. Life brought no emotion more pure, more intense,
more selfless, nor, when it was unrequited, spurned, more
painful. It was a blow not just to your pride but to your whole
personality and made you not just distrustful but self-doubt-
ful. It left wounds into adult life. His had been healed by
Cathy but he still carried old scars. Daily: that was the fre-
quency of his opportunity for observation of them, for not a
day was allowed to pass that summer without those two seeing each other and it was at the Curtis home that they spent
their time. Anthony preferred always to wage his campaigns
on his own terrain. And it had been sweet to see him offer his
parents as one of his attractions.

Alice on her horse cantered alongside as he jogged. Afterwards they cooled off with a dip in the pool. On it he taught
her fly casting. He took her with him to fly Jezebel. Alice
must have known then that she was being put to a test.
Anthony was discovering with daily delight the differences
between himself and the pretty half of humankind but his
long-lasting indifference to them had not been without some
causes, one of which was their usual squeamishness toward
nature in the raw. He did not expect Alice to share his enthusiasm for falconry but had she been what he called silly about
it she would have slipped in his esteem. She passed the test.

Alice soon sounded the depths of Anthony's devotion to
her, and while she could not return it measure for measure,
she knew its worth and was grateful for it, knew its vulnera-
bility and was protective of it. She told him of a boy before
him in her life. This boy had loved her with a love she could
not return. He had turned out badly—maybe because of her.
This she told him almost pleadingly, as though begging him
to be cautious with them both. The essential thing about a
first love was to come through it with your self-regard and
your trust in the opposite sex whole and healthy, and Alice
was charting Anthony safely through the shoals. Watching

them canoeing once had given him that comparison. On her side Alice had to paddle hard to keep pace with Anthony and steer them straight; in doing so, however, she was helping to accelerate their speed.

When Anthony wanted a thing he went all out to get it and he had never before wanted anything as he wanted that girl. He was willful, impetuous, importunate, possessive. Much as Alice liked him there must have been times when she would have liked to get out of the boat, when she felt they were going too fast, in depths over their young heads. But to have tried to slow him or to urge a passage through shallower waters would have had the opposite effect. Anthony did nothing by halves. Any suggestion that he ought perhaps to think again before plunging into something only made him the more headlong, and even a hint that he was too young for it was a challenge to prove you wrong.

On that canoeing trip they had had a long hot day on the water when, at the close of it, they beached their boats, Cathy and he in theirs, Alice and Anthony in his. As the first cool of the evening came down, while the men brought the gear up the strand to the woods' edge, gathered fuel for the fireplace which they themselves had erected there years before, and stretched and pegged the tent, the women took towels and went out of sight around the bend to bathe. At the time it had seemed to his father that Anthony's excitement, evidenced by his unaccustomed talkativeness, came from titillation at the thought of his mother's seeing Alice naked— the next best thing to being there himself. What was to happen later would be so incomprehensible, such a distortion of everything, prompting thoughts so wild as to make him wonder whether Alice were not, in the jaded jargon of abnormal psychology, rather the person to whom Anthony had transferred another, unnatural passion and that the thrill he was vicariously enjoying was her sight of his naked mother. That abomination gave the measure of what had happened, how far it could derange, poison, and pervert the mind and fill it with suspicions revolting to itself.

But that was later—a lifetime later. That evening while the

women made camp and prepared the food that was to accompany the trout they were confident of catching, the men went fishing. They were rigging their rods when Anthony, lining up the guides on his and pushing together the two sections, said in a tone as offhand as he could summon, "Dad, it's none of my business, of course, but if you don't mind telling me, when did you propose to Mom?"

"I reckon it is your business," he said. And he told of that evening on the terrace of the clubhouse with the Thayers—Anthony's godparents—present, and something of the feelings that had prompted him then. He could see that as he listened Anthony was making some personal comparisons. Some contrasts, too, he trusted. Not wanting to discountenance the boy, he made no mention of his age at that time, but he hoped it went without saying. Yet he would not have been greatly surprised had Anthony, feeling, as they sat around the campfire, as though this moment, here in this place, with these people, was one *he* wanted to prolong for life, said in imitation of his father, "Alice, marry me, will you?"

Anthony boyishly thought it was boyish to let your feelings show, especially your pleasure, but his that evening were too great for him to dissemble. Watching Alice and his mother working together on the meal and then cleaning up afterwards, washing the utensils at the streamside in the dying light, he was enchanted. His father could study him because he had eyes only for Alice. He glowed with pride in her as though she were already his own, pride in her camping competence, her ease with his parents, her grace and prettiness, her little sallies of wit. Above all he was enjoying the sense that the four of them were two couples on this outing together—especially when they all bedded down together in their sleeping bags. For the first time that evening Anthony's father pictured himself as a grandfather—without, of course, picturing himself a day older than he was.

In the night he had awakened, had slipped out of his sleeping bag and gone down to the water to listen to it and to stargaze. There he found Anthony.

"Oh? You awake, son?"

With uncharacteristic openness Anthony said, "I'm too happy to sleep."

From too much happiness could come deep disappointment and Anthony was awfully young to make his happiness dependent upon another person herself equally young. But this worry that tinged his father's satisfaction that starry night was no more than that: a tinge.

*

One day early that August, looking up from the letter in his hand, Anthony asked, "Dad, supposing I was to get admitted to one of the Ivy League colleges, could you lend me the money to go?"

"Lend you the money? I'd give—"

"It's an awful lot. And there's more to come. After I got out of college could you lend me the money to go through Cornell University School of Veterinary Medicine?"

"What's this about lending? You get yourself admitted to college and—"

"I've done that. Read for yourself. Here's my letter of acceptance."

Thus was explained the true purpose of his recent hitchhiking trip to Princeton. No word about changing his mind, about having applied for admission to the university. Never a word until he knew the result. Nor would there ever have been a word if he had been turned down. That was our Anthony.

"Congratulations, son! But I thought—"

"I changed my mind. You know, Dad, life is a serious business and time is short. You aren't given enough of it to go goofing off any."

"True. All too true. Have you told your mother about this?"

"Not yet. First I had to speak to you about finances."

"She will be very pleased. So now what about this year? Are you still planning to spend it out west?"

"No. I'm going to Princeton."

"This year? Does it say you've been accepted for *this* year? It's unheard of!"

"Well, my school record is pretty good" (in fact, it was outstanding) "and I came away thinking I had made a pretty good impression on the admissions officer. Now, I have checked this thing out, and here is what I'm up against. Veterinary schools are hard to get into, as hard as medical schools, maybe even harder. Veterinary medicine is a closed shop. Vets don't want any more vets. Before you can get into veterinary school you first have to work for a vet for six months, and many of them won't take on a student helper."

"How do you propose to get around all that?"

"One step at a time. And here," he said, brandishing the letter, "is the first. Not many applicants come to them with a degree from Princeton. The schools have to stay in business. They turn down many applicants, especially Cornell, but they accept the best. I mean to be one of those. The only problem is money. It's going to cost a bundle. So here is what I propose: you stake me and I'll repay you out of my earnings."

"No more of that."

"Dad—now don't take offense—in a few years I'll be making more money than you ever dreamed of. If I was going into something impractical it would be a different matter, but I'm not. You're probably thinking: animal clinic, distemper shots, boarding pets while people go on vacation. Forget it. Dad, practically our whole economy depends on vets. The meat we eat. Our water supply. Commercial fishing. Champion bulls. Thoroughbred horse breeding. Laboratory research for the big drug manufacturers. You've done enough for me. No more freeloading. Past a certain point in life a man ought not to have to work anymore for his kids. I'm asking you for a loan. The arrangement is the same one I'm going to make with my son when he's college age."

There was a final note.

"Suppose I had said no, I couldn't afford it? What then?"

"Matter of fact, that was what I was expecting you to say."

He overlooked on grounds of youth this second slight to his ability as a provider. "And?"

"Oh, then I was going to get a bank loan. And I mean to pay you the interest I would have had to pay on that."

That was still just months, one might even say just weeks, ago. What went wrong with all those far-reaching plans? From an aimless kid tired of school to professional man, even the father of a son: there could be no doubt that all this was founded on hopes centering on Alice Clayton. Theirs was the kind of youthful romance that might well have resulted in marriage, in time. That the affair had had its little ups and downs they had seen, for although Anthony had disciplined himself never to display his feelings, he had only half succeeded: he could conceal his satisfactions but not his disappointments, though, with evident annoyance that it could be asked, his reply to the question, what was bothering him, was always "Nothing." Now his father wondered whether perhaps the boy's mother was right, after all. Right not in thinking it was a stunt that went wrong, for it was no stunt, it was in determined and deadly earnest, but right in thinking it was meant to throw a scare into somebody, and she knew who. If that were so, or even if the poor child only imagined it might be so, then of all Anthony's victims Alice was the most mistreated. Linked hand in hand with that thought was this one: was it possible to come to hate a suicide? Not pity the poor lost soul but hate him for the pain he had brought upon you and his blighting of the lives of all who had known him, loved him? If that were so, if he were to make you end by hating him, and suffering the self-hatred that would entail, it would be a revenge too cruel to bear. Was suicide the one death that ensured your never being laid quietly to rest in the memory of your survivors? It was horrible to impute to such vindictiveness even a fraction of the motive, but was that one of its attractions?

*

Because she had said over the phone that she was expecting to hear from him in a tone that caused him to interpret "expecting" to mean "dreading," and because there had been a long wait and the dead silence of a hand being held over the mouthpiece while the sister who answered told Alice who was calling (not by his own name but as "Anthony's father" was how he had identified himself), then another long silence, long enough for quite a lengthy family council, even an argument, even a scene, he was totally unprepared for what happened when they met. He had reckoned that her parents would be unhappy over this meeting but would not oppose it, rather would insist that it was her duty, however painful. So he could not have said just what sort of reception he went expecting, only that it was not what he got, and he was moved by it, chastened, humbled, more than ever sorry for his own part in her unhappiness and angry at his wife for her underestimation of it—and maybe also for not having done herself what this child did on sight: throw herself into his arms sobbing brokenheartedly.

Child? If until now she had been a child, she was one no longer, she was a woman, like it or not, one put to a test reserved for few and deeply shaken by it. The word that leaped to his mind at the sight of her was *widow,* and though no child, she was pitifully young to look like that. Far-reaching and rough were the waves Anthony had sent outward in scuttling his own boat. He thought he had counted up the losses to himself; now to the list was added Alice and all that she might have been.

He was not so simple as to think her outpouring was pure unmixed grief for his dead son, neither was he so selfish as to resent its admixture. What did it matter which among the welter of her feelings was uppermost: sorrow, shock, bereavement, bewilderment, mistrust of the life that lay ahead of her after this discovery of its deceptiveness, its treachery? Or stark terror? For as he stood holding her close and feeling her throes, the thought crossed his mind that had she been anywhere nearby at the time Anthony lost his balance there might have been not one violent death but two, not one family in mourning now for a child but two. How hard it was at moments like this to keep in mind that the boy had acted irrationally and excuse him, not add to the bill of indictment against him what he had done to this poor girl. Despite all he could do, a growing resentment toward his dead son was building up in him.

Much passed through his mind as he stood holding Alice for what was to be the first and the last time. Among his thoughts was this one: out of an instinct only too human, Anthony's mother sought someone to put the blame on; was it the instinct of only a mother that she blamed the one girl in her son's short life? And himself? Had he requested this meeting half in hopes of trapping her into some revelation that would put the blame on her and relieve him of his share? Whatever Alice had done, if anything at all, she could not have foreseen this outcome. For his part, knowing all that he knew now—and not knowing all that he would never know— he supposed Anthony was capable of twisting and magnify- ing some little tiff they had had into a motive for what he had done; if so, he only hoped it had been something so trivial, so insignificant that she would be unable even to remember it, much less imagine that it might have been the cause and have it come back to haunt her. What if she had very sensibly said no to a proposal of Anthony's that they get engaged? That she vow while he was away at school to go out on dates with no other boy? Was she to make a nun of herself at her age? Was she to blame if Anthony were mad enough to kill himself over the thought of her going to a movie with some other boy? The calamity would be compounded if she were to allow some such thing to cloud her life. She had been shown a glimpse into the human mind, its unknowability, its penchant for self-torture and destruction; young as she was, she would never outlive that. Misfortune enough, her mere encounter with such disaster. Enough that she felt, as he felt, rejected. The help and comfort she might have given had been judged useless. Now to the list of his self-reproaches must be added this meeting. He had subjected her to it and his profit on it was further anger toward Anthony on behalf of this victim of his rashness. Perhaps the worst thing of all about unnatural death was the total confusion of feelings it caused.

It was this young woman's children he was vaguely thinking of when, not long ago, he had pictured himself for the first time as a grandfather—without then picturing himself as any older than he was. There was nothing vague about his realization now that he would never be a grandfather. Anthony had killed his grandchildren. He had never longed for any before. He had assumed that he would have them, and that had been a pleasing if somewhat indistinct prospect, but he had never longed for any. He did now. Now that he could only mourn for them he did. So much so that, holding in his arms his might-have-been, his almost daughter-in-law and looking over her shoulder, he could see, hand in hand, the grandchildren, a girl and a boy, whom he would never have —could even see their resemblance to himself. He felt old enough to be a grandfather now, many times over.

There passed through him as if a switch had been thrown a shock that was electrical, and like the polar charges of which an electric current is compounded, it produced in him feelings diametrically opposed but which in their combination flooded his mind with illumination. It flowed from her to him like an electric charge. He tensed with the sense that he held in his arms not one person but two and a part of a third, blood of his blood, flesh of his flesh. She was pregnant. That explained everything. Even now, ripening in her, was his fatherless grandchild. She was a widow without ever being a wife. She was pregnant with Anthony's child; guilt for that was his motive for what he had done, and the calamity was extended into the next generation. Yet though half of the charge that coursed through him was a sickening dread, half of it was hope. A fantasy born of fear and longing, it left when it passed feelings half of relief, half of regret.

Her first words when she was able to speak were to inquire after Mrs. Curtis. How was she bearing up? Her consideration was an added accusation against Cathy.

As well as could be expected, was his reply. Better than that. Courageously. She was setting an example for them all.

"My parents asked me to tell you how terribly sorry they are for you both," she said.

"Thank them for us both. And say that we deeply regret the unhappiness which your association with our family has brought into theirs. We hope you will be able to put it all behind you as quickly as possible."

"Was it something I did? If I said something to hurt him why did he never tell me so? Give me a chance to explain. Apologize."

"You must not sift your memories for things you might have said or done. There was no way of your knowing that you were dealing with a person incapable of weighing things properly. Don't let your conscience torment you. Put Anthony away in your memory and keep no reminders of him. If you have letters from him, destroy them. Live. When the right man comes into your life, marry him. Have children. Be happy."

"I thought I loved him. I thought he loved me. We were too young for it now, of course, but I really thought we might get married someday. Now it's as if I never really knew him, never knew what was going on in his mind, and I'm left not knowing how I ought to feel."

"You should pity him but that doesn't rule out a good dose of anger, a sense of being unfairly rejected. A person's life is not all his own to be reckless with, not when he has involved others in it. Whatever was troubling him he owed it to you, to all of us, to give us a chance to help, to account for ourselves. But then pity him, because whatever it was he felt it was too much for even us to be of help."

At the end there were promises to keep in touch, expressions of lasting mutual interest in what became of each other. In their longing to feel that the bond between them was durable, not perishable, both were trying, as much as to keep alive the memory of Anthony, to put a stop to time and its inexorable erosions, to deny the transitoriness of all human life, a glimpse into which she too had now been given. On his side he intended to keep none of these promises, for he knew that reminders of him would soon begin to be burdensome to her, and he knew that she would renege on them too after a time. She was young, and while he was not one of those older people who thought the feelings of the young were short-lived because they were shallow, he knew that they were rapidly replaced, that the wonderful recuperative powers of youth and its unquenchable appetite for life and above all its irrepressible self-delight, all the saving instincts his Anthony had somehow lacked, would soon take Alice's thoughts away from this unfortunate experience. In his memories she would always occupy a place all her own as the one girl his poor doomed boy had loved, and as the daughter who had almost been his, the mother of the grandchildren he might have had.

Why? Why did he do it? she asked again for the last time, and then for the first time he felt a moment's irritation with her. She asked it as everybody did, as if there could be no answer. Yet it was not so bizarre, not so unaccountable as that tone of wonderment implied. His son was no one-of-a-kind freak. He was not alone in judging the world unfit to live in. Every day many young people did what he had done and each one found a different reason for it. And still people wondered at them, thought their behavior mysterious. How did that old joke go? If you can keep your head while all about you men are losing theirs—then maybe there's something wrong with you.

But he swallowed his bitterness and to this young person with her life before her said that she was seeking a reason for an act that was unreasonable, an explanation of the inexplicable, and he wished that he himself could believe what he was saying and not that he was seeking an escape from self-interrogation and blame. "We'll never know," he said.

It was what she needed to hear and the sigh with which he said it was what she needed to have it turned off with. By putting it beyond hope of ever being understood one put oneself beyond the obligation to try to understand.

"We'll never know," she echoed him. And Anthony's ghost receded a step deeper into the shadows, faded a shade less substantial.

His last long look at her was his good-bye to all that she
embodied for him: a fulfilled and contented old age—an old
age that seemed to have arrived ahead of schedule and to
have brought him little contentment, no fulfillment.

*

Et in Arcadia ego.

The setting was pastoral, the mood idyllic. Beside the silvery stream they sat like characters out of Walton. And their
dialogue was about death, for even in Arcadia it was there.
Ah, if only there were a spray against people! One that like
the insect repellent promised on the label hours of protection.

"I have a confession to make," Ken Howard was saying.
"My feelings right from the start were mixed. I pitied my
poor father. Of course I did. That was my overriding feeling.
But at the same time I was angry. Hurt and angry. I felt sorry
for myself.

"In those days I believed that parents the age of mine—
they seemed awfully old to me then—had all long since lost
any romantic attachment to each other and lived only for
their children. Their private lives were over. That was foolish, of course, and also very selfish, as only children can be. I
paid the price for thinking it. Believing as I did that my
father lived only for me, I was bound to believe that only I
could have been the cause of his death. What had I done to
disappoint him so? We had been great pals, or so I thought;
now our good times seemed like a sham. He had only pretended to love me. It cast an ugly light on all our lives together. I know now that my father did think of me, up to the
end, and that if his love for me and mine for him was not
enough to go on living for, it wasn't personal, if you know
what I mean. But I was many years coming to understand
that. His doing what he had done made me different and at a
time when every kid longs for one thing above all and that is
to be like the others. I tell you, awful as it is to admit, for a
long time I secretly hated the memory of my poor father.
And of course I suffered tortures for that."

It was not against people that he needed protection. What he needed was a spray for protection against himself, against the stings of remorse. He had had many, and he did not shed the venom. In him it accumulated.

＊

Each morning when he selected clothes for the day from his closet and again each night when he hung them back up he saw on the shelf the carton containing Anthony's ashes. He might have put it somewhere else and spared himself the sight but he felt he ought not to be spared. Meanwhile, the time had not yet come to discuss with Cathy what was to be done with it. She was still not ready for that. She had never asked what disposition he had made of the body. In this he saw not indifference but dread of the subject. She still shrank from any mention of Anthony. Only yesterday he had found the family photographs all gone from the piano lid and from the shelves and the walls of the living room. Not just the ones of Anthony or including him but also those of just the two of them. Reminders of her former life were all painful to Cathy and she was hoping by putting them out of sight to put them out of mind. Bare patches in the dust where they had stood and unfaded squares of wallpaper where they had hung, the ghosts of photographs, were reminders more haunting to him than the photographs themselves.

Indeed, the whole world was already erasing the traces of Anthony Curtis's short, unhappy stay and getting on with its many affairs. It seemed determined to flaunt its goods and attractions to prove his wrongheadedness. Spring came almost impudently early. One balmy day succeeded another and trees budded as though winter had been called off that year. All the more imperative then that he not forget for a moment. Alas for good intentions! Though the spirit be willing, the flesh is fleshy. He felt a stirring in him and recognized it as a renewal of interest in his work. He felt other stirrings as well and was loath to look closer for fear of recognizing them. He noticed things around the house neglected and in need of his attention. He read the newspaper, wondered what was

for supper. In short, time passed and, willy-nilly, did its work
of healing. Seen so often, Anthony's carton became a familiar
sight, ceased to be a continual reminder, sometimes even
went unnoticed as he chose a pair of pants for the day or
undressed for bed. One morning he was appalled to catch
himself humming a tune as he shaved. Was he growing indifferent, callous? Perhaps it was just a part of general deterioration. You couldn't go on forever feeling things as intensely
as you might once have done. The nerve ends numbed, you
turned in upon yourself, your range of vision shortened, you
cared less for causes, more for creature comforts: that was
what it was to last—dying young you died good. He need not
have worried; his too-quick recovery was merely a remission.
He was in for a relapse. Anthony's ghost had not been laid; it
was just biding its time.

A constant preoccupation with Anthony: that was his due
and to endure it patiently his duty. An eternal flame must
burn to that wronged and reproachful memory and he must
be its vestal. To have assumed the awesome responsibility of
bringing a person into the world and then to have contributed in whatever way and to whatever extent to that person's
early rejection of life deserved a life sentence of repentance
and atonement.

But that was reckoning without the old Adam in him. For a
man just going on fifty, in robust health and with better than
normal appetites, to foresee an end after a while to a regime
of self-denial and castigation of the flesh was only human, all
too human. There was no more poignant admission of our
distance from the state of grace than that contained in the
words "Life goes on." One survived calamities that ought to
have killed one out of sheer shame of surviving them. One
ought to have perished of bereavement and grief but one
indecently didn't, one grossly didn't. Broken hearts beat on,
and they longed like none others for company and comfort.
What ought to have been a tribute to human resilience and
recuperativeness became a reproach for our animality, our
insensitivity and our impudence. One not only survived but,
shameless creature that one was, looked again with quicken-

ing interest at the world around him, only recently so desolate. Even over land seared black the little shoots of fresh green grass reappeared in time, grew, and grew rank. Penitential abstinence defeated its aim by arousing a ravenous appetite. Flesh of his flesh had destroyed itself, but his own too too solid flesh shuffled on, and where there was life there was lust.

But if he thought that time enough for this had elapsed then he and his wife were living by different calendars, almost, it would seem, on different planets. She repelled his overtures, timorous and exploratory as they were, as though she were repelling them for all time to come, for all time past, both as though the two of them were now strangers to each other and also as though they were too close akin, as though he had proposed something not only illicit, indecent, but incestuous, though the full realization of this was to be delayed for several minutes, came when he heard the faintest of noises, heard it for the first time ever yet knew instantly what it was and what it signified. Infinitesimal in duration, barely audible the actual sound, yet to him it was explosive, reverberant. He knew what it was the way, in battle, a soldier knows the sound of the shot destined for him, the one he cannot dodge. It was the click of the lock on her bedroom door.

She had put him off before, but then she had said, "Ask for me tomorrow, Romeo."

And he: I've been Shakespeared!

And she (switching to the drawl of her native Ozarks): Tonight, ole hoss, I've got a sore between my two big toes.

And he: The hurt cannot be much.

And she: 'Tis not so deep as a well, but 'tis enough, 'twill serve: ask for me tomorrow.

She was past all that, past childbearing now.

To his own bed he slunk that night like the cat he had just put outdoors.

After this he waited for her to make the next move toward a resumption of their conjugal relations. He waited and waited.

*

> They flee from me, that sometime did me seek
> With naked foot, stalking in my chamber.

Wyatt's bitter lines and Job's lament. *My breath is strange to my wife* ran in his mind like a refrain. And its being strange to her made his breath strange also to him.

His wife had given him a slap in the face and his cheek burned red from the blow. She had fouled him with a far more grievous blow below the belt. But shame a man for something, however innocuous, and he will feel ashamed, and anger soon succumbs to shame.

Although his immediate reaction to Cathy's repulsion of him had been indignant, resentful, and defensive, it left in his mind, already envenomed by doubts and regrets, the toxin of self-contempt to swell and fester long after the sting had worn off. To have his advances repelled in so brusque and final a manner was to make him feel beholden for all those she had ever submitted to. That was how he must think of it now: submitted to. Those had been many and so he had much to feel beholden for. Made to feel dirty, disrespectful of both the living and the dead, crudely ill-timed, both stung and shamed he shriveled into himself and the distance and the silence between them lengthened and deepened. He was afraid to look at her lest his look be misinterpreted—or rather, interpreted rightly.

Rejected by the woman who had been all womankind to him, he felt rejected by the entire sex. Having vowed to forsake all others for her, he had seen himself as a man through that one woman's eyes. He had done so ever since she accepted him; that was what had made a man of him— until then he had been a boy fumbling under skirts; he could not stop when she spurned him. No other woman now lent him her eyes to see himself with anew. Because of Cathy's love he had thought the better of himself; without it he thought the worse. He had not known that his amour propre was so dependent upon her, but so it was, and when she left his bed she took with her his self-respect and his manhood. The possession of them having been the undisguised source of pride that it was, their loss must be just as evident. He had felt that people pointed him out behind his back as the father whose son had killed himself; now he felt that to this they added, and the husband whose wife does not sleep with him. To men his despicable condition must show in his face. Women must scent his rancid musk.

He felt both detached from and yoked to his big unwanted body. Without the partner whom he had shared it with for most of his adult life it was useless, gross, and ugly to him. He neglected it. He stopped shaving, brushing his teeth, washing his face so as not to have to look at himself in the mirror in the morning. Thus he made himself still less attractive—or would have if she had noticed. Whenever he did catch sight of his reflection it seemed to be that of another person bearing a close resemblance to him, and its hangdog look made it seem that to that other person the resemblance was an unwanted one. At such times he felt rather as though he had living in the house with him a twin brother, identical and inimical, one who detested him and detested his likeness to him. Not wanting to see anybody was now joined to not wanting to be seen, and his isolation was complete.

He was learning that the humiliated and despised have nobody to protest their mistreatment to but themselves. Nobody wanted to hear about it, and besides, you would have died of shame to tell anybody. You yourself wanted not to hear about it. Nothing was more shameful than the consciousness of having endured mistreatment. Not to have protested it was to admit having deserved it. Being despised made you despise yourself. Indeed, such a person's sole defense was to reject himself before the other person could do it. One was riven in hostile halves.

The estrangement between his wife and him was aggravated by their physical nearness and the constancy of their association. The freedom from an outside job and the independence to work at home for which he had thanked providence daily these twenty years was now a curse. A little absence might have made hearts grow fonder. As it was, she was always within sight or sound: a longing, a loss, a heartache; while for her, there he was: a reminder, a revulsion, and a self-reproach. Just as when—this after several drinks—he was driven to look into the mirror and there saw double, so did Cathy when she looked at him, only for her the second person was Anthony. He could tell from her irrepressible shudder. She might almost have been seeing the sight he was shown in that undertaker's basement in Princeton. He came almost to believe he was that sight. The resemblance between father and son had been a strong one and with the boy no longer present to make the comparison it had grown all the stronger in memory; he thought so himself. It was as though Anthony were now his shadow. He was glad then that he had never told her how her son had died; her shudder when she looked at him was sufficient without that. His desire and her distaste, his guilt over his desire and hers over her distaste, made for an intolerable situation. The measure of that was that the break, when it came, would be a relief even to him.

Meanwhile his torment of the flesh grew upon him daily. It might be inappropriate, ill-timed, unseemly, but it was not to be denied. He took refuge from shame in the knowledge that this longing was a common way of compensating for the loneliness and grief caused by the death of a loved one, even of a spouse. In that and in the conviction that his longing was not entirely of the flesh. An affirmation of her love was what he longed for, an assurance that with the death of their child that love had not died too. Who but his partner in the union that had produced the boy could share and assuage the grief and the guilt that tormented him?

Yet the once-living proof of his manhood was dead by its own hand. The life he had engendered had wanted no more of that life. Was his manhood threatened or had it been extinguished? For all his longing, he was not at all sure that given the opportunity he could perform as a husband again.

He found himself blushing now like a pubescent boy at any mention of sex—and how often it got mentioned! It was still another reason for avoiding contact with the world. His condition gave him a sense of—surely premature?—agedness, decrepitude, of being finished, burnt out. The callow youth he had been, the old man he was to become: he felt like either or both of those, not like the man in his prime that he was used to feeling. The sexual craving of a dirty old man (was there any other kind?) accompanied by the shame of an adolescent—the shame that every man looks to marriage to relieve him of. Cathy was teaching him by example to loathe himself, particularly that ungovernable appendage of his, or rather, that part of him to which he now felt the rest was an appendage.

How could she not see that their situation was intolerable? That man and woman could not live around the clock under the same roof in married celibacy? Of all sexual perversions that was the most unnatural. It was indecent. It was grotesque. And she had always been so sensitive to his wants. Whenever he desired her she knew it telepathically. She knew it often before he did. Had she no sense of his humiliation now? Could she not feel in wavelengths throbbing on the intervening air his constant longing, his smoldering resentment?

It was not a question of her "duty" to him. He had never thought of it as a duty. He never took her for granted. Twenty years of it had not diminished his wonder and gratitude at having a woman of his own. He never fully believed in his good fortune. Each time she responded to him was a surprise and a joy. "She's going to do it! She is! She really is! She's going to!" he said to himself. The sight of her body made him feel he was about to die of heart congestion and constriction of breath and not care if he did—what better way? Now to taste the ashes was to recall the fire.

*

"*Must* you have *another* drink?"

It was another of their evenings, another of those now routine conversationless evenings heavy with silence, until now.

To what he had already poured he defiantly added a dollop. "Just one more before I have another," he said.

"How many is that now?"

"I haven't been keeping count."

"You mean you've lost count. I haven't. It's four."

"Well, as they say 'way down yonder in New Orleans on their way to the graveyard to bury a man, 'Ashes to ashes and dust to dust; if the women don't get you the liquor must.' In my case, God knows, it won't be the women."

She aimed at him a look of disgust and disdain, rose from her chair, and went upstairs. He watched as Anthony rose from his chair and followed his mother up to that bedroom the door of which was locked to him.

He was seeing slightly double but this he saw clearly, and just as clearly saw himself and was appalled at the depravity of his mind. Yet why should he be? It was a modern-day commonplace that sons lusted after their mothers and resented their fathers' possession of them, subconsciously wished to destroy their rivals, feared castration by them as punishment for their incestuous cravings and to prevent their consummating them. Another commonplace: afraid to destroy their fathers and tormented by guilt for their wish to do so, some destroyed themselves instead, perversely triumphing over their rivals from beyond the grave. "Long before you, many a man has lain with his mother in his dreams," Jocasta tells her son and husband, Oedipus. "Who does not desire his father's death?" cries Ivan Karamazov. Once considered criminal psychopaths, both characters were now accepted as spokespersons of normality. Like books that started out as literature for adults and within a generation were children's classics, these once unmentionable conjectures were nursery school knowledge now. Often it was the child who brought them home from sex education class for the enlightenment of a parent born to a more naïve and inhibited generation.

But did he really think that something like this had been a factor in Anthony's case? Was he jealous of his wife and the ghost of his poor misbegotten son? Never mind what he thought. Whether or not an unnatural love for his mother and an attendant guilt toward his father had been, consciously or unconsciously, a part of Anthony's motive, the fact was that he had come between his parents. He had alienated his mother's affections. It was he whom she now took to bed with her.

While overhead his wife of twenty years slept, he sat long into the night staring into the flames of the fire and then into its embers and then into its ashes, reviewing the feelings that had been accumulating in him. Despite what he had drunk, he was sobered by the realization that he had been weighing his grief against Cathy's and, with his finger on the scale, had tipped the balance in his own favor. She had recovered much sooner than he, therefore it had gone less deep with her. She had not viewed the body; he had. The truth was, though she showed it less, she felt it more. He himself was the measure of that. For her Anthony had become the sole reason for their union and with his untimely death that had ended. The combination of their genes, the home they had made, the example they had set, one or more or all of these had gone wrong, calamitously wrong, and in him she saw embodied their failure; she shrank from his touch, from his very look.

For this he blamed the dead, defenseless boy. He blamed him for the sorrow, the self-accusations, the isolation that had been brought upon him, and now for the estrangement from his wife. He blamed Anthony for inconveniencing him, for disturbing the routine of his life, for interfering with his pleasures, his peace of mind. He begrudged him his unassailability. Only another drink prevented him now from following this out to its inescapable conclusion.

Had his son died of a disease or in an accident or in combat, in a word, blamelessly, then his memory might have been properly interred and grass allowed to grow over it. It might have been visited on appropriate occasions and otherwise left unvisited without any self-reproaches. But Anthony had died by his own hand, through his willful decision, not deterred by any consideration for those who had loved him, and shameful as it was, his father's pity was giving way to a sullen resentment. Anthony had "placed his psychological skeleton in his survivor's closet." In the one book on suicide that he had since looked into he had gotten no further than that preliminary statement. The author of it seemed to have peered inside him like a surgeon probing to verify the presence of an inoperable malignancy.

Meanwhile, diseased though he might be, he was still alive. Life did go on, and he had had a lot of it in him. All his appetites had been big ones, some might say gross ones, and though this blow had suppressed them for a time, it was only for a time. Like Hardy's observation, pertaining to his Tess, that, moralists notwithstanding, fallen women do not usually die of their humiliation, they live through it, and regain their spirits, and again look about them with an interested eye; so might a failed father look again at his child's mother. He might shame himself with the inappropriateness of his passion while their child's ashes still sat on the shelf in his clothescloset, but that did not put down the passion.

To be resentful at being made to feel there was something dirty in his desire for his lawfully wedded wife—surely that was only human? Was it heartless of him to feel that while Anthony had of course been the main thing between them he was not the only thing? His coming had interrupted their romance; now his going had ended it. All she could see now whenever she looked at him was their failure, and shudder with remorse and revulsion. His mind kept returning to that shudder of hers. And she had not seen the sight he had been shown in the undertaker's parlor.

And suddenly there it was before him. Seated in the armchair where nobody had been just the moment before, given an appearance of embarrassment and self-apology by that twisted neck which forced him to look askance at his father, was Anthony. He had come to ask his father what kind of brute he was. Pity, pity was what his son deserved—not resentment, pity; all he could summon would still fall short of enough. Pity and penance, and if a lifetime of married celibacy was his sentence, it was still insufficient atonement. In killing himself Anthony had not acted alone; his father had been an accomplice. Never mind that his mother had, too; be that on her conscience, let his father attend to his, it was burdened with more than it could ever be purged of and he added to the load with his every thought. Anthony came to ask if he really wanted more of what had engendered him. Could he ever again take pleasure in the act? Was he resentful at being denied that?

When he reopened his eyes it was still there and he realized then that this visitation was not altogether unexpected. The sense of something unwanted in the house, as though they had a lodger, one uncertain of his welcome and thus shy of declaring his presence: he had felt that already.

He had felt it first one night just recently. Alone downstairs, he had switched on the television set and found himself viewing a drama about anorexia nervosa, another of the many novel scourges afflicting today's youth, another expression of their widespread wish not to live. When the heroine had starved herself into a state of such emaciation that she looked like an adolescent inmate of an extermination camp she was committed by her desperate parents to an institution. There she was spotted by and taken under the wing of a sister inmate, a veteran of perhaps seventeen, an accomplished hunger artist, one wise to the ways of the grownup world of food junkies and pushers. A vampire who sucked air, a self-destructive narcissist enamored of her own ethereality, she enlisted her all-too-willing pupil into her cult of *la belle dame sans merci pour elle-même*. She was foiled in her design of leading her disciple to her death by dying first herself. Something in the atmosphere of the darkened room that evening had made him feel he was not alone in watching this, had made him wonder were suicides, especially youthful suicides, who in forswearing so much set you to questioning whether they had forsworn anything worthwhile, like that: sirens luring the living to their shoals? Did their unquiet spirits return with the design of enticing those whom they had left behind down the path they themselves had trodden? Loners in life, did they afterwards long for company in their limbo, especially for the company of their kin?

On that night nothing had materialized, but now here it was. Speechless on account of that scarred and twisted neck, that protruding tongue, Anthony conveyed his message by his aspect. He was eloquent, he was sly, he was insinuating. Patient, patronizing, scoring points without uttering a syllable. Dad's drinking oiled *his* tongue while tonguetying Dad, so, unlike his mother, he was uncensorious about the booze. Didn't bother Anthony one little bit how much old Dad drank, despite the fact that his was a generation that disapproved of the favorite drug of their decadent elders. Tolerant of smoking pot, popping pills, sniffing coke, but down on drink. Not Anthony. Go ahead, Dad, have one more before you have another.

Just sitting there he was exhibit A in evidence of a state manifestly preferable to yours. He would leave it to you to say whether yours was so enviable. Suicide: nothing like it, Dad, for getting your way with the women in your life, and let's face it, old man, you've struck out with yours. His own had been Mom and Alice, right? Well, look at them now! Contrite? Remorseful? Devoted? Let them live to a hundred, nothing would ever exorcise him from their minds. They could no longer give him what he wanted, even ask him what it was, so they gave him their all. Climb a mountain, win a trophy, get your name in lights: mere competitions—put yourself beyond competition and they were yours for as long as they lived. You became their unappeasable god. Mom was his, all his. Of course, if Dad were to do it too, why then he would have to move over and make a place for him on the bench. Having another? That was a slow but sure way of putting an end to your pain but if that was your aim was there not something to be said for stealing the march on time? It could be done in a minute. And on that note, good night, Dad, and pleasant dreams.

And so he was left alone to wonder where all this was leading and where it would end. How much longer could man and wife go on living in this cage of a house like specimens in a zoo daily disappointing their attendants' expectations that they might mate? Upon that question the light of false dawn shed no illumination. What it did show him was that for the memory of the dead son with every claim upon his pity and his penitence what he had come to feel was jealousy, suspicion, and hatred. To justify himself he had created for Anthony a ghost that was vengeful and vindictive, one who relished the misery he had inflicted upon his survivors, one whose motive had been just that. How cowardly of him to attribute unnatural, unspeakable desires to the dead boy who could not defend himself, and to take refuge from blame in the type-castings of what he himself called abominable psychology.

*

When a man married for twenty years awoke one morning to find himself alone nothing looked the same to him, not even himself. He had lost the eyes through which he had seen himself. In his own case the change affected his every moment. His and Cathy's had been a very different married life from that of most couples one or both of whom went out to a job by day and who saw each other only in the evenings and on days off from work. For twenty years they had spent their every hour together under this same roof. He wrote in his study within her call. Whenever he was stuck for a word or when he needed to straighten his back or stretch his legs, he strolled around the house or out to the garden, where he found her. It was a life of routine and rituals. They drank their preluncheon sherry, their predinner martinis, ate their every meal together. His first few days alone in it, he wandered around the house like a man lost. He was only half the man he had been and he was looking for the lost half.

Yet when the time came he was half relieved to see her go. The loss of her was fully as painful as losing the boy; but the humiliation, the unnaturalness, the perversion of living celibate under the same roof with his own wife—at least that was ended. He was relieved for another, related yet contradictory, reason, as well: her repulsion of his perhaps poorly timed but certainly licit longings had seemed to make them illicit, the most criminal he had ever felt, as though she were

Anthony's now, or felt herself to be, and his own longings for her were taboo.

Now whenever the phone rang he let it go unanswered. For now that he no longer wanted it to ring, it did. Its sound to him was like the shrilling of some noxious insect reemerging from its period of dormancy. His mourning duties had been paid, he had served out the term of decorous withdrawal from the world, and people felt the time had come to extend a hand and welcome him back to their society. That unfortunate incident could be put behind them all and the misguided not to say misbegotten boy who had chosen not to live could be treated as though he never had and life be resumed where it had been so rudely interrupted. He imagined the party on the other end of the line saying to his wife or she to her husband, "I'm calling the Curtises. We've let time enough go by. Their wounds will have begun to heal and they'll be ready for company now. Life must go on." He let the phone ring until it stopped and the house was steeped in silence once more. If he never saw anybody again it would be too soon.

To Tony, when he called with the news of Christy's death, he himself had said, "I'll come at once."

"No, Ben," Tony had said. "Thank you all the same and, please, don't be hurt, for it isn't personal, but I don't feel like seeing anybody. I want to be alone."

He had been hurt, deeply hurt, at the time. He had never taken anything so personally as Tony's telling him it was not personal. For while he understood Tony's not wanting to see anybody, he was not anybody, he was he, Ben. Experience had taught him better now. It was not Tony on the line when the phone rang now. Tony knew that he was the last person he would want to hear from. Tony knew that when you longed for a certain person whom you would never see again the sight of anybody else, even a dear friend, was painful, almost distasteful. Yet Tony knew only of his loss of just one of his old familiar faces.

On the very morning of his first day alone the long-married man was faced with a domestic problem which underlined his new state and would be a reminder of it three times every day. He who had not eaten a meal alone for twenty years was now to savor the tastelessness of food consumed in solitude and silence. To be sure, his and Cathy's meals of late had hardly been festive affairs. But recalling them now brought to mind the old saying, the man without shoes complained until he met the man without feet.

He joined the ranks of a class he had once been privileged to pity, a class that Cathy had found particularly pathetic. Those men along in years seen shopping alone in supermarkets and looking as lost and helpless there as in a jungle. Men for whom that most familial of occasions, mealtime, had become a mere bodily function and a chore. Men who might have been builders of bridges, bosses of gangs, managers of millions, but who had gone home every night to a waiting supper served them by a wife who knew their tastes and whose first waking thoughts were on planning, buying, and preparing that supper, men as incapable of taking care themselves of their most basic need as a suckling babe.

"How awful to be all alone like that when you are old," Cathy was moved by them to say. "To have nobody to turn to, share your feelings with. Nobody to whom to say such little things as 'Come to the window, don't miss this sunset' or 'Look! A hummingbird.' Worst of all, to get and eat your meals alone. A solitary old age must be even more painful for men than for women. They are so unable to take care of themselves, most of them." He had thought it was feelingly, now he realized it was self-complacently, that he concurred, that he added, "As for me, I'd be hopeless."

That was now being tested and proved. He had been thoroughly spoiled. Cathy had accustomed him to eating very well. The dishes he attempted to make for himself now were overseasoned, either burnt or overdone, and no two of them were ever ready in time to be eaten together. The results were not worth the effort. And how much of his time it took just to keep himself fed, and badly fed at that! He soon came to understand why those old men whom before he had pitied picked items from the supermarket shelves with just one

thing in mind, not how tasty but how easy to prepare. Thus
when they checked out it was with a dreary sameness of diet,
no fresh produce but rather preprepared, heat-and-eat, one-
man meals in boxes. In a word, TV dinners. The TV dinner
represented a whole way of life—if you could call it living.
The very sight of one of them with the deceptively mouth-
watering photo on the lid brought to mind pictures of loneliness, alienation. Food of America's unloved, her widowed,
her divorced, her unwanted, her elderly, her pensioners, her
kitchenless millions in bed-sitting-rooms with one-burner
hotplates, whom rejection, age, the loss of teeth had—merci-
fully—robbed of appetite. Something to be thawed and
chawed without paying any attention to it while watching
television alone, for even if you did pay attention, close attention, there was no telling one dish from another; they all
tasted, if that was the word, like chicken pie without any
chicken, so no wonder one saw old men at the checkout
counter buying stacks of a week's worth of the same frozen
beef stew.

He had become one of those, and it added years to his
sense of agedness. To avoid being seen by anyone of his
acquaintance at this unmanly and humiliating chore he
drove to a town thirty miles from home to do his solitary
shopping. His clumsiness in the kitchen would have been
comical to watch. To see a man near fifty, trying to mop up an
egg dropped on the floor, suddenly seeing in it the wreckage
of his life and, on his knees, with tears in his eyes, begging,
"Cathy, come back to me," would have been amusing to
someone else perhaps but not to the poor fool himself. He
masticated his joyless fodder as mechanically as a cow in its
stanchion munching hay. He passed up meals. Although
mostly owing to what came later, his loss of weight had its
beginnings then.

Cathy's room was open to him again now and one day he
found himself in it.

There had been no settlement of property between them,
no communication of any kind. He was not expecting her to
ask him for a divorce. He hoped he was wrong, hoped she

would, for it might be taken as a sign that, unlike him, she reserved for herself the possibility of remarrying one day. But even though she was past the threat of childbearing, he doubted that she would. Once burned, twice shy, and she had been badly burned. To him she meant married life, always had, still did, always would, and, he feared, he meant the same to her. When he felt up to it, he would find himself another house, in another town, clear out of here and inform the lawyer that he was gone and that she might now return. He suspected that Cathy would sell this house along with the reminders of their life together and find herself another one somewhere else too. Meanwhile, but for what she had packed to take with her, all here was as she had left it.

On her mantelpiece stood the pair of Meissen candlesticks they had bought at a country auction in upstate New York, the seashells they had brought back from the Bahamas, above it the Callot etching she had spotted in an antique shop in Edinburgh and that had been his tenth wedding anniversary present to her.

He was afraid of being overcome by memories and regrets through even so much as a glance at the bed.

By the window that gave onto the garden sat her chaise longue. He had often brought her tea on a tray there in the afternoon and read aloud for her criticism and comment his day's production of pages.

There on her sewing table sat the carved red lacquer box—the traditional wedding present to Chinese brides those were—in which she kept buttons. *Pray you undo this one. Thank you, sir.*

There stood the Jacobean marquetry stand-on-stand—another of their finds—in whose many small drawers she kept her stockings, her scarves, her handkerchiefs, her gloves.

There was an African violet, dead from lack of watering.

On her desk a revolving calendar showed the date on which she had left. He reset it not to the day's date but to that of Anthony's death. It was like the inscription on the burial vault of a family that had perished all together, for this room

in which he had been conceived was now the tomb of the
love that had died on the day Anthony killed himself.

*

The moving van set off for Stone Ridge at quarter past nine
in the morning. A crew of two had sufficed to do the packing,
and it had taken them less than an hour: aside from his personal possessions he was taking with him only his desk and his
bed. Now he had only to leave and Cathy would find a house
from which, except for the articles they had owned jointly,
every last trace of him had been removed.

Those traces had been many, and removing them was a job
that had occupied him for weeks. All day long for days he had
emptied closets and drawers, sorting out his things from hers.
He had toiled endlessly up from the cellar and down from the
attic carrying cartons full of stuff. Twenty years he had lived
in this house, and he was one of those people who never
threw anything away—just the opposite of Anthony, who
took after his mother in this. From a trip to the town dump he
would return with half the load he had carted there, appalled
to see the perfectly serviceable things that Cathy was dis-
carding, and to her exasperation, back in place it all went.
You might not have need of a certain thing right now but you
never knew when you would, or if not you then somebody
else. Old? Yes, but for certain jobs that was what you wanted,
not a new pair. That was not working now but one day he
would see whether he could fix it. He had saved everything,
and he had a lot to save, for he operated on the principle that
if you found something you liked you had better lay in a
lifetime supply because they were going to stop making it.
Not until now had he asked himself what was a lifetime.

He must have supposed he was going to go on living forever. Had he had no sense at all of the passage of time, of the
narrowing of prospects, the waning of enthusiasms, of the
inevitable decline of his strength and the weakening of his
faculties, of the fickleness of fortune and the folly of presum-
ing upon the future? How thoughtless, how selfish of him!
What a rat's nest for other people to have to dispose of when

he was dead and gone! This accumulation of goods, the naïve trust and the blighted hopes it represented, now mocked him, sickened him with the evidence of his fatuity. If only Cathy could see him now! Daily the Salvation Army truck came to haul it all away—the rag-and-bone shop of his heart.

Cathy had been impatient not only with his saving of things, she was impatient with things. Something lying around unused, taking up space, angered her as a lazy person might. She endowed it with a being, with a personality—shiftless, sly, good-for-nothing—and treated it, when she spied and pounced upon it, as though it had been lying low and living off her without earning its keep. Seeing for the first time now that for him this accumulation of things had been a promise, an illusory promise of life always to come, he wondered whether Cathy's hostility to them might not have been because for her they were just the opposite: a memento mori —that this was behind the rage that came over her whenever another spring rolled around to clear them all out, get them out of her sight. He was sentimental about old creels and picnic baskets because he associated them with good times and foolishly expected the good times to last forever; in her contrary way Cathy was sentimental too, resenting such things because they could not go on indefinitely repeating the pleasure they had given her and because being old and worn they made her feel old too. Since changes in women's clothes were so much more radical than those in men's, an old dress of hers with its hem too low or too high or a pair of shoes with tall spike heels angered her because they dated her, far more than an old suit of his with lapels half an inch different in width from those of today did him.

With shoes, clothes, hairbrushes, tennis rackets the division was easy enough, but separating some of his possessions from Cathy's had been like unraveling warp from woof, like separating the yolk from the white of an egg. What, for instance, to do with one document from the carton in the attic labeled Vital Statistics: Anthony's birth certificate? Cut it in two, half for him and half for her, like the disputed child of Solomon's judgment? His decision was to tear it in pieces: nothing for either of them.

Every house was a gamble; this one had been a long shot and on it they had staked their all, for it represented the decision to give up both their jobs, leave the city, and trust in his by no means certain ability to support them by his writing. Not just a house, it was a career as well. Or rather, two careers: his and the one she was giving up for the sake of his.

They had liked this area, which was still totally rural then although it was only an hour by train from the city, but if it had been up to him they would not have bought this house. They would not even have gone inside to inspect it. Having inspected it, they would certainly not have bought it. Crumbling garden walls, rank weeds, untended flowerbeds gave evidence of a once well-to-do family gone to seed. Inside the neglected grounds sat the neglected house. Even to him there was dimly discernible the showplace it once had been, as the pretty girl is discernible beneath the wrinkles and the stoop of old age, but to restore it to its youth seemed as hopeless an undertaking as restoring the old lady to hers. Cathy's was the eye that had seen beneath the hideous wallpaper, the bilious paint, the fussy fretwork with which the Victorian grandchildren of its builders had gussied up the stately old structure, and hers the dauntlessness to tackle all that dilapidation.

Laughable now, the price they had paid for it, the wages of workmen then, but for them it had been a burdensome commitment and for the first several years a steady struggle, a nest of inconveniences. The carpentry, the masonry, the plumbing, all the jobs requiring skill, they had hired done, getting around to them as the money became available, living with things as they were until such time. His first book had put new cabinets in the kitchen, dampers in the fireplaces. The second bath had had to wait for the second book. Meanwhile, years of their own toil had gone into refurbishing the place inside and out. They planted shrubs, seeded a lawn (no three words ever stood for more work), laid out a rose garden and beds for cut-flowers. Five feet tall when they set them out, the hemlocks topped twenty now, the willows fifty. They stripped, scraped, sanded down through as many as a dozen coats of paint, spackled walls, grouted tiles. There was no rest; as soon as one project was completed they undertook the next one awaiting them. The baby had had to wait for the third book. When it was born a room was ready for it. He decorated the room in blue while waiting for the two of them to come home from the hospital.

Meanwhile they were furnishing the house, starting out with nothing, for until then they had lived in a furnished apartment, and God knew, neither of them had inherited anything from anybody. In this task they were lucky in their time and place. In shops in nearby towns and at household auctions could still be found fine antiques at affordable prices, especially of the period they developed a taste for, early Empire, then overlooked not to say despised, for this was before Mrs. Kennedy renewed interest in the style through her televised redecoration of the White House. For ninety dollars a dealer had parted gratefully with a rosewood washstand stenciled in gold with a running Greek key that had belonged to Joseph Bonaparte, deposed king of Spain, during his years of exile in Bordentown, New Jersey. A carved mahogany window seat by McIntyre of Salem, with cornucopia arms and kneed, winged, and clawed feet, had cost thirty-five. Another dealer, in whose shop it had sat gathering dust for a decade, let them name their price for a Launnier pier table. They were proud of their cleverness, their sharpness of eye, their uncommon taste. As part of the pretense of being landed gentry they dressed for dinner— except on those warm summer evenings when she came downstairs dressed in nothing at all and transformed the place into a bordello out of the Belle Époque.

At the auctions and in the shops they were attracted by things other than furniture: oriental rugs, jewellike in their tints and in their intricacy of design but displaced by the fad for wall-to-wall carpeting, cut crystal, also old-fashioned and worthless, and above all by pottery and porcelain. The hiero-glyphic makers' marks on these became another language to them. In one unlikely shop he spotted a pair of Chelsea *putti*. She found a charger monogrammed by Lambertus Cleffius, one of the earliest makers of delftware, in a stack of dime store dinner plates. He found a T'ang bowl at a flea market.

It had been an education and for two people brought up poor, children of the post-depression, and in her case only a generation removed from southern sharecropping, living surrounded by their instant heirlooms had made them feel like the lord and lady of the manor. At the same time it remained always something of a joke. Out of the people in the primitive portraits they brought home they made themselves a family tree—hollow for generations—and gave their ancestors biographies which accounted for not one penny of the once vast family fortune's having come down to them. A youthful disappointment in love was what had so soured the features of Great-aunt Hortensia and caused her to leave her millions from the China ginseng trade to a home for unwanted kittens. Cathy's great-great-grandparents, Jubal and Matilda, shown on the pillared portico of Taradiddle, had sold the silver and the jewels and had mortgaged the old plantation to put everything into Confederate war bonds. Already at the age of four pinheaded Great-granduncle Leonidas gave promise of his fecklessness. Sole heir to Cincinnati Guttapercha, manufacturers of condoms and babybottle nipples, he allowed the holes to get put in the wrong one of the plant's two products and after lawsuits and receivership and a life of vagrancy had ended up dead of anemia when, as ringmaster of a traveling troupe of trained fleas, he was reduced to nothing but himself to pasture his performers on.

Just as his books were built into the house, so the house was written into his books. It and its furnishings had been his storehouse of metaphors. Whenever he felt the need of one to convey his meaning, a stroll outside or a session in the kitchen usually suggested one. To recall all these now would have been like recalling several models of defective cars back to Detroit, but otherwise he had done a thorough job of effacing himself, and the place was Cathy's now, all hers. If their joint possessions were painful reminders to her of him then she was free to do as she liked with them, for he had consigned his share in them, along with the house, to her. The small carton he picked up now in leaving was the one thing he was taking that had belonged to the two of them and it was a thing in which she had shown no interest. It was the carton containing Anthony's ashes. "A light kind of cinders," in Sir Thomas Browne's phrase, his son's remains weighed less than the newborn child had weighed.

With the carton under his arm he pulled the front door shut behind him, locked it, and slipped the key under the doormat. In his letter to the lawyer he had said he would be out of the house by noon. Cathy probably planned to allow some little time beyond that to ensure their not encountering. He was getting away at an hour that would spare them meeting even on the road.

Cathy had left without their ever discussing what was to be done with the ashes. Anthony might have left no mortal remains to be disposed of, so completely had he taken himself out of her life. If she even knew they were in the house all that while she never said so and for fear of having her show any repugnance he never told her they were. Her indifference made him all the more conscious of their presence.

It devolved upon him to choose a burial site. He felt no attachment to his ancestral cemetery plot back in Kansas. Orphaned at ten when both of his parents, along with his little sister, died in a fire, he had hardly known his family. The grandparents who had taken in the orphan boy had been dutiful but were too old to be much more than that. Anthony and those people had never laid eyes on one another. Cathy was disinclined to return to her native Arkansas dead or alive. Blairstown had been home to him for longer than any other place, but he was severing all ties with it now, leaving no forwarding address. He predicted that Cathy would sell the house and everything in it and quit the area too. Anyhow, Anthony had disassociated himself from his family.

What would have been his wishes in the matter? None, probably. Blank indifference. Scatter them to the wind. Disperse them and let it be as though they had never been. But an instinct of his own, so primitive it amounted to superstition, kept him from this course. Free as the wind to wander, Anthony's spirit would roam; laid to rest in some spot where he had been happy, it might lie quiet.

His prep school: he had been happy there—at least he had seemed to be; what he had done made you wonder whether Anthony had ever been what he seemed to be, how long he had been secretly unhappy. But there he had seemed to be happy, and the school had its own cemetery. It was on the edge of the campus, on a hilltop overlooking a river. In it were buried long-tenured faculty members and a few old grads. It was a quiet spot where, in good weather, students came to study, stretched on the ground in the shade of the old oak trees. There Anthony would be spared ever having either of his parents alongside him.

Over the phone the school's headmaster had told him there would be no objection, which was coolness enough to make him think there really was and to say there would be no ceremonies, the space he required was small, and attention would not be drawn to it afterwards as no marker was contemplated. The headmaster repeated that there would be no objection. And so, on this painfully pretty day, with the sun shining so bright it hurt your eyes and with people everywhere eager to get out of doors and enjoy themselves, he drove northeastward to bury in Massachusetts the last relic of his former life before assuming the one awaiting him.

*

Possibly the headmaster had wanted to guarantee him his privacy, spare him the embarrassment of having any of Anthony's former schoolmates or teachers present out of a sense of duty or morbid curiosity; more probably his way of assuring that there would be no objection was to keep the matter to himself. Whatever his motive, that he did, and the outcome was that the funeral, that one-man ceremony in which he himself was the entire cortege, the gravedigger, the preacher, and the congregation, ended in his being apprehended by the campus cop on charges of suspicious behavior. There could not have been a more telling commentary on the furtive, hole-and-corner, outcast and excommunicated character of the proceeding.

Arriving on campus in early afternoon, he used the service entrance, driving past Dormitory Row and the tennis courts, up the hill past the headmaster's house and the library, through Faculty Circle to the cemetery gate. There he left his car and with what must have been unconvincing nonchalance took a stroll along the paths to make certain he had the place to himself.

Uneasy he must indeed have appeared, for no criminal with evidence to rid himself of could have been more anxious to encounter nobody, to do his job and get away unseen, but in searching out a spot in the remotest part of the cemetery, away from the bustle of the campus and as far removed as possible from the nearest occupied plot, he was following what he judged would be Anthony's wishes as well as trying to meet any objections to the nearness of a suicide by the survivors of those interred there. To the faculty wife watching him from her window or to the unseen student whose curiosity he had piqued he might well have looked like somebody searching for a spot to cache his loot or to bury the body of his victim.

Since what he planned to do was of the starkest simplicity he had thought he would be done with it before he had time to feel much. He had not foreseen that in the starkness lay the pity of it and in the brevity the pain. Funerals were for the living, to let them assuage their grief by giving expression to it, take leave of their dead and receive the condolences of relatives and friends, but in this one at which he officiated there were none of these customary consolations. This had been a death desperately desired; to mourn it would be a mockery, to embellish it hypocrisy.

He knelt on the ground and with his pocketknife cut a square of turf. He lifted it out and placed it on a newspaper. The dirt he dug with his knife he piled on another newspaper. He had his reason for wanting to disturb the appearance of things as little as possible, to leave no traces, but his doing

so could only have quickened suspicions already aroused, as
would what must have been his evident agitation as he returned from the car bearing the carton. If he looked guilty,
remorseful, distraught, was it any wonder? Indecisive, too.
For until now his one thought had been to get it over with
quickly; now he felt the contrary urge to slow it down, do
something more, dignify it, not let the boy go so unregretted,
put forever out of sight with this indecent haste, this lack of
ceremony. Until now he had been fortified by the sense that
he was dutifully doing Anthony's bidding. If a part of that
bidding was to deprive his father of the consolations of company, offerings of flowers, music, remembrances by those
who had known his son, then it was his duty to bear that too.
And so he had, until now. It was as he came back along the
path carrying the carton that the sight of his shadow on the
ground struck him with the full force of his loneliness. Perhaps that had been a part of Anthony's intention too. Pitiless
toward himself, Anthony could not be expected to spare
those whom he had left behind. He was overwhelmed by the
bitter appropriateness of this bare, bleak ceremony to that
lonely death. He longed for his wife, the boy's mother, and
her absence mortified him.

He set the carton on the ground beside the hole, rose,
looked around him with feelings of desolation and anguish,
lowered his head, cleared his throat, and said what he felt
Anthony would have chosen for him to say.

Let the day perish wherein I was born.

All the more ironical to think now that he had been impatient for his birthday, could not wait for it, came before he
was due. His father had been in the kitchen that morning
preparing breakfast as usual when his mother came down to
say she thought maybe they ought to go to the hospital. Her
face had been like one of those days described as mostly
sunny, only fleetingly clouded by fear. They were glad to
have their expectancy shortened by her being three weeks
premature.

*Let the day perish wherein I was born, and the night in
which it was said, There is a man child conceived.*

Let that day be darkness; let God not regard it from above, neither let the light shine upon it.

As for that night . . .

As for that night, that enchanted night, it had been one of a thousand and one when, himself a literary King Sharyar, done with his day's storytelling, his Scheherazade spun him her wordless tale of love as if her life depended upon it, that night different only in being one of those on which they had hopefully left off using precautions. That spasm in the groin had begotten this boxful of ashes.

As for that night, let darkness seize upon it; let it not be counted unto the days of the year; let it not come into the number of the months. . . .

Because it shut not up the doors of my mother's womb, nor hid sorrow from mine eyes.

Why died I not from the womb?

Just possibly because his father had been there to prevent it. There had been fresh-fallen snow on the ground that morning and he had bundled Cathy into her old raccoon coat and over slow roads had driven the fifteen miles to town, learning only when he parked and helped her out of the back seat that her labor had commenced. Halfway down the walk she stopped, said, "I'm afraid I'm not going to make it," turned the color of the landscape, gave a gasp and a groan, and sank to the ground. There in the snow, with his bloody hands, he had delivered the child, himself delivered toward the end by hospital personnel summoned to the scene by someone's having spied it from an upstairs window. Always in a hurry, that boy, both in coming into the world and in leaving it.

He had knelt there pinching shut what their cleaning woman (in recounting how an infant of her acquaintance had been strangled by his) called the biblical cord so that blood would not drain from the baby back into the afterbirth, waiting for help. It came at last and he was relieved.

"Nothing much for me to do but tidy up after you," the doctor had told him afterwards.

Had this unexpected role of his in the birth made him bask

with even more pride in his first sight of mother and child together? Of course it had and he was grateful that he had had the good sense, the immodesty, the shamelessness to admit it and enjoy himself. She thanked him, kind sir, and he said, shucks, ma'am, it was no more than any fellow who happened along would do for a lady in distress.

Why did I not give up the ghost when I came out of the belly? For now I should have lain still and been quiet, I should have slept; then had I been at rest with kings and counselors of the earth.

He knelt and lowered the carton into the hole. With those hands of his that had been the first and the last to hold his child he crumbled a clod of dirt on the lid of the carton, saying, "Earth to earth, ashes to ashes, dust to dust." He filled the hole and replaced the square of turf. It had been the work of five minutes.

This season's growth of grass would heal the cuts made in it. Even now it was hard to tell that the ground had been disturbed. Within days it would be impossible. Indeed, he himself, just minutes later, had some trouble finding the spot when ordered to do so by the campus cop, who marched him back from the car and made him dig the box up again.

*

By being cut back to one, martinis had regained their potency. He felt the old anesthesia dull the edges of his mind. Ken Howard capped his flask. Ken had disposed his lunch among the pockets of his vest; now he assembled it and spread it before him. From out of nowhere the picnic wasps appeared. Ken casually waved them away.

He took his lunch from his creel and opened the box to see what Pauline had packed for him. Breakfast at the club was served at fisherman's hours and Pauline came to work early enough to find him there this morning in her kitchen putting together a sandwich for his lunch.

"Ah, there, Mr. Curtis, I will do that for you," she said.

He had to turn from her to hide the tears that sprang to his eyes. That happened to him often now. The least little thing

could cause it. A snatch of old song, words that carried an
import for him of which the speaker was unaware, photographs—to them he was so susceptible he had to keep them
out of sight—small courtesies like Pauline's that touched him
to the quick. Or often for no cause at all, out of nowhere, like
a sudden shower on a sunny day. His new skin was thin, his
self-command shaky. Nerves, his doctor said; he would get a
grip on them in time.

What Pauline had packed for him now brought tears to his
eyes again and he had to turn away to hide them from Ken
Howard. In the box was the kind of lunch he used to consume
before: two hard-boiled eggs, two thick sandwiches, a slab of
cheese, pickles, potato chips, an apple, and a slice of cake. It
was a long time since any woman had tried to tempt his
appetite, feed him back to his old self. He was touched—why
was he also saddened, shamed by such consideration? He felt
it was wasted on him. For he too had insulted life, and having
attempted to sever his bond with humankind he felt himself
undeserving of its care and concern.

PART TWO

So, while he was purposely avoiding paying a visit to the Thayers, somewhere in the ice-jammed waters below him, maybe directly underneath, as he drove over Hudson's Rip Van Winkle Bridge that afternoon en route from Massachusetts to Stone Ridge, lay Tony's body, tossed by the tides to and fro for months already then. Upstream the river was still breaking up, the glittering shards of ice a broken mirror big enough for seven times seven years' bad luck. From that day it was three weeks yet before Pris would write him her two letters, three weeks before the body would surface and be found and laid to rest along with the other Thayers, Christy among them, in the hilltop churchyard looking across the blue water to the chain of blue mountains brooding above it. New troubles would be beginning for him then. Not those brought by the news of Tony's death. Not until some three months later, with another year's herring come and gone from the river by then, would he receive the first of those letters and learn about that. But within just three weeks, in that troll- and elf-land where old Rip before him had gone to get away from the world and a loveless wife and had fallen out of time, a mind once scornful of all spiritualism, one firmly rooted in the realm of the real and the accountable—his own mind—already wavering, would have darkened superstitiously and be convinced that for all he had buried and all he had left behind that day, he had brought with him to this lonely house and this out of the way place a passenger, an uninvited, permanent, and most pernicious guest.

It was a place from which visitors could be seen coming a mile off but with nowhere to hide if you did. The holding of which it was now a part was a dairy farm of four hundred acres spread across a valley. The flat fields surrounding it were sown to hay and the long dirt road leading to it had neither dip nor bend to conceal anything taller than a turtle. The road ended at a creek and there, that evening for the first time, he left his car. The car was not the only evidence of modernity he felt he was leaving behind, for it was as though time itself came to a stop there. For more than a century the big fieldstone shed that stood at the edge of the creek had served to house farm implements, for two centuries before that it had been a gristmill. The waterwheel was long gone but the millrace, the work not of man but of nature, a flume of seamless rock, remained, creating a waterfall with a ceaseless crash. A narrow footbridge of some twenty feet spanned the creek to an island of one solid rock about a quarter of an acre in extent. Scoured by the periodical flooding of the creek and cleared of silt, the island was naked of growth; there was not so much as a blade of grass anywhere on it. Resting on the rock like the Ark on Ararat was what had once been the miller's house, his now on lease for the next three years, surrounded on all sides by the waters of the creek like a moat. A fastness, a keep, was what he had found for himself here.

A house so old it had seen everything, he would be no novelty, it could shelter him, too, might, if walls had tongues as they have ears, even have told of some former tenant out of all the generations that had dwelt within them in a situation more similar than not to his own. Gray though they had been from the beginning, its stones looked grayed with age. The thick slates of its gambrel roof were ragged and flaky at the edges like the worn scales of an old, old fish. Even from outside one knew that its doors, its shutters, its floorboards would creak arthritically. The house was severe, even dour, of countenance, unadorned, ostentatiously unostentatious, the architectural projection of the plain people its builders, the Palatine Huguenots who had settled this valley of the Esopus stretching southwesterly from the old state capital of Kingston down to New Paltz. This was not a house to welcome home a prodigal son. Its doorway one could imagine a fallen daughter once upon a time being ordered never to darken again. Its windows, deeply set in its thick walls, were few and small, as befitted long harsh winters and fireplaces fueled by wood—felled and split with hand tools and hauled by oxcart and sledge—and the threat of Indian attacks. Their little panes, mullioned with lead, were diamond-shaped, and now in the light of late afternoon/early evening those of the facade, permanently tinted purplish by the rays of many a rising sun, glimmered opaquely like the facets of gem-cut steel. Windows not for letting in the world but for keeping it out. To avoid flooding of the ground floor the foundation rose high and the steps of half-round stones, once millstones, leading to the low Dutch door were stacked like pancakes. So worn hollow were the stones by generations of feet they might have furnished half a dozen churches with holy-water fonts, a mischievous thought pleasing to him because it would have been such anathema to the rigid Calvinists who laid them up and because as he climbed them that first evening it seemed to him that he was entering something like a one-man monastery. For he was forgetting that it is in solitude that we are least alone. It would have been humanly impossible to have shut the door before admitting his uninvited guest, for it followed as closely upon his heels as his shadow. However, it would be a while in making known its presence. That night, with Anthony twice buried and with the death of Tony not known to him, he was allowed to go to bed thinking he had left everything behind him and was as isolated on his island as he seemed to be.

*

He knew that in work lay his one hope of salvation, hard, absorbing, daily dawn-to-dusk work, but he knew too that he must now make a complete break with the past. He had brought with him copies of none of his books. The Cathy to whom one of them was dedicated, the Tony another, were no more (the terrible irony of his rightness about Tony he had yet to learn); for that matter, the person who wrote them was no more. Always one to move on, never one to reread his books once the proofs had been corrected, he wanted now never even to see their spines on a shelf again. Another life, one lost, irretrievable, was reflected in their every phrase. He could not return to the half-finished story he had been working on before his troubles; the point of it had been lost. Lost too was the eagerness he had felt then to get started on several other projects. Reexamined in turn, each of them now seemed unpromising, illusory. Yet no new ideas fired him. He forced himself to his desk daily but the writing he did was just that: forced. It was not that it came hard; what was wrong with it was that it came easy, and, as one of his favorite bon mots went, a writer was somebody for whom writing was harder than it was for other people. At day's end, without Cathy to discuss it with, he threw away his production.

The fault was his and he knew it; therefore he blamed the house.

Yet the setting was nothing if not peaceful. The house itself, in its own way, had charm; indeed many if not most people would have found it altogether charming. No amount of puritanical asceticism could quite stifle the native good taste of the age of its builders, nor uglify the virgin materials they had found to work with: chestnut paneling for the walls, wavy-grained, wide pine floorboards, massive oak beams with the mark of the adze on them, all now honeyed with age. The very determination with which they had sought to exclude beauty from their lives had created a style of stark simplicity sure to appeal to a later generation whose aesthetic credo was that form followed function.

But that rich patina had been acquired from the touch of human hands, and "happy the people without a history" went for houses, too. History groaned in every board of this one. The worn treads told of how many had climbed those stairs another night with a heavy heart, had wearily watched another day break through those windowpanes. Over such a long span of years how many had waved for the last time to a loved one as he crossed that footbridge to die alone in some

distant place? Whose they were and exactly why they had
been shed he could not know, but he could be sure that tears
had flowed within these walls enough to fill that brook from
bank to bank. The rafters must have shivered time and time
again to words that could never be unspoken. It was not
depressing just to think of how many had died here, though
that was depressing enough; rather it was to think of how
many had lived here and of what they had had to endure only
to die at last.

And so when he first began to imagine—fantasize—halluci-
nate—a presence in the house he thought he was endowing it
with some composite spirit of the place, one afflicted with all
the accumulated sorrows and disappointments ever felt beneath its roof. And that was bad enough. That was silly, sim-
pleminded, childish enough. It was not like him. At least, it
was not like the him he knew, the one he had always been
before. Now he hardly knew himself, so greatly and in so
many ways, all for the worse, had his life changed. Yet surely
his mind had not so far deteriorated that he was ready now to
believe in ghosts. "Ghosts" was merely a name for the dead
one accumulated in life and carried inside oneself—including one's own dead selves. He did not believe in haunted
houses. Or rather, he believed that all old houses were
haunted, which came to the same thing. You could not live
for long in one without peopling it with its former tenants
and weaving tales around them, and for this isolated and
ancient house one's imagination had full license to make the
tales gothic and gruesome. But he heard no footsteps in the
night nor saw nebulous shapes lurking in the shadowy corners of the rooms. Bats fluttered around the eaves in the
evenings and deathwatch beetles ticked away in the walls,
but there came no midnight tappings on windowpanes.
Above the everlasting rush of the waterfall he heard nothing,
he saw nobody, living or dead. No one came near the place.
The hayfields surrounding his island sanctuary required no
attention from the farmer at this time of year, would require
none until the one week, in July, when they were mowed. He
had dropped out of the world in coming here. His mailbox at

the end of the lane was over half a mile away and he stopped to empty it of the junk addressed to "Boxholder" only when he passed it on his way in from shopping. This he did in nearby Kingston so as to avoid becoming known to the merchants of the village and preserve his anonymity. His occupancy of the house, his very existence, were unsuspected. Why then this irrational sense of there being somebody skulking about the place? Why, sometimes, was the very air of the room he entered still palpitant with the presence of someone who had fled from it on his approach? Why, when he knew it was not so, was the conviction overwhelming that that doorlatch had just been lifted and then softly put back in place? His scalp tingled at times when he felt himself being watched; the mind inside the scalp could only wonder at itself, at its inability to prevail with its unassailable reason.

Maybe the genie was one he let out of the bottle along with the booze, for it was in the evenings, after his third or fourth, that he was most conscious of it. By day a lone castaway on his island, by night his companion was Jack Daniel's, Jim Beam, Old Grand-dad. He drank up such a storm, the island rolled and pitched like a boat—his *bateau ivre*. Mountainous seas of alcohol he bobbed upon, yet while the shoreline of sobriety receded from sight, the snug harbor of obliviousness remained always inaccessible. Then, the house unmanned, the presence stalked at will. Like having a dead rat somewhere inside a wall, it began as a faint suspicion, grew more noticeable, subtly filled the atmosphere until it came to pervade the place, and could not be traced to its source and eradicated.

Presence? Sober again, he knew that what he sensed was no presence, it was an absence. He was alone and all was still, and nothing was so populous as solitude and nothing so full of sounds as silence. The place was not accountable for his imaginings born of liquor and loneliness. "Spirits," the British called hard liquor; those were the spirits he let loose by night. He might have been anywhere in the world. It was not on this barren rock that he was castaway, it was on an island all his own. No need for him to borrow other people's ghosts;

he had his. He had brought them here with him and he would take them wherever he went. He had deluded himself with the notion that in leaving the house in Blairstown he was leaving behind him a life, that in coming unencumbered to this house he was beginning a new one. That was nothing more than the other side of the mistake he had made with the accumulation of things in the attic. A life was neither preserved in keepsakes nor shed along with them. The door here had been opened to him by a Cathy as real as the real one, wherever she might be, and an Anthony more real than he had ever been in the flesh. Conspicuous by their absence: never had a worn and empty phrase seemed to him more fraught with meaning.

*

He had lost, or had mislaid, his eyeglasses. Not just his working pair; this time he had lost his reserve pair, the ones he used whenever his working pair were lost, as well. He had searched every nook and cranny of the house, every inch of the island, and when that failed to turn up either pair he had gone systematically through the whole search again. He had looked under chair cushions and behind car seats, had sorted through the contents of wastebaskets, the laundry hamper, had emptied the pockets of every piece of his clothing, poked beneath radiators, rearranged the litter on his desktop, all this not just once but twice, three times, with mounting distaste for his own dirt and disorderliness.

It was not that he was helpless without his glasses—far from it; without them he was able to do everything he had to do except the one most important thing, namely, work. But that was not all that important now either, for his work was going so badly it hardly mattered whether or not he did it. But his fruitless search soon became an obsession, and the longer he was without his glasses the more deplorable seemed the loss of time from his work.

Nor was this the first time he had ever lost his glasses, even both pairs at once, yet the effect of it upon him now had no precedent. Perhaps this was at least partly because of his consciousness that it was the first time he had neither Cathy nor Anthony to whom to say "I've mislaid my glasses. Be on the lookout for them, will you, please?" But maybe the mood about to pounce upon and overwhelm him had been just waiting for something, anything, the more trivial the better, to provoke it. Whatever the explanation, the depression he was plunged into was out of all proportion to its immediate cause.

The reason for the fervor of his search all too soon became evident. It had been to stave off feeling like such a fool—but an utter fool, a hopeless fool. How could anybody with half a mind lose two pairs of glasses? Lose them here in this uncluttered, this sparsely furnished house, on this postage stamp of bare rock where even a needle could not have gotten lost for long? Having lost them, how could anybody not have found them, at least one pair of them? Somebody who knew full well that without his glasses he could not read a word. Somebody to whom words on pages were his livelihood, his life? Not just one pair: *two!*

Such a fool was not fit to live; to be such a fool and know it was not to want to live. He knew this was wildly excessive, irrational, ridiculous, even comical, but it was how he felt nevertheless and nothing he could do could shake off the feeling.

His glasses were often, if not always, a cause of mild depression. He had not worn them long enough to be thankful for them. His eyes had served him so well until so late in life that he had been spoiled, had taken them for granted—nor had he then realized that it was quite that late in life. It was still only a few years since the day in New York when, trying to make a call from a public phone, he had had to stop a passerby and ask him to find the number in the directory that he himself could suddenly not read. He resented this dependency upon his glasses, and since they were an unwelcome appendage at best, he was angered whenever the sly things, seemingly with a will of their own, hid from him. But only angered, of course, nothing more. Now as he sat on the front steps of the house defeated in his search, the loss of his glasses seemed the final failure in a lifetime of futility. With this he seemed to have reached the end, to have stepped off the edge of the world and fallen through space and when he landed to be at the bottom of the bottomless pit.

It was at that moment, as he searched himself frantically for some defense against the desolation and despair he felt about to overwhelm him, that there entered into his mind the most despairing utterance known to him: *When salt has lost its savor wherewith shall it be salted?* It was that propensity of his for quotations all too apt to his predicament, and which was ultimately to prove so perilous. It struck such terror to his soul that had he not felt so childish he would have recanted with "I didn't mean it. I take it back." Actually he had been at the bottom of the pit for a long time; only now had he looked up and measured the full depth of his fall, only now had he ventured a cry and learned that it could never carry all the way back to the brink.

The incongruity between the present moment and the one immediately preceding it was too great to be grasped. He sought to liken it to something familiar. What he likened it to was not something familiar to him but was something he could all too easily imagine, for, though it always happened to someone else, it was a fear that nagged at us all. What it was like was a visit to your doctor when you had no specific complaint, when probably you would not have gone to him but for the fact that it was time for your regular checkup. However, it was just as well that the time for your checkup had come, for you had been feeling rather out of sorts lately. Nothing serious—just not up to snuff, not your old self. Sleeplessness, loss of appetite, lack of energy, of interest. What you might call a general malaise. What you might better call the blahs. Middle age, my friend, middle age: welcome to the club. For there was nothing really the matter with you; the routine tests all proved it: blood pressure, EKG, prostate, blood, urine. Why then was the doctor so unaccustomedly grave? That was unsettling. Like making an expression in the mirror and the mirror not returning your expression but instead some other, quite different, more sober reflection.

The doctor, who had been your doctor for years and knew you in some ways better than you knew yourself, looked at you now as if he did not know you, or rather, as if he knew you but was seeing you in such a novel aspect that he must find another slot to file you in. It was not at you but into you with X-ray eyes that the doctor was looking. And suddenly you had a sinking premonition, which instantly became a certainty, that you had ceased to be you. What you were about to become the doctor knew as surely as though already you bore upon you the chart that soon would hang from the foot of your hospital bed. You now—not someone else, but you—were in the medical textbooks and your progress marked as though with mileage signs along the route to your unavoidable destination. You had just been sitting in the waiting room with nothing wrong with you, or with only a minor indisposition; now you were told that what you had was fatal, inoperable, and already so far progressed that you had better quickly settle all your worldly affairs. Actually you were no more ill than you had been just moments before; the difference was that now you knew it and knew the name and nature and extent of your illness. The diagnosis in his case was an advanced and irreversible sclerosis of the soul.

He believed in the existence of the soul. He believed it was the most vital of vital parts. It animated and informed the others. Without it they were mere matter. It was the one for which no transplant was possible. To him it was not less but more precious for not being immortal. Rather than believing it was immortal he believed the soul was the most perishable of human parts. Rather than outliving the body, in many, if not most cases, it died before the body did. Such casualties were everywhere to be seen, as apparent as amputees and far commoner in this age of medical miracles and spiritual stagnation: the legions of the listless, the living dead—those for whom salt had lost its savor.

An impulse beyond his power to resist impelled him to go and look in the mirror. It was the first time in weeks. Dorian Gray in his locked room communing with his telltale portrait could not have been more appalled by what he saw. He was a stranger to himself. Lackluster eyes stared indifferently out at him, past him. His features had settled into a fixed impassivity. His skin was colorless and creased. His hair and his beard—still black then—were a tangled and tousled pelt.

He sensed that now to him had come a time that came to one and all. To some sooner, to some later, but in the end to everyone. The feeling itself declared its impartiality. A census taker at the door could not have been more impersonal. But it was to number one among the living, to gather vital statistics, that the census taker came; the one at his door now, from a bureau not of this world, came to count him among another, far more numerous, population. He felt his sense of selfhood slipping from his hold. He felt himself fall out of time as the earth in its turning spun on and left him behind.

*

When the appetites burned out, ashes were left on the tongue. That raised a thirst. It was midafternoon of that day of self-discovery, or rather, of self-loss, when he began drinking. Between him and the bottle it was always a bout, generally a mismatch; by early evening he was down for the mandatory count.

He lay on the couch, half-opened eyes relaying to a half-closed brain the slow suffusion of twilight throughout the room. As colors faded and the forms of things grew indistinct, it seemed that he was merging into that gray impalpability, into a crepuscular netherworld, a limbo in which past and present, being and nothingness, life and death, lost their distinctions and fused in some universal solvent. The sensation was a novel one and, like all novel sensations, both alluring and alarming—a dangerous, possibly fatal languor into which he drifted unresistingly. Trying later to describe it, he would liken it to the time he passed out from sunstroke. There had come to him then and there came to him again now a moment that was not a moment but an unmeasurable interval outside of time, both brief as a breath and long as life, when values were all reversed, when from a positive image with the darks dark and the lights light the world was trans-

formed as though chemically into a photographic negative.
The time he had had the sunstroke he had thought he was
dying. He thought so because this was the opposite of everything he had ever experienced, and was that not death's
definition: the opposite of living—the only way we could
comprehend it? He had not been frightened; on the contrary, it had seemed to be life's last, supreme surprise, a gift
kept to the end and revealed only to those who could never
tell anybody: how painless, how easy it was—a simple reversal of things. Now in his mind, as he would remember and tell
the doctor afterwards in tracing the end back to this beginning, a phrase that seemed both banal and unbearably poignant ran like the refrain of a poem of which one cannot
remember the rest. The phrase was "With the death of love
the love of death begins."

In that state of suspended animation, his gaze strayed over
without at once registering the figure standing beside the
table in the center of the room. More like the shadow of a
man cast upon a wall than like a man it was. Indeed, he could
be seen only by not looking at him but by looking to the side
of him and seeing on the periphery of vision.

That this, come out of hiding at last, was his shy and elusive
houseguest, the fellow who had been hanging around the
place, there could be no doubt. Whether he was real and not
some figment of the imagination, of that there was room for
considerable doubt. But real or imaginary, ghost or flesh-and-
blood prowler, he was a modern one, not a creature in dou-
blet and ruff collar out of the house's past; he was his, come
for him. Even in mere shadowy silhouette there was something instantly familiar about him, disturbingly familiar,
more than familiar: familial; and having experienced it once
already, then too under the influence, he took it to be another visitation from the spirit of his dead son, an impression
reinforced by the inclination of its head to one side as it stood
regarding him.

"You're drunk," he said to himself, and that was certainly
the case; no disputing it; the question was, had he said that to
himself or had his visitor said it to him?

Did he pass out then? Did he ever pass out? Was what
followed a dream or a waking fantasy? Did it matter? Either
way it was the product of his own mind, or rather, of the
mind that had been his but which seemed now to have
slipped his grip. Either way it was enough to give him the
fright of his life. Of his life up till then.

"Hallucination," the psychiatrist would label it. "Maybe
delirium tremens." And that would be irritating—no, it
would be infuriating—for although that was his own explanation, he resented the doctor's classification of it, his professional, pat way of dismissing the experience with a label, a
knowing nod. Of course it was hallucination! That was what
was so terrifying about it, that you could see something as
real as life with one half of your mind while the other half
told you that you were seeing things.

For he thought he saw, or dreamed he saw, in any case he
saw, this stranger, this now definitely sinister stranger—who,
however, seemed thoroughly at home—move closer, stand
looking down at him where he lay. Still in shadow, his features could not quite be made out; nonetheless, he was familiar, and he was not Anthony. He was a lot like Anthony, but
yet different enough not to be mistaken for him. It was somebody he knew, and this was disturbing because, strong as that
sense was, he could not for the life of him place the fellow.
Because he wanted not to? The man must know he was
unwelcome. Welcome guests knocked before entering, were
invited in. After playing hide-and-seek for weeks, this one
had waited until today, taking advantage of his condition, his
defenselessness, to come out into the open.

The man drew nearer, slowly bent down for a closer look,
as though to ascertain whether he was awake, whether there
was life in him. He said, "Don't I know you?" He had the
feeling that he was being tested, taunted, though whether
this was because he really did not know the man and ought to
know him or because he knew him very well, perhaps better
than he cared to, he was unsure. "I know you," he said,
though it was more in hope than in conviction, as a child
might say it to someone masked and trying to frighten him.

Then the face was thrust into his range of vision. But even after the features fell into place he could not identify the fellow—or could not believe what he was seeing. Then, yes, he knew him, all right. There, returning his stare of startled recognition and utter repudiation, was none other than himself.

It was as if the two of them had turned and fled in terror from each other, so suddenly did the apparition vanish and a rush of rational explanations, almost irrational in their rush, come to fill the vacuum left by its departure. Nothing otherworldly about this. It was a memory recurring to a drugged and semiconscious mind of that shocking sight of himself earlier in the mirror. It was a specter out of the mists of his depression. It was the drink. Mainly it was the drink, not just today's but the cumulative effect of all that had preceded today's. Fueled by alcohol, he had been headed toward a crackup. That way lay madness, his mind was now warning him. Then and there he swore off drink. The memory of the experience made keeping his pledge easy. He never even bothered to throw away his last, half-full bottle. In fact, the occasional sight of it was cautionary.

*

So when the same thing happened again a week later, with him thoroughly dried out and cold sober by then, there was no blaming it on the booze. The bottle that had gone untouched since he set it on the shelf had the innocent look of a reformed delinquent falsely suspected. But the apparition had appeared again, as though curiosity had impelled it to come see whether he had the effrontery to have gone on taking up living space.

After that reappearance it became a regular visitor, though making it plain always that the pleasure of his company was not the attraction. Or rather, not regular, for there was no predicting the time of its arrival, most irregular, but frequent. More and more so—too much to be called a visitor. It took up residence. It became his lodger, his boarder—his shadow.

No longer was it just a creature of the night and the twilight hours. It entered his room without knocking and made itself at home while he was trying to work. It sat across the luncheon table from him. It rode beside him in the car. Perhaps it was tonguetied with amazement. However, there was no need for speech. The expression on its face said all it had to say: with nothing to live for, why do you go on living?

This, he told himself, is a textbook case of what is called disintegration of the personality. If an echo could be heard before the sound that had produced it, this was such an instance, for just so would the psychiatrist later say it: disintegration of the personality. Both patient and physician were trusting that, thus identified, labeled a malefactor and a phantom of the mind, the malady would shun the light and seek the shadows, would slink away, go haunt somebody else. But delusions knew no shame. Their impudence was incorrigible.

A woman of his acquaintance once had a nervous breakdown. Even after the worst of it was over and she was again back in circulation one delusion of hers persisted. She was convinced that her teeth had turned black as a result of the tranquilizers she had been dosed with; nothing could disabuse her of this absurd and obviously painful self-deception. The poor soul's struggle with herself to be sensible, not to ask the question that tormented her, was evident, was painful to behold. She could actually be seen biting her unruly tongue. At last, unable to stand it any longer and, sick with self-disgust, personally far more exasperated with herself than her husband and her friends were with her, but in the grip of a drive beyond her power to resist, she would blurt "My teeth. What color are they?" One suppressed a groan and told her. Told a thousand times, she persisted in her folly. It was not just exasperating, it was maddening, the spectacle of a mind so impervious to sense. Delusions: all right, a person sick in her mind could not help herself; they were to be expected. But this one was ridiculous. She had eyes in her head, didn't she—or did she?

So it was with him now. Reaching out to touch, which was

to say *not* to touch and thereby dispel, his phantom, he
touched only air, yet there it was. He might feel his body,
pinch it, look into reflecting surfaces, but what his eyes re-
layed to his mind his mind did not receive, just as that poor
disturbed woman, all the while praying "Dear God, please, I
beg you, let my teeth be white. I know they are. I know it.
Everyone tells me so. Please, God, let them be white to me,"
with fear and trembling had looked and, between herself and
her a veil of illusion intervening, had instead of white teeth
seen black ones grinning hideously, mockingly at her. Looking over his shoulder as he looked at himself was another,
implacably hostile, second self. This the mirror could not see,
but there it was.

What he needed was a change of scene, some company; he
needed to get out of here and be among people. But in his
listlessness he made no move, and the thought of being
among people, at first distasteful, grew more and more
frightening. He feared seeing in their responses to him evidence that he had become peculiar, that he had lost his mind.
He was unsure of even his most ordinary gesture now. Was it
that of a sane man or was there something about it to which
he himself was blind, and which betrayed a state of mental
alienation?

With the death of love the love of death begins.

What would it be like not to be?

One who could ask himself that question had arrived, by
whatever route, at a point where there could be only one
answer.

*

That *au fond* reversal of natural order, of life's values,
when a man took his archenemy, death, for his best friend,
upset everything. Stand on your head and all the world was
turned topsy-turvy. But just as an artist could learn certain
things about his composition in no other way than by placing
his picture upside-down on his easel, this odd angle of view
could be uniquely illuminating. Though to be sure, the places
into which the light was shone were places better left dark.

Thus was answered his old question about the suicide's choice of method, why one person chose to do it one way and another a different way. One did not choose, one was chosen, predestined. For this person a gas oven waited, for that one a razor blade and a warm bath, and of those two each would have said of the other's method "Oh, *I* would *never* do *that!*" Birds of a feather? No, birds of altogether different plumage. What did the means matter when a man might himself his quietus make with a bare bodkin? He might, but only if bodkins were his thing. One had a choice only when one had no choice, like the prisoner in his solitary cell with nothing but his bedsheet to make himself a hangman's rope. Seneca homilizes, "Wherever you look there is an end of evils. You see that yawning precipice? It leads to liberty. You see that flood, that river, that well? Liberty houses within them. You see that stunted, parched, and sorry tree? From each branch liberty hangs. Your neck, your throat, your heart are all so many ways to escape from slavery. . . . Do you inquire the road to freedom? You shall find it in every vein of your body." A fine flourish of Roman rhetoric! Vanity to think one was free to pick and choose. Considerations operative throughout the life about to be willfully ended dictate the mode of death. The lifelong hydrophobiac will not drown himself nor the hater of firearms blow out his brains. Of these enemies of theirs they, who are their own enemies, remain afraid to the end. The swimmer will do it, the hunter will. The woman praised for the beauty of her neckline will not disfigure it in death by hanging herself. Only in that last line of Seneca's speaks the man who when his time came did not jump down a well or hang himself from the limb of a tree or even consider these alternatives but who used the dagger he had saved for the purpose. The means was provided before the intention was discovered, just as before the question "What have I got to live for?" was asked, the answer was ready and waiting. The answer had prompted the question. In his case he had been filling prescriptions for sleeping pills and hoarding them for weeks without questioning why, without letting himself observe what he was doing.

One effect of this reversal of things was shortly to make you feel that you no longer belonged to the human race. Its interests were not your interests, and because they were not yours and because yours were so much more serious and otherworldly, theirs seemed to you mundane, petty, frivolous, and vain. Time came to a stop for all men; the man who had stopped his own clock could look down upon others in condescension and pity.

He learned at least to doubt that suicide was ever truly impulsive, spontaneous, altogether rash. It gestated. In even the seemingly most impulsive cases the tendency toward it had been there, dormant, waiting for something to catalyze it, like that insidious killer, cancer, painless until past cure. Maybe not for long, maybe virulent and headlong almost from its inception, with the shortest of incubation periods, a galloping consumption of the soul, but there already, silently at work. He doubted that even the very young did it the first time they ever considered it.

Suicide was an addiction. It resembled alcoholism. In a mood of desperation one turned to the bottle. The contemplation of a painful but speedy and certain way to put an end to one's pain was like one's first drink of raw whiskey: one shuddered, gagged on it, nearly threw it up, but choked it down and it brought relief, anesthesia. Next time two drinks were needed to produce the desired effect. The habit grew, fed upon itself. Soon one was drinking in secret and on the sly and at unapproved hours of the day for drinking. Then came the time when, suddenly, it was you who were doing this to yourself. Not "one"—*you*. And realizing that the cure was killing you, you swore off, and the mere thought of that was enough to send you to the bottle ravening for a drink—a last drink—the first of many last drinks. So with the contemplation of suicide: you ended by becoming dependent upon it as your only way of keeping alive. You hugged it to you, afraid that it might be taken away, as the drunkard hugged his bottle, fearful that someone concerned for his health might take it from him.

Another thing he learned by standing on his head—

learned it in advance of the lesson itself: the actual doing of the deed was made easier, was made possible by a reversal in which time was made to run backwards. The effects of things were their causes. He would have been dead for some time already when he got around to killing himself. That would be an anticlimax, almost incidental. To die then would be, if only for an instant, to live, to experience sensation after the long coma of emotional insentience.

Concentrate exclusively upon any one thing and the light shed upon that thing cast everything outside its circle in shadow. Now in the courtroom of his mind the advocate for death held center stage. He became a monologuist, a filibusterer, refusing to yield the floor. The objections by the voices that might have spoken in defense of life were drowned out. Discouraged from trying, they gave up.

The voice of reason and restraint is always muted and moderated, level. Should reason become passionate and loud in its defense it ceases to be reason. Yet of all things reason is the most impatient. It can tolerate no disagreement. It finds it opponent's claims too absurd to argue with and quits the field in disgust. One quiet and soon discouraged voice beset by the raucous mob which populates the mind of man: no wonder it is not much to be depended upon in times of most need.

One could generalize about suicide as one could about any human activity, so far and no further; each case was the work of an individual and thus unique; but now he was finding answers to at least some of the questions he had asked when he was trying to explain Anthony. (And many times he could see that death's head, so close in favor to his own, nod approvingly as he gained some new insight, as much as to say "Now you know. It was the only way you would ever understand: by following the path I cleared for you. To learn more, carry on. To learn all, go the distance.") He had supposed that at some point Anthony's personality had split in two, like those unicellular organisms that multiply that way, and that the halves had then turned against each other in a fight to the death. Now he disbelieved that, for such was not the case

with him. Instead of into two, he divided into at least three
distinct parts: the two between whom the deadly contest was
waged and a third who was their audience, a fascinated,
terrified, and helpless audience of one such as he had been
when as a small child at the Saturday movie matinee he had
cried out to the unsuspecting hero on the screen to beware of
the villain's designs upon him.

For in his drift toward danger he had not lost his fear, his
instinct for survival; on the contrary, it had never been
sharper. One part of him lived in constant, unremitting fear.
But it was as though the other part were hypnotized. He
could not get through to himself, break the spell, any more
than he had been able as a child to make the actor on the
screen hear and heed his warnings.

Also, he was drawn on partway out of curiosity. Personal
and professional curiosity. He was beginning to gain some
insight into a thing which had long intrigued him and which
before he could only try to imagine: the workings of the
criminal mind. It was disturbingly close to the workings of
the fiction writer's mind, the kind he had always had: the
shedding of his own personality and the projection of himself
into an imagined character, the excitement of doing vicariously things one would never have done oneself, and he
wondered whether his métier had prepared him for, even
predisposed him toward this—and whether he had unknow-
ingly manipulated the child of his flesh as he had done those
who were the children of his imagination.

To another of his old questions the answer was yes, suicide
gave depth to a person—or the illusion of depth. To split
oneself into identical halves was to gain the third dimension
of stereo. To say to an unsuspecting world, I have potentials
in me that you people do not dream of. Would-be killer and
victim in one, he was twice the intellect he had ever been
before. His destination determined and his course fixed, he
was free to observe and study himself. This he did with the
fascination and surprised enlightenment with which he followed his fictional characters whenever—as always occurred
with the successful, the convincing ones—they themselves

took over their destinies from his direction and went their own self-willed ways. This was fiction brought to life, with himself as all the cast. He had lost interest in himself; now his interest was renewed. He had thought he knew himself; he was more complicated than he knew. His death gave him something to live for. He had never plotted a story as successfully as this one. Each day was a chapter. What would he do next? To be continued.

For as long as it lasted, this self-sustaining illusion that he was directing it gave to it a sense of make-believe and thus the comforting sense that his fear was synthetic, self-induced. Up to the end he would never quite fully believe that he was really going *all the way*. The preparations, yes; urged on by his helpful houseguest, up to the uttermost one, but then . . . Then something would intervene. The telephone, so long silent, would ring, a salesman would knock or some self-appointed door-to-door peddler of salvation, and the illusion would be shattered. The urgings of some cultist to mind his eternal soul would teach him how final a fate he had been flirting with. An airliner would pass overhead and he would look up and wonder where it was bound and that would remind him of places he had been to and make him sense once again how wide the world was, then wonder at himself, how he could have fallen so deeply into this deadly charade. Then to return to life would have the tonic shock of coming out of a matinee into the light of a day still to be fulfilled.

This lesson he would learn only after it was all over, but one self-protective mechanism was at work for him all the while —or was it not rather the most self-destructive, the most self-deceptive of all? In the case of suicide the consequence trammeled up the deed. Obscured, lost in the soft seductive promise of the end was the hard means required to attain that end. Never in all that semisomnambulant time did the unpleasant business toward which this was tending present itself to his mind's eye in all its grimness. Not one shred of pity or even of fellow feeling was he moved to by his occasional glimpses of his victim, his dead body, destroyed by his own hand. It was all preparation, a chase without an end in

view, only a view of the sweet oblivion the other side of the
end. So carefully planned, so long expected, the end would
come as a surprise, almost an impertinence. Some unpleasant
duty awaits my doing and only I can do it, a nasty chore to be
gotten through and out of the way: of this he felt a dull,
insistent but distant sense; however, the details of it were
kept always out of mind.

Meanwhile the self-hatred required to do the deed was
administered in small but ever-increasing doses like the ho-
meopathic inoculations of the venom of some insect to which
one was allergic in order to build up immunity. Death would
be robbed of its sting. Now whenever his lifeless body did
intrude upon his thoughts it inspired him with no feeling
other than distaste. Its piteousness did not plead its cause but
further condemned it. It could be thought of only as a thing.
The owner of it himself had judged it worthless, a burden
upon him and upon the world. Imperfect as the knowledge
was, who better than the man himself knew a man's worth?
How could anyone else feel for that inert and already de-
caying object anything but contempt and revulsion? Sweep it
out of sight, put it out of memory.

But it would never come to that. And afterwards he would
never speak of it to a soul. For it would have been all make-
believe, playacting, bluff, of a certain immaturity, a childishness then if you will, of which, even at the time he was most
deeply engrossed in it, he was perfectly well aware, and even
acutely aware. And he was painfully embarrassed by it. To be
quite truthful, in its antisociability, its secrecy and furtive-
ness, it had all the attributes of adolescent self-abuse. Blame
it on bad company; he had been enticed into it by that uninvited lodger of his. Meanwhile, however, his very embarrassment was, perversely enough, an incitement to carrying on
with it. It was mischievous, naughty, a prank played by two
bad boys on the world. He was curious to see what came next.
That was an encouraging sign, a healthy sign. As long as you
were curious you were safe. It was when you stopped caring
about what came next that you were in real danger.

And he could not have kept from taking the next step,

foolish though he knew it to be, if he had tried. For it was not he doing it. Or rather, it was he and it was not he. It was some two-dimensional character projected upon a screen. Gone now was the rich sense of roundedness he had felt for a time. Now he could only watch. So sometimes did a crowd of people surrounding him like an audience in a darkened movie theater, watching him do such things. Such things as? Such as sorting and labeling things in parcels as though—As though what? As though to be found afterwards. He would be anxious, desperate to disassociate himself from that unreal character, to convince the crowd that what they were watching was him playing a role he had been cast in. Once the show was over and the lights went up he would step down from the screen and join them for a drink, a swim—whatever everybody was doing. And yet a feeling of ethereality, of otherworldliness, as though he were nothing more substantial than transparent celluloid, told him that he had ceased somehow to be like other people.

Meanwhile, knowing how the story came out did not lessen the suspense, the tension; still to be discovered was the timing. How would he know when his time had come? Anthony, availing himself of the temporary absence of his roommate Jeremy that his method required, had had it settled for him. How many times during those days had he rehearsed it: put the noose around his neck and tightened it and stood on his chair? The end of that absence nearing and Jeremy's return imminent, a voice had said to him "Now!" and he had kicked the chair from under him.

Perhaps his time would come when the playacting, the sham of it all, his shame for his procrastination, simply overwhelmed him with embarrassment and he would not be able to face another day of it. He would not need courage. The staginess of it all would sicken him and that would steel him to do the deed, and do it right.

He was learning much. Was that a part of the fascination of it? Much that otherwise he would never have known, could have learned in no other way. Maybe such knowledge was granted only to those who were not to be allowed to take it

back with them from beyond. Others must learn it for themselves, as he had. Forbidden knowledge, revealed only to the
daring, the unconventional, the dauntless, the self-explor-
atory few. One lesson was this: when a man became his own
sworn mortal enemy a kind of inverted narcissism set in. By
the world's standards worthless, untouchable, he became to
himself a prize. When never before had he—that was to say,
his continuation, his future—been of so little consequence to
him, a matter of utter indifference, he found himself studying himself with as much respect as a pathologist nurturing in
his laboratory a microbe he hopes to wipe out, as a hunter
stalks his prey, a fisherman plots his strategy against a trophy
fish. Priest and sacrificial victim in one, like those of the
ancient Aztecs: the knife would be driven home and the
throbbing heart cut out whole, but in the meantime the
doomed one was the chosen one and was a living god.

Not that it would ever come to that. Not that he was going
through with it. Not really. Once he had gone to that penulti-
mate step and shown that he *meant business* then death
would lose its allure, for that was based on fear and ignorance
and he would have dispelled the mystery and proved his
fearlessness. He could despise death then. It would be to gain
a species of immortality, for no man could die twice. Only
maybe by then he would have grown so weary of the game it
would seem the only way to regain reality. Maybe when that
point was reached, that absolutely last moment, and you
were alone with the death you had courted as with your new
bride, then it would lose its terror and between you and it the
barrier would drop and there would be nothing to prevent
you from stepping over the borderline to consummation.
How to express the terror you were sure to feel on discovering that you had lost your capacity for terror?

As with the man resorting regularly to the bottle, who
believes he can always quit and who discovers one day that
he cannot, so with him: at some point the game ceased to be a
game. Daily his fear of himself mounted. His took his alert-
ness for inescapable vigilance. He despaired of outwitting an
enemy so clever and so determined, one bent on his annihila-

tion, who knew him so intimately and who foresaw and forestalled his every twist and dodge. When a man's mind was luring him to destruction it became devilishly ingenious.

Blinders had been put on him: he could see nothing to the side of the straight and narrow path he was on. Should he pause for a moment in his progress and try to get his bearings, he was prodded on by the watchful presence always at his back. It came to seem that he would be putting an end not to himself but to it, and that that would be the only way to do so.

One consideration deterred him: Tony. He hesitated to hurt him, but more than that, the thought had passed through his mind before, apropos of Christy and Anthony, that to someone close to the event, a suicide might set an example, point the way, and he feared setting an example to his friend suffering from the same loss as himself.

Then he made his last discovery, the one that triggered the timing. He found that he cared less about that than he should have. He found how selfish the would-be suicide was. Or if "selfish" was not quite the word for someone planning to destroy himself, then how incapable of consideration he was of those of whom he should have been considerate. His absorption in his own misery did not entirely numb him to the misery he was about to inflict upon them, but their voices fell on muffled ears. And in his case they hardly amounted to a chorus.

It was then that he heard Anthony say to him, "I'm waiting, Dad."

*

Daunted by the prospect of the traffic on the State Thruway, he drove across the river thinking to take a less heavily traveled route. He was in flight.

The pills, some three dozen of them, along with the water to wash them down with, were waiting. He took one last, leavetaking look at the world. And that was his mistake. Given one more chance, life fought for itself. Never as in that instant had his vision been so sharp, his hearing so keen, the

surge of his pulse so powerful. After weeks, months of sub-
tlety of mind, the most involuntary, the most unintellectual
of human urgings asserted its hunger. He could have wept,
he could have laughed over this defeat of his will by an
impulse so elemental. What he did was a bit of both as his
body propelled him out of the house and across the footbridge to the old shed that housed his car.

He drove to Poughkeepsie so fast he was in danger of doing
on the road the very thing he was fleeing from home to
escape doing, and he was a menace to others as well. A
change in his plans was called for. So in Poughkeepsie he
stored his car and from there took a train to the city.

From Grand Central Station he went directly to the
Princeton Club, and then directly back to the station. For at
the club, on signing in, he was handed by the desk clerk the
first of Pris's two letters.

To the clerk he said as he put the letter and the envelope in
his pocket, "It seems I won't be staying after all."

He had time to kill before the next train back to Poughkeepsie, so in Grand Central, onto the roof of which Christy
had leaped those forty-seven stories to her death, he went
out of old habit to the Oyster Bar, source of the scallops he
always used to bring for the first evening of those cruises
aboard *Pandora*.

"Are you alone, sir?" asked the headwaiter.

He absently replied yes. Then, "Yes. I am alone." And, now
a man the door to whose future had been flung open on a
vista as flat and featureless as an arctic waste, he turned and
walked away.

It must have reverberated in his mind a dozen times, like a
clock bell tolling the hour of midnight, that worst of words:
alone. Throughout the wait for his train, in the midst of the
crowd, it tolled on. Throughout the ride upriver, throughout
his conversation about the baseball season with the driver of
the taxi he had decided to take home—tearing up and tossing
out the window the claim check for his car as they crossed the
Hudson—after he had paid his fare and tipped the man with
the liberality of someone with no further need of money and

heard him drive off, as he crossed the footbridge, mounted
the steps, it tolled on. By then it had become a knell. It had
attached itself as an echo to these lines supplied him by his
fatal fund of verse:

> When true hearts lie withered
> And fond ones are flown,
> Oh, who would inhabit
> This bleak world alone?

PART THREE

Life too was a club in which your membership was kept active even when your dues had gone unpaid. From this most unexclusive of clubs you were not permitted to resign. Once a member, you were kept on the roll for as long as a breath was left you.

Should you try to opt out, you were never afterwards a popular member; you were ostracized as an ingrate and shunned as a renegade, a traitor to the side. It began at once. A team of army doctors working to save the life of an enemy soldier must do so with the same detachment, the same professional disinterest as those working to save the life of a would-be suicide. What they were working to save was not the person but the principle. The principle was the one to which they had sworn their Hippocratic oath, the sanctity of all human life, even an unwanted one. And just as the enemy soldier saved from death was not repatriated but was kept a prisoner for the duration, so with the thwarted suicide: it was restricted life to which he was restored, it was those comrades of his for whom hostilities had ceased, the army of the dead, whom he was not permitted to rejoin.

Once he had been critical of Cathy for supposing that Anthony had taken an easy out by swallowing an overdose of sleeping pills. Now he was to learn how uneasy an out that was when you tried it and barely failed and how grievous the aftereffects could be. You did not just wake up from a longer and deeper than usual sleep.

He had very nearly succeeded in his intention. He had snuffed out the flame of life, only the pilot light burned on, a pinpoint of vitality that flickered like a match in the vastness of a cavern. He could see nothing, hear nothing, could not

move a muscle. Was he in a coffin, in his grave, mistakenly
thought to be dead? In a straitjacket to restrain him from
further violence to himself? He would be told later of times
when he had shown no outward sign of life, no pulse, no
discernible respiration, no reaction to the prick of a pin. He
did not know where he was or at first who he was. His mind
was a blank. It held no memories, received no stimuli. It
might have been a disembodied organ kept alive in a culture.
In this comatose condition he was like the victims of certain
venomous spiders, paralyzed, wound in webs, preserved
from spoiling by the barest circulation of their own blood
until such time as they were wanted to provide a meal.

Sounds reached him, human voices, words in a language he
had once known, reminding him of living, of the pain of
living. He tried to speak, to say, "Please, let me die. I want to
die. Please, leave me and I will be able to die." Even after his
sight had returned his tongue remained partially paralyzed
and his speech slurred like that of a person who has suffered a
stroke, but at some point he must have managed to make
himself understood because he was told no, he was not blind.
His eyelids were paralyzed—temporarily—but he was not
blind. Later he would learn that no one knew for sure that it
was only temporary or that he was not blind as well. He could
have been. He could have been totally, permanently paralyzed. He could have suffered incapacitating brain damage.

Out of the milky mists a world slowly took shape in which
everybody was twins. A world in which people, ghosts of
people, all in white, all silent in their rubber-soled shoes,
were all in the endless process of doubling as though through
binary fission. He gestated. The room, white, unrelieved by
color, uterine, was his womb, the oxygen tent his placenta,
the tube attached to his arm his umbilical cord. Most of the
time he slept. Later he pretended to sleep so as to avoid
contact with the nurses and the doctors. As these gained in
substantiality they saddened him all the more. He longed to
die. He dreaded having to make the excuses and the apolo-
gies, to tell the lies, that would be expected of him for having
tried to do so.

Even when, as in staring at the halves of a stereo picture until finally the two images merge and become one, people ceased to be twins and became single individuals, the expressions on their faces remained split by their mixed feelings toward him. He was not your ordinary patient recovering from near death through accident or disease. They were wary of him as though he might be contagious, yet they were intrigued by a specimen different enough to reject the gift of life and anticipate the universal dread, the very thing it was their profession to postpone.

The humiliation of being dependent upon others, in his case upon strangers, was compounded by a sense of his unworthiness of their care and his ingratitude for it, his indifference to the life they were working to restore to him. He was expected to feel contrite and lucky to have escaped the consequences of his rashness and folly, to have learned his lesson and be thankful to these good people for having saved him from himself. He was supposed to feel like a chastised and chastened child spared by mere chance and by the mindfulness of his elders from the consequences of some childish not to say mischievous act of his. What he felt was that he had been thwarted in his purpose by busybodies, do-gooders who had invaded his privacy and interfered with his careful and terrible plans. He wanted not to know the name of whoever had found him. These people were not trying to save him out of any love for him. He was nothing to them. Less than nothing. No, he was something to them: he was a fool and a troublemaker. They had enough calls upon their time and talents from people really sick, really hurt, eager to be helped and cooperative, appreciative of the concern being shown for them—in a word, sensible people. He sensed beneath their noncommittal exteriors a hostility toward him for his disloyalty to the race of which they were the guardians. They had sworn to preserve human life; he called into question the reason for their professional dedication. How much trouble he had gone to, how much pain he had endured, and it was all for nothing! And for this he was expected to be

grateful. Yet such was the force of human tradition and training that he felt ashamed of his ingratitude.

Oh! Dreadful is the check, intense the agony,
When the ear begins to hear, and the eye begins to see;
When the pulse begins to throb, the brain to think again.

The parts of his body reassembled bit by bit like an army
put to rout, with scattered detachments straggling in and
reporting day by day. They brought details of their defeat, of
their losses. His perceptions remained dulled and distorted.
Long after he had stopped seeing double the outlines of
objects remained indistinct, blurred, colors muddied, distances deceptive. His body felt as though it had cracked apart
like the pieces of a jarred jigsaw puzzle, or like the splinters
of a broken mirror.

Just as his eyes would not focus properly nor his limbs
coordinate, so his feelings fluctuated wildly out of his control.
To the hospital staff he was a vandal who had damaged a
work of art by the greatest of masters, and with the patience
of a team of restorers they had pieced him together again.
But he could see into himself as through a fluoroscope and
knew his every crack. Fits of unprovoked rage shook him,
tears of self-pity flooded him. Angry self-justification changed
in a twinkling to self-loathing. To be sorry to be saved from
death was too confused a feeling to cope with.

Even while he lay prostrate and helpless in bed there was
one thing he knew. He would never be the same again. What
he would be he did not know, just how he would differ from
before, but he would never be the same again. He had tres-
passed a forbidden boundary and had returned a man transformed. They might restore him to life but he would be a
person who, while he had failed in his attempt to kill himself,
had succeeded in killing a vital part of himself, that which
was his key link with his kind. As murderers did, so did
unsuccessful self-murderers: he had cut himself off. He was
cut off even from others like himself, survivors of suicide
attempts, from them perhaps most of all, for if they were
shunned and feared by everybody else they were feared and

shunned the most by their own sort. They knew as did nobody else the burden of incommunicable experience and the guilt for having transgressed the primal taboo. The faces of his fellow patients with hopes for themselves and dread of death, their relatives coming to visit them, concerned for their well-being, cheered by their recovery—he was no part of that world.

As for him, his first and only visitor, when he was able to receive them, was Anthony. He found him seated in the armchair beside his bed waiting for him to awaken. It was the first and would be his last visit and he stayed just long enough to say by the contemptuous expression on his ravaged face, "Well, Dad, you botched it."

There was something contemptible about a man who tried to kill himself and failed. Some incommensurable gap between so grim an intention and such ineptitude of execution. What could be easier? What *could* a man do who couldn't do that? What was more comical than would-be tragedy? Anthony had meant business. The method he had chosen, or that had chosen him, left no chance for failure. As for himself, he must never from the start have had the nerve to do the job efficiently. He must have meant not to succeed. He was an impostor, a faker.

He felt he had earned all mankind's mistrust. Never again would he be accepted as a reliable member of the race. Despite his efforts to conceal it, the doctor suspected that as soon as he was able he would make another attempt upon his life. Would he? Once, before trying it, he would have said no. At a later time, just before trying it, he would have said yes, and if at first you don't succeed, try, try again. Having tried it and failed taught you that you never knew what you might do. He could rely upon himself now no more than others could rely upon him.

However, he doubted that he would. He doubted that he would ever again have the strength, the determination, that he could work up a deep desire even for death. He feared failing a second time and making even more of a fool of himself. It was the sense of failure of a man who had botched a job that, if anything, would make him shy of another attempt. That: not relief, not thankfulness for his reprieve, his second chance. Yet even of this he was not sure. Even to him the appetite for life might yet return. That it might was, in fact, his greatest dread. That his fragile frame might be shaken at eve with throbbings of noontide.

For now, he lacked the strength of will to fight the return of his bodily strength, to resist the ministrations of his keepers. "Swallow this," they told him. "Make a fist. Repeat after me." And he did as he was told as docilely as a child. Compliance was easier than defiance. He watched the life-giving fluid flow drop by drop from the bottle, down the tube, and into his veins with a passivity born of weakness and indifference.

If he had marveled before at man's ascendancy considering that of all creatures he was born the most helpless and dependent, so slow to mature and with so much to master, he understood nature's provision now. If an infant could know beforehand all that it faced it would say with its first words, "That's not humanly possible." It was only after it had invested too much labor, had fallen and hurt itself too many times, that to the already bruised and weary and disheartened being was shown the long road it had to travel and the burden it must bear. In learning again to talk and to walk his added burden was the knowledge that he had inflicted this upon himself.

When he first saw his reflection—and he was deliberately kept from this for a long time—he thought again that he had actually succeeded in his intention. It was a startling experience to look into a mirror and see someone other than yourself. But the hand that reached out to touch the glass for verification, though it trembled out of his control, was his hand, and by staring long enough he could detect a resemblance between himself and the pale, puffy-eyed, white-haired old man he saw reflected. It was the resemblance between himself and his ghost.

It was not too much to say that he had succeeded in his intention. Between his after and his before an unbridgeable gulf had yawned. They told him he had been unconscious for four days and that during that time his hair had turned from black to white as though by a killing frost; to him it seemed like the twenty-year sleep of Rip Van Winkle with the difference that it was he, not the world, that had changed out of all recognition during his absence. "Mr. Curtis," the nurses called him, every twin pair of them; it was the name on the chart at the foot of his bed and he answered to it. The name was his one connection with a life that had ended as surely as if he had accomplished his aim and destroyed himself.

Or so he thought, and so he later wished, when his memories, like those seeds preserved with the mummified pharaohs in their tombs, even after thousands of years, germinated and bore fruit. Bitter fruit it was, and the bitterest were those that had been the sweetest. Amnesia was what he had sought; total recall was what he had attained. How contrary memory was! How it teased and tantalized and eluded us when we tried to summon it, how it mocked us by coming unbidden, unwanted! The life he had lost was preserved under glass, every evidence of it; no archaeologist could have been more meticulous in his excavations, and he was a prisoner inside the museum.

*

He awoke now from his nap, alarmed to find that he had slept and even more alarmed at the thought that he had been awakened by an insect bite. If so, he must act quickly but not too quickly. He must not panic. He must not confuse the two kinds of pills, one of which he was to swallow six and of the other to let one melt under his tongue. He lay very still, attentive to every cell of his body. He lay until all danger was past and he could be sure he was safe. Then with a sigh of relief he sat up and armored himself afresh with repellent. As he waited with his eyes shut for the time when he might open them again he considered this example of inconsistency: a man once unafraid to swallow three dozen sleeping pills, now in terror of the sting of a honeybee. To reassure him that he was only human there came to his aid a line from an old song: I'm tired of livin' an' feared of dyin'. It was a rueful amusement but the irony of that old contradiction amused him. Meanwhile, as the song went on to say and as he could hear for himself, ol' man river, he just keeps rollin' along.

Left napping on the riverbank by his companion at lunch, he had slept for several hours. The shade of his tree had shifted and he shifted with it and sat there thinking further. No longer fearful that he had been caught off guard during it, he was able to appreciate the refreshment his nap had brought him. Into his rested mind now came a new, a novel conception of himself. An odd conception it was, and even odder was the fact that it should be not only not troubling but rather soothing. It struck him that his life was like a child contested in a divorce. Both his old contending selves had been judged unfit and the court had awarded custody to a guardian with responsibility for the infant's welfare. He was now that guardian. Not even in the days when his hostile halves were warring had he felt more detached from himself, but now there was no sense of friction, rather there was the sense that decisions were out of his hands. Things were as they were and what would be would be and the end would come when it came. He would just keep rolling along—no rest till the Judgment Day.

The attraction of death was diminished by the thought of how very little we could ever gain on it. By shortening your years yourself how few at most you were able to subtract, how few add to the many you would be dead. Man that is born of woman has a long time to be dead. There was no such thing as a long life. There was such a thing as too long a life— eighteen years could be a weary lot; but there was no such thing as a long life.

He got into his gear and waded into the water and began fishing his way upstream.

*

Now he was back at the pool where he had set out in the morning. He turned for a look at the stretch of water he had twice traversed today. Above it now hovered a layer of mist like dust above a road after the passage of a vehicle, or like a visible exhalation, a sigh at the end of day and the coming on of evening. Shaded, the water was turning chillier.

A hatch of mayflies, the evening rise, was beginning to come off the pool in ever-thickening numbers. Splitting and shedding their nymphal shucks in their swift ascent from the bed, they exchanged elements, surfaced, and rode the current for the seconds required to dry their wings for flight. A miniature armada about to take off. It was these seconds in their life cycle that the dry-fly fisherman imitated with his artificial, for it was then, during their period of immobility and helplessness, that the trout preyed upon them. Those that escaped found perches for themselves among the leaves and branches of the streamside bushes. There overnight they attained their maturity. One last function of their brief lives remained to them. Hovering above the stream out of reach of leaping trout, males and females, a cloud of them, met and mated on the wing—fulfillment fatal to the males. The females dipped again and again depositing their fertilized eggs upon the surface, rose when all were shed in a last flutter of release, then fell thick as snowflakes to the water, spent, their carcasses now feeding the fish. Their winged lives would have lasted for a day. Next year's trout, those of that third of their kind that survived the winter, would feed on the nymphs and the duns that hatched from those eggs, they in their turn to feed the fishermen who made it back, licensed for another season. Ol' man river, that ol' man river, he don't plant taters and don't plant cotton, and them what plants 'em is soon forgotten, but ol' man river, he just keeps rollin' along. The water he had waded through this morning was miles downstream from him now and somebody else was fishing it. By this time tomorrow it would be part of a different river and by next week an ocean wave. And even now, over his native Kansas, were forming clouds that would replenish the stream with raindrops that once before, even more than once, times out of number, had mingled in it, when one of those old mustachioed members of the club, and after him his

son, even that latter worthy's last cast framed and hanging on
the wall, had stood where he stood now. The amount of
moisture in our atmosphere and on our planet was a constant, fixed at the creation, perpetually being recycled, ours
on loan in our time and place. Izaak Walton, fishing his River
Dove, had fished this very water. And what was it we were
told? That the human body was seventy-five percent composed of water. Around his feet now flowed a droplet con-
densed from the vapors of that one, flesh of his flesh, reduced
to its components in Princeton on that October day. As it was
in the beginning, is now, and ever shall be: world without
end. Amen.

Now as he watched, fish began to feed on the emerging
flies, though unless you knew how to interpret the signs you
might not have known what was occurring. The rise came on
like a summer shower, the surface of the pool dimpling here
and there as though struck by large drops of rain as the fish
slyly sucked the flies under from below. Soon, like a quickening shower as the flies began to take flight, there were rings
made by rising fish all over the pond. Then the first one broke
water, followed instantly by a second, a third, a troupe of
them, as though a baton had been raised and brought down
and a ballet corps of trout had made their orchestrated entrance. Pursuing the flies in their flight, they rose into the air
and hung quivering there in defiance of gravity.

It was at times like this, when a large hatch was on, that
trout, though most voracious, were at their choosiest. The
fisherman had to present them with a fly the exact replica in
color, shape, and size of the real thing on which they were
feasting. The March Brown that was the only pattern they
would take yesterday at this time was worthless today when
the Gray Fox was on the evening menu, though the difference between the two was microscopic. Out of the swarm all
about him he grabbed a fly on the wing, held and studied it.
In size it was a number 16. Its pale, straw-colored body,
mottled wings, and ginger tail could best be matched, he
decided, with a Light Cahill. Among the rising fish he had
seen several good ones, but as he was tying on his fly a fish

leaped that he determined to try for. It was a fine one, over two pounds. He plotted his strategy.

His first consideration was not to hook some smaller fish and in fighting it disturb the pool and put down his fish. But his was a fish big enough to keep any challengers out of an extensive territory of its own. He watched it rise and rise again, clocking its timing, meanwhile studying the currents, positioning himself. He kept his line in the air with false casts. He reckoned the fish's resting station to be a yard downstream from the spot to which it consistently rose. Now immediately following a rise, as the fish was reentering the water, he dropped his fly a yard above that spot. Slowly it floated downstream. With a twist of his wrist he mended his cast. As his fly neared the fish's feeding circle he tensed for the strike. It was allowed to drift by untouched.

He let his fly float well below the fish's lie then gently lifted his line from the water. To dry his fly with false casts for a fresh float he turned aside so that the drops shed by his line would not fall where the fish might see them and take fright. He cast again, and again with no telltale drag, his fly drifted past the critical spot. Had he spooked his fish after all, put it down despite his care? He rested the water. During his recess the fish rose again. It was still on the feed. Was something suspicious about his fly? Was his leader too coarse?

The light was fading fast, and knowing that the hatch would soon end and their dinner end with it, the fish were feeding with abandon. Maybe in the frenzy his would lose its caution. Meanwhile, remembering the adage that a fly could never be too small, he changed his for a number 18. It was no bigger than a gnat, and to thread the leader through the eye of the hook with his trembling hands he had to hold it silhouetted against the sky. Again as he rested the water his fish fed.

The failing light now came to his aid, obscuring his leader, hiding any shortcomings in the faithfulness of his fly. He himself could just follow it. As it entered the target area he tensed in anticipation.

"Take it!" he said to the lurking fish.

And it did. Launched like a guided missile from underwater, it hooked itself in gorging the fly—no need for him to strike nor was there time to—and instantly it was as though a switch had been thrown and his line became a live electric wire crackling with current. Clear out of the pool and up-stream into the narrows the fish shot, and in the shallow water its passage raised a bulge on the surface as a torpedo does. Fifty feet it ran before the opposing current and the rein of the line brought it to a halt. There it hung, and as it recouped strength, the vibration of his rod, the strumming of his taut line by the flowing water gave him the sensation of feeling the very heartbeats of the fish, frightened but still full of fight.

The rod allowed the fish no rest but, like the other tine of a tuning fork, responded to its every motion, forcing it to strain continuously against the tug. Now the frustrated fish turned and rushed downstream. Past him it went and, catching sight of its tormentor, fired its auxiliary rockets. In the depths of the pool it sounded. There for fully five minutes it sulked. Then the changing slant of his line warned him that the fish was surfacing, about to leap. Out it came, threshing, tossing its head, trying to shake the hook. It danced on air, its spots sparkling, its golden underside flashing.

Twice more the fish leaped and twice more sounded, but nearer to him each time as he regained line, reined it in. It was as though he were connected by telegraph wire to the fish: he could feel its distress signals weaken steadily and at last sign off. His rod ceased vibrating, his line leveled, and the fish, on its side, floated slowly to the surface. He scooped it up in his net and sloshed ashore.

The fish could be saved, and game as it was, it deserved to live. It looked lifeless but it was not, it was just exhausted from the fight, and if he held it head first into the current and gently rocked it back and forth its respiration would be restored and it would revive. He extracted the hook from its palate using his hemostat and submerged it. Then he changed his mind. Holding the fish as he would hold a club, he knocked its head against a rock. It quivered, then stilled and stiffened.

He changed his mind because into it had come thoughts of the moment on the clubhouse porch when everybody laid out his day's catch. If he appeared there with nothing they would all feel sorry for him, and God knew, people were tired of having to feel sorry for him. But if he brought in the day's finest fish—and it was unlikely that anybody had caught a better one than his—it would seem that he was proud of himself and pleased with his day. Nobody would envy him his luck. They would all be relieved. They would congratulate him and want to stand him to a drink. At supper Eddie would serve the fish to some party with his compliments and from across the dining room they would gesture with thumbs up and he would respond in kind. Then it would seem to all that he had really rejoined the club.

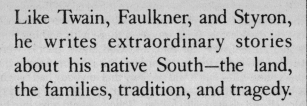